# CHAMPION OF LOST CAUSES

*Frederick Faust*
*(Max Brand)*

*Blood Ritual:*
*The Adventures of Scarlet and Bradshaw, Volume 1*
BY THEODORE ROSCOE

*The City of Stolen Lives: The Adventures*
*of Peter the Brazen, Volume 1*
BY LORING BRENT

*The Complete Cabalistic Cases of Semi Dual,*
*the Occult Detector, Volume 2: 1912–13*
BY J.U. GIESY AND JUNIUS B. SMITH

*Doan and Carstairs: Their Complete Cases*
BY NORBERT DAVIS

*The King Who Came Back*
BY FRED MacISAAC

*The Radio Gun-Runners*
BY RALPH MILNE FARLEY

*The Scarlet Blade: The Rakehelly Adventures of*
*Cleve and d'Entreville, Volume 1*
BY MURRAY R. MONTGOMERY

*Sabotage*
BY CLEVE F. ADAMS

*South of Fifty-Three*
BY JACK BECHDOLT

# CHAMPION OF LOST CAUSES

## MAX BRAND

INTRODUCTION BY

## WILLIAM F. NOLAN

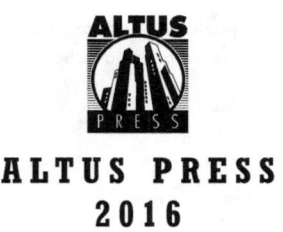

## ALTUS PRESS
### 2016

EDITED AND DESIGNED BY
Matthew Moring

ASSOCIATE EDITOR
Ray Riethmeier

THANKS TO
Everard P. Digges LaTouche and William F. Nolan

ISBN
978-1-61827-227-0

Visit *altuspress.com* for more books like this.
Printed in the United States of America.

# TABLE OF CONTENTS

Introduction *by William F. Nolan* . . . . . . . . . . . . i

Champion of Lost Causes . . . . . . . . . . . . . . . 1

About the Author . . . . . . . . . . . . . . . . 307

INTRODUCTION

# WILLIAM F. NOLAN

**FREDERICK FAUST LAUNCHED** his early career with the Munsey pulps when editor Robert Davis brought Faust into print in the March 31st, 1917, issue of *All-Story Weekly*.

Unable to sell his poetry (classical verse was his great passion) Faust turned to popular fiction, writing initially for the Frank A. Munsey pulps, creating his enduring pen name, "Max Brand," in June of 1917. During this early period, beyond *All-Story*, his fiction appeared in a variety of Munsey publications including *Railroad Man's Magazine* and *The Argosy*.

The novel at hand, *Champion of Lost Causes*, was serialized in late 1924 in *Flynn's*, a Munsey crime magazine (which, in 1927, became *Detective Fiction Weekly*). As he did with *The Darkness at Windon Manor*, Faust spins a tale of mystery and melodrama embraced by pulp fans of the era. This formula, quaint and stylized, and very much in the tradition of the "murder in the rose garden" school of crime, best exemplified by Doyle's Sherlock Holmes, is dated by today's standards—but Faust knew his audience and delivered exactly what they were seeking.

Proof of his success was the sale of *Champion of Lost Causes* to Hollywood, produced as a Fox film in 1925. (Edmund Lowe and Barbara Bedford were featured in what Motion Picture News described as "well done with an eye to entertainment values." (In all, Faust works formed the basis for some two dozen silent pictures, providing a solid secondary income.)

Therefore, relax, and allow your imagination to transport you back to the 1920s when a fatal gun shot in the library of a great mansion ignites the action.

*Prolific award-winning author William F. Nolan (best known for* Logan's Run*) is the leading global authority on the life and career of the legendary Frederick Faust ("Max Brand"). Celebrated as "The King of the Pulps," creator of Dr. Kildare and (among 250 Western novels)* Destry Rides Again, *Faust was killed in action in 1944 while serving as a war correspondent during the Italian Offensive in World War II. (Kildare was named after county Kildare in Ireland—and Faust had used the name earlier for his pirate hero Ivor Kildare.)*

*William Nolan has edited six books on Faust: three volumes of his best Western stories, two collections of classic Faust tales, and a book of his best crime stories. His pioneering volume,* Max Brand: Western Giant *(1985) lists all of Faust's 25 million words of fiction, his plays, non-fiction, verse, films (adapted from his works), radio, stage, and TV productions, and compiles memoirs and essays relating to Faust's life and career.*

*Since the 1950s Nolan has written extensively about Faust (and his 20 pen names) for a wide variety of markets. He has seen his work appear in each issue of* Singing Guns, *a magazine devoted to Faust, and in* The Max Brand Companion. *For many years he was a close friend of Faust's eldest daughter, Jane Faust Easton, and her husband, writer Robert Easton, now both deceased. Nolan's novel,* Rio Renegades, *is an homage to Faust. Also, working with the Eastons, he compiled* Max Brand's Best Poems *in 1992.*

*Nolan's collection of works by and about "Max Brand" includes 1,100 books and nearly 600 full-issue pulps, and remains the world's largest.*

# CHAPTER I

# THE MAN WITH THE OPAL

**THE NERVOUS MAN** muttered something about a breath of fresh air and left the table. When he was gone the other three exchanged glances, but only the man with the opal smiled. His long white fingers began to mix the cards for the new deal and the great stone in his ring flashed red and blue and green and yellow, or as he packed the cards together the jewel quivered with all colors at once.

It was characteristic of this fellow that he smiled down at his hands; instead of sharing his amusement with his companions, he seemed to be mocking them as well as the nervous man who had just left them. One might have called him a type of the gambler, but even in the gambling house he was unusual; a man to be looked at, perhaps, because he was such a perfect type. As for the other two, they spent a moment relaxing, recovering from the strain which the nervous player had imposed on them.

Then the fat little man spoke. He was a matter-of-fact person who took his winnings and his losses with the same puckered brow of thought; his baldness gave him a tonsured effect. He thrust out his clenched fist; between the thumb and forefinger the flesh bulged.

"What I want to know is this: Is our fidgety friend coming back?"

The ugly remark made Loring's lip curl a little, but he readily forced an expression of nonchalance. The man with the opal

*Loring could never
forget the white
anguish of her face.*

had been addressed; indeed, it seemed natural to appeal to him
for judgment in all matters at a gaming table. He did not answer
until he had smoothed the edges of the deck so that it was a
solid flash of gilt. Then he dismissed it with a farewell touch
and raised to the fat man, eyes as cold and gray as water under
moonlight.

"Why do you ask?"

"He's taken the big money out of this game, and I'm not
going to stand by and see him welch. He's taken out twelve
thousand if he's taken a cent. I've watched, even if you haven't!"

Loring smiled. It was ridiculous to conceive the man with
the opal not watching. Now he was smoothing his short mustache with the white, calm fingers. He answered: "I haven't seen
him take your money."

The fat man for the first time felt that his grumbling might
be out of place. He flushed a little, but he continued to growl:
"I don't like it. A fellow I've never seen before. Don't know his
name, even. Do you?"

*He stopped the rush of men
with outspread arms.*

"Nobody asks about names at Buttrick's," said the man with
the opal, deftly turning the point of the question. "But you can
be sure he'll come back; everyone comes back to Buttrick's—
comes back sooner or later."

"Sooner or later! That may mean a year from now."

"Patience! What is a year?" He spoke with a voice as low as
if he were explaining to a child, yet there was not a shade of
gentleness. Loring had been covertly examining him all evening
and his interest had grown.

The fellow was perfect in type and yet he was full of contrasts;
imagine a gambler wearing an opal, the jewel of ill luck! Loring
was a fighter; he fought the cards just as he boxed with a man,
cool, keen-eyed, attacking eagerly always, and yet ever poised
to take advantage of the first opening and shoot home the
finishing punch. Because he was a fighter he recognized power
of all kinds at once and admired it; all evening he had been
admiring the man with the opal.

"Patience!" the latter was repeating. "A minute is eternity; a
year is a minute. It depends on the point of view."

"I'm not a star gazer," snarled the little man, passing a hand over his tonsured head.

The man with the opal smiled at this implication and then with a shocking suddenness looked at Loring. His delicate finger tips continued to pass over his mustache, but his eyes held, for a second, as many lights as his great opal. "You've lost quite a bit," he remarked almost gently.

"Rot!" burst out Loring. He was glad of a chance to turn the talk from the nervous man and the possibility that he might have definitely withdrawn from the game taking his winnings with him. To even sit patiently and listen to such suspicions made him feel tainted. "I've lost a little," he went on, smiling, "but I still have a little left to throw after the rest. Not much, to be sure!"

As he spoke he took a wisp of bills out of his pocket and flicked the corners of them; there was a little over a thousand dollars there.

"Not much," nodded the man with the opal. "The price of a man's life, I'd say."

Loring looked down at the money with a new interest and then his hand brushed the bills with a shudder of distaste. "The price of a life, did you say?"

"A cheap one. Men are like greenbacks—they have different denominations, eh? A million would hardly buy the death of one man; a hundred dollars would get another. All tagged with different prices."

"Not in the eyes of the law!" cried the little fat man.

The glance of the man with the opal departed from Loring for the split part of a second and flicked across the bald head.

"Ah, no," he said. "Not in the eyes of the law."

Loring found himself staring at the pale man with the black mustache as he had stared at a cobra behind plate glass when he was a child. What he had said about the purchase of human life had been shocking enough, but it did not seem out of keeping. He had to wrest his mind away from that handsome, implacable face.

"Here we are again!"

He nodded across the room. The nervous man had just brushed through the curtains and stood with one hand gripping the stiff folds. He scowled at them from beneath his brows and now that he was in view seemed to have regretted his return. He was terribly in earnest; he had been terribly in earnest ever since the game began.

At length he made up his mind, crossed the room hurriedly, and took his place. Beneath the table Loring saw him lock his hands together while he looked fixedly into the faces of his companions, one by one, as if he suspected that they had "framed" the game during his absence.

"Begin," he said dictatorially. "I'm ready!"

The little fat man rubbed his chin with his knuckles and glanced at the nervous man across his shoulder in apprehension; plainly he was as nervous as the winner. Loring felt that the old air of constraint was settling back upon the table and he loathed it. He hated this businesslike atmosphere. He could not to save his soul "work" with the cards. No matter what the stakes, it remained a game to him.

All life had been a game to Loring. He had played it with all the strength of his powerful body; he had rioted through every emotion. He had gone through scenes that would have damned other men and he had come out clean. He was one of those men who are always making new starts. His hair, as a result, was decidedly gray over the temples, and in repose his face aged by ten years; but his smile was all boy. He smiled now, shook his wide, thick-muscled shoulders, and raised his head.

"I warn you, my friends," he said joyously, "that I'm tired of this dull game. I want action, action, action! Out with the cards, sir. By the Lord, I have a tingle in my finger tips that tells me I'm going to win!"

"Damnation!" exploded the nervous man; he avoided the

volley of glances by adding hurriedly: "Why the devil do we have nothing to drink? I need a nip. Nothing to eat since— where is that waiter? Is the fool deaf and dumb!"

Buttrick, in furnishing his gaming house, had retained many mid-Victorian features, and among others he had left the bell cords instead of installing electric buttons. Now the nervous man whirled in his chair and wrenched at the silken rope until it came taut with a hum and they heard the silver tinkle far off and faint.

The outburst brought a sneer from the fat man; the man with the opal presented his usual blank face; but Loring overflowed with pity. He felt that this game was beginning to make him unclean. He determined on the spot to be rid of it even at the price of the rest of his money, though where he would go for more was a mystery. Such mysteries, however, were too old to greatly disturb him. When the round of drinks had been brought and passed, he began wagering heavily on the first hand that was dealt him.

Starting with a miserable pair of deuces before the draw, he held up three cards, and then bumped up the bidding in lumps of two hundred. The man with the opal stayed to the second raise; at the last raise of which Loring's thousand dollars was capable, the nervous man bit his lip and laid down his hand. Pure bluff; but Loring raked in the chips without joy. He wanted this thing to end.

He kept on playing like a madman; and he kept on winning. He could not lose, it seemed. When he bluffed, the others stayed with the betting only long enough to fatten the stakes. When he held a full house someone was sure to call him when the bet had reached a dizzy height. Usually it was the nervous man. Finally the fat man slapped down his cards with the violence of an oath and withdrew from the game, his pudgy back daring them to ask questions.

Loring had won again. He cashed in piles of chips to clear the table and flung himself into the game again, joylessly. For the face of the nervous man was becoming a horror. Obviously he was meeting each loss with his life blood, but how could Loring stop while he was winning?

The crash came. Loring had opened a jackpot with queens and filled miraculously with three nines. The betting swept up; the nervous man "called" with a straight, and as Loring drew in the chips the beaten player rose slowly. He propped himself on stiff arms above the table, his shoulders thrust back into ridiculous points.

"Gentlemen," he said, "I'm done. Good-night!"

And turning, he crossed the room with a slow step, as though he feared that if he hurried his legs might crumble beneath him.

# CHAPTER II

# CONCERNING MERCY

**BOTH MEN TURNED** to follow him; Loring, with a sick look, faced the man with the opal again in time to see him raise his hand until it was level with his forehead and make a significant small gesture with his forefinger.

"No, no!" groaned Loring. "Not that! I feel like a murderer!"

He started up, but the voice of his companion cut in on him, stopped him, as though with a hand.

"Would you pity a jackal that was poisoned by dead meat?" he asked. And when Loring turned the man with the opal added: "Carrion, sir; nothing but carrion, mind and body."

Loring blinked.

"I forget. The game has to go on?"

"Not at all. For this evening I have had enough." He admitted defeat with a calm that made Loring respect him more than ever—a respect with a touch of fear in it. "But I wish," continued the man with the opal, "to know you. My name is Nicholas Zanten; but that does not in any way imply that you must tell me yours." He went on gracefully, giving Loring time to think it over and drop the subject.

"In Buttrick's, of course you've observed that names don't matter. Men lose their personality and become merely bags of money with hands to spend it as soon as they come within those soft closing doors downstairs. For all I know, it may spoil your pleasure to identify yourself; spoil the game, eh?"

But Loring was flattered in spite of himself. He felt at once that he was receiving an attention which the man with the opal paid to very few, indeed.

"I'm Samuel Loring," he answered readily. "Very glad to know your name, Mr. Zanten." He thought the foreign twang of that name fitted perfectly with the fellow's exterior. "As for the game—I think it's been a rotten mess! Won't get the face of that chap off my mind for months of nights."

"Give me your ear for one moment and then forget what I've said," returned Nicholas Zanten. "The name of that man is Joseph Wilbur. Does that mean anything to you? I see it does not. Very well, then. Take my word for it that Wilbur is lost. He was lost before this game began. And I give you my word of honor that he is not and never has been worth saving."

They crossed the room together as they spoke. Zanten stepped out to the curtains first and drew the heavy tapestry well aside for Loring. In spite of himself the big man slipped through hastily. He did not relish having those moon cold eyes behind his back, unwatched. On the farther side of the curtains he was sharply ashamed of himself and glanced at his companion. Zanten was smiling at the floor and Loring knew that he had understood. The thread of their friendship was cut even before the spinning had well begun.

"Roulette, by Jove!" exclaimed Loring, for in the depth of the long apartment he made out a group of players and heard the hum of the spinning wheel. "All this under the very nose of the law."

"The law is not omniscient," returned Zanten, "and sometimes it is even discreetly blind. I remember—"

"Look! Look!" broke in Loring, and he pointed out the lofty, meager figure of Joseph Wilbur playing the wheel. It was a form as somber as a skeleton playing dice. Out of the very back of the man appeared his ghoulish eagerness to win, his desperate determination.

Once more the gesture of Zanten recurred to him. He saw Wilbur at the end of the evening's play retiring to his room—

perhaps to a brightly lighted mansion—and drawing a revolver from a secret drawer. The shocking part of it was that
Wilbur was no hungry, common gambler. In every respect he
suggested the man who had handled large destinies. It was as
horrible to see him wince under the loss of a few thousands as
it would be to see a stalwart white man cringe before a Negro.
The horror repelled and fascinated Loring.

"Very well," he heard Zanten saying, "I thought you would
be stronger minded. But if you are determined, go ahead."

He turned in surprise to his companion. There was always
something freshly interesting in the white and somber face and
in the remarkable eyes. He was touching his mustache with the
hand that bore the opal and the jewel flashed with redoubled
brilliance across the colorless face. He seemed to Loring dis-
tinctly the skeleton at the feast, the warning at the gaming table.

"What did you mean?"

"That you are going to help Wilbur lose his own money and
yours as well. But nothing can stop you. Good-night."

"You have no pity?" asked Loring curiously.

"I? Nonsense! Of course I have pity. A man who hardens
himself to pity has closed one door to happiness. I am as full
of pity as a ten year old girl. I am as soft of heart as that
Madonna."

He nodded to a crumbling limestone statue taken from the
ruins of some Gothic church in France. From the broken arms
of the Virgin the infant Jesus had long since fallen, but the
half-obliterated face was still bent with pathetic tenderness.
How much Buttrick had spent in furnishing his little palace of
Chance behind its sober, brown-stone front, not even Nicholas
Zanten, probably, could guess.

Loring looked about him at the marvelous browns and blues
and reds of a tapestry which seven centuries had softened; at
the andirons of the monstrous fireplace, wrought after the
fashion of two gargoyles of Notre Dame de Paris; at a bottle of
green Venetian glass, semi-translucent, netted over with gold

filigree which framed four cameos of microscopic workmanship. He looked at this beauty and then stared back at the hard face of Nicholas Zanten, knowing that the gambler could appreciate all this beauty tenfold more than he, Samuel Loring, who had kept his hands clean and his heart pure.

"I pity him," said Zanten, "but I judge him. Beware of tenderness, Mr. Loring. It leads a man to damnation as surely as the path of the Prodigal Son." He relieved this moralizing with a smile as cold as ice. "A man who pities others is apt on occasion to pity himself," he concluded. "And what a fall is that, eh?"

Loring flushed in spite of himself. This man was surely not ten years his senior, and yet he made him feel like a child. Then he tossed up his big head as a fighter should.

"You are fortunate, Mr. Zanten," he said. "I see that you have learned the great lesson and understand how to say 'no.' I, however, have had a less classic education." He took the sting out of this remark by saying frankly: "Good-night, Mr. Zanten. I look forward to seeing you again."

"You will," said the other, and trailed his bloodless fingers across the palm of Loring's hand. But when Loring had turned, Zanten looked after him with a smile that made his white face, for the moment, almost beautiful. Then he went thoughtfully on his way.

In the meantime Loring had reached the group at the roulette wheel.

"The devil take Zanten," he muttered on the way, "unless he is the devil come on earth, which I half suspect. Besides, what am I when it comes to thinking? A child!"

Therefore he followed his impulse. He had hardly placed a bet on the red—and won—when the clawlike hand of Wilbur closed on his arm. He turned his head but discreetly avoided the face of the gambler.

"My friend," said Wilbur, forcing a hideous chuckle of good-fellowship, "you had a remarkable run at the cards. Remarkable!

Do me a favor, now, and let me share your luck. Take my money; place it!"

"If you wish."

A ten dollar bill was crammed into his palm by cold, shaking fingers. He played the red again, and won again.

"Once more," whispered the voice at his ear.

Again on the red and again a winning. Still, with the whisper directing him, he let the bet ride. The ten dollars had grown to a hundred and sixty.

"God bless you," gasped Wilbur. "God bless you, lad. Now—a single number. A single number!"

Which meant, of course, one chance in thirty-six.

"Not that," protested Loring.

"By God, I say yes!"

"Then, play it yourself."

"No, no, my friend! The luck is yours. You're in a run. You can't be beaten! Bet all on one number."

He obeyed, played the nine, and saw the money disappear. Turning to Wilbur he found a face like death. He took the man by the arm—his fingers bit through the skinny muscles to the bone—and helped him to a chair.

"It's done," the other kept repeating. "It's done!"

A criminal in such a voice might echo the verdict of guilty.

"Listen to me," said Loring, mastering his shudder of contempt, of pity, of disgust. "I have eight thousand dollars of your money. It came to me across the card table. It's yours."

He held out the stiff handful of bills. It seemed at first that the other was paralyzed. Then he drew in his breath as one drinking and clutched the money with both hands.

"Is it all here?" he stammered. "All here?" He counted it feverishly. "Yes, eight thousand!"

The life went out of him again, and he sank deeply into the cushions of the chair.

"What is eight thousand? Nothing! Nothing! So much rustle of paper; dust on the wind. Nothing!"

"Good-night," muttered Loring, feeling a mortal cold draw into his heart.

But the birdclaw fingers of the other seized him again.

"Not yet!" pleaded that hollow and tremulous voice. "My young friend, my dear young friend!"

In spite of his effort, Loring could not keep the disgust out of his voice.

"I am sorry," he said, "but I am leaving Buttrick's at once, Mr. Wilbur."

All the hysterical hope went out of the face of the man and he shrank into his chair as though seeking protection.

"You know me, then?"

"I know your name. Nothing more."

"Zanten told you. I see. Don't believe Zanten. He lied. He lies about everything. He's a devil. A cold devil. I hate Zanten—for reasons. In reality, I'm a man wronged by lies and rumor. Public opinion has crucified me. Look on me, my dear fellow! You see a man stretched on the cross and bleeding from the wounds of rumor!"

He clutched his breast with one of those ugly hands as he spoke and tears of self-pity misted his eyes. They were instantly clear again, probing Loring to see what effect the speech had made on his auditor.

"You believe me?" he went on, raving in the same hurried whisper, and letting his wild glance rove as though he would frighten away eavesdroppers. "Yes, I see that you believe me. When two men meet—in a crowd or in a desert—heart speaks to heart and they know each other at once. The moment I laid eyes on you, I knew you to be such a man!"

The flattery sickened Loring. He silently cursed Buttrick's and the moment he had entered the place.

"And as surely as I knew you then," rushed on Wilbur, retaining his clutch on Loring to drag himself to his feet, "I know

now that you will continue to aid me—a man oppressed. You will take this money of mine and play it. All on single numbers—all on single numbers. What is eight thousand? Nothing! Divide it into eight parts. Play each part on a single number. If one part wins, it will be enough. More than enough. Enough? Ay, salvation!"

In vain Loring argued that even with eight trials at a single number the chance each time was still only one out of thirty-six. He could not press his point effectively against this hysteria, and he dared not meet the eye of a man whose soul was naked in it.

Reluctantly he chose a number and played the first pile of bills. It was gone, and the hand on his shoulder contracted and relaxed. Again, again, again, again, and always he lost and always that pulsing grip on his shoulder, eating toward the bone. The man was gibbering at his ear; not advice. He listened. Wilbur was praying swiftly, whispering the invocations.

And then the last pile of money, all save a few small bills, was placed, and it followed the rest. Loring turned with his eyes on the floor, but to his astonishment there was no cry of anguish.

He found that Wilbur was buttoning his coat close to the throat. He had become appallingly calm.

"Very well," he said. "You, my friend, I thank. For the rest—"

He left the curse unspoken and hurried out of the room. As for Loring, for a moment he hesitated, then he strode after Wilbur and stopped him at the door.

"The rest of your money," he said.

He put it in the nerveless hand.

"Now, Mr. Wilbur, take hold of yourself. If there is anything I can do for you—"

"One thing. Let me have peace, sir. Let me have silence."

The dignity of that speech roused in the younger man a sudden eagerness to save him.

"But your friends! I shall find your friends, any you may name, and—"

"Friends?" echoed Wilbur. "Friends, did you say?"

He broke into hideously soundless laughter and fled down the stairs. Loring waited until the hiss of that laughter had crept out of his ears, and then followed. No matter where the unfortunate Wilbur was fleeing, it would be to his destruction, and in the little interval Loring had vowed solemnly to save the man if he could.

# CHAPTER III

# THE FUGITIVE

**IT WAS ABOVE** all things necessary, however, that he pursue Wilbur without the latter's knowledge. Self-destruction, he felt, must be the goal of the losing gambler, but something told Loring that there was not in that shambling, fear-ridden skeleton, enough courage to end his own life. By every glance of his eyes, by every whispering or thundering tone of his voice, Wilbur bespoke the fear of others. For them he had played his desperate and losing game in Buttrick's house. And now, hopeless, and terror stricken, he was going to them.

It was amazing to Loring. He had seen the wildernesses of three continents. With such a multiplicity of places to hide, what was the power which seemed so inescapable that a man gave himself up to it without a struggle except to meet and pay its demands?

Something of all this rushed through the mind of Loring as he went down the stairs. Opening the door, he was in time to see Wilbur disappear into the blackness of a taxicab. It was a freakish spring night. The evening had set in clear, with only a tumble of clouds in the northwest. Now the sky was a solid gray of low-hanging mist, with the stain of Broadway's lights upon it. The rain was a steady dripping except when the wind picked up an armful of it and flung it rattling against the windows or into the face of some bewildered pedestrian. Such a gust of water whipped the skin of Loring before he could raise the collar of his overcoat.

It was literally a dash of cold water in the face, and he paused on the verge of this adventure. He saw the huddle of people going down the pavements under their umbrellas; he saw the black windows across the street and the pale, wet roofs; looking up, the wind carried a drift of fog that tangled about a skyscraper. An unseasonable night for adventures of any kind, thought Loring.

Then he saw the taxicab which carried Wilbur, picking its way delicately through the traffic, fearful of skidding. He started as the hound when it sees the flaunting tail of the fox. In a bound he was down the steps. He passed three taxicabs with the drivers huddled shapelessly in the front seats, enduring weather as only chauffeurs know how to endure it. At the fourth machine he paused, examined his man again, and then tapped his arm.

"You see that machine?" he asked quietly, giving the number.

His man grunted.

"I want you to follow it. I have ten for you above the fare if you keep in touch with it—but not too closely, you understand?"

The taxi driver had slipped from his place to crank his cold engine. Now he paused with one foot on the step and a grin spread slowly on his pale, square face. One eye closed. It was an expression of infinite understanding, infinite cunning, and Loring climbed into the body of the car with a sigh of relief. He felt that he had chosen his driver well.

He was sure of it when he noted the manner in which the chauffeur, for all his hurry to overtake the quarry, eased in the gears and put his machine in high; he was entirely convinced as they slipped through a twisting pack of cars and nosed into a more open stretch again. Loring bedded his heavy shoulders in the corner of the cushions, and having lighted his cigarette he made his mind a blank and waited.

That was his habit in crises. But presently he opened his eyes. The machine had stopped and now the door was opened and a hurried voice muttered.

"I lost him, governor. About a thousand machines on Seventh Avenue. Dunno whether he turned down or went ahead."

"Find him," said Loring.

"I dunno—I'd sure try—but I'd only be taking a chance."

"Find him," said Loring.

"I can't read the mind of the traffic, governor."

"Find him," said Loring.

The door closed with a crash and the machine pitched ahead, while Loring smiled behind the veil of smoke and closed his eyes again. The engine lowered to a hum and a purr abruptly as they were stopped by traffic at corners; it shot up into swift crescendos as they gathered speed again, or whirled around cars which led them. Assuredly, Loring thought, he had picked his man well. And after a time the speed of the car decreased. It fell to a smooth, jaunting pace, and the door was opened.

"Got 'em!" cried the driver.

"Of course; I knew you would."

To uphold this reputation, there was nothing the chauffeur would not do. Knowing this, Loring smiled again, but now he sat up and took notice. They crossed the scattering lights and the noise of Fourteenth Street, that cheap imitation of Broadway; they were running swiftly south. Now they angled into lower Broadway in the shadow of huge walls of office buildings. Far away he saw the dancing back of the taxicab which they were pursuing. Traffic was slight in this quarter at such a late hour and his chauffeur took no chances of being observed in his pursuit.

At Chambers Street they stopped.

"Here we are," said the driver, opening the door.

"Has he left the cab?" asked Loring.

"No."

"Then wait till he does."

After a moment the fugitive car started on again from its

halting place close to the Municipal Building. It changed direction.

"Brooklyn, I guess," called the driver, as they drew close to Manhattan Bridge.

But in the square at the entrance to the great bridge, lifting over East River, the other machine merely paused again, though this time Loring observed Wilbur get out and walk about with the wind whipping the overcoat about his skinny body.

This time they veered straight north.

Loring was beginning to think that he had taken up the trail of a madman. What earthly connection had the Municipal Building and Manhattan Bridge in the mind of a man who seemed about to die? Perhaps the fellow had been under the influence of a drug, and his despair had been as false as his flight was now without reason.

They had cut back into Broadway again and the fugitive raced at high speed through the shadowy lower part of the famous street; reaching the thirties he slowed again and entered the zone of the night lights at a creeping pace. Whether the traffic was heavy or the street vacant ahead of him, the first driver kept his machine at a snail's pace. In spite of that slow gait it was soon difficult to trail the car without coming close so many times as to attract suspicion.

Every now and then a side street poured a host of traffic into Broadway, and Loring's man was crowded back. But he was never left long behind. He kept as accurately in touch with his engine as a fine rider does with the mouth of his horse, and whenever a narrow gap showed in the mass of automobiles he was instantly scooting toward it and closer on the heels of the quarry. Yet it was precarious and nervous work, for at any time they might lose their man down a side street.

Luck, however, stayed with them. The fugitive kept to Broadway until the bright lights fell away to a duller glow at Columbus Circle. The traffic, also, was now lighter, with less feeding into it from the side streets. They kept easily in touch with their

man as he rounded the subway station at Seventy-Second Street
and shot swiftly down toward the Drive.

Up Riverside Drive the fugitive maintained the same rate of
speed, dodging recklessly around the leading cars until he
reached the swinging crest at Eighty-Fifth Street. There the
taxicab stopped once more, and again the tall, scarecrow figure
emerged and stood with the wind in his face, looking back
where the Drive dipped down to Seventy-Ninth and then rose
leisurely and twisted out of sight at Seventy-Fifth.

Again Wilbur drove on, swerving back from Riverside to
Broadway at One Hundred and Tenth. They sped swiftly again,
the tires catching the water and sending it with a steady swish-
ing against the mudguards. At One Hundred and Twenty-
Second they dived into the gloom of Manhattan Avenue and
here Loring half expected that the journey would end. It seemed
fitting that the doomed gambler should go to his fate in that
dark hollow; but through the shadow they sped out and up
toward the hill beyond.

They had settled back into a steady pace, by this time. The
nervousness of the leading driver had apparently worn off.
Resigned to his long, odd journey, he kept his machine well
under its top notch and jogged quietly on with Loring's cab far
behind, sometimes losing the other over a hilltop, or in the
shadow of a hollow.

Far out Broadway, in the early Hundred and Forties and
again in the Sixties, they entered dense waves of traffic as they
crossed uptown amusement and business centers. After that
the going was comparatively clear, and presently they struck
into a suburban road. They had threaded the whole length of
the great city. Open spaces began to grow, touches of green
under the road lamps. It was like another world to Loring.

Then big estates, formal gates opening on tree-lined drives.
Into one of these the taxicab swerved. When they came opposite the gate the machine had disappeared among the poplars
and beyond the black treetops loomed a great mansion with

the clustered chimneys of Tudor times. This, at last, must be the end of the trail—and what an end! The possibility that that skeleton-faced man might be owner of this estate turned Loring cold to the heart. He was not a moralizer, but a gloomy premonition of the vanity of human endeavor came to him as he stood on the ground at last, stretching until he got the feel of his muscles again, and listening to the wind in the trees.

He gave the driver the promised tip and the necessary word of praise.

"Besides," said the chauffeur as he thanked Loring, "I'm mum, governor. You can count on that."

"Nonsense. You can talk all you please. But this joke has cost me a devilish lot of time."

The chauffeur allowed a smile to grow around his eyes and never reach his lips. The eyes looked steadily at Loring out of the huge, pale face.

"Sure," he said, "a joke. Sure it's a joke."

And he laughed mirthlessly.

When he had gone, Loring stopped a woman scurrying past with a boy's hand clasped in hers, tugging him against the wind.

"What place is this?" he shouted into the gale.

"Lord, sir!" she cried, shrinking from him, and when she saw it was not a highway robber: "The Charles place, I guess."

The name of the owner, for some reason, was a great relief to Loring. There was something clean and manly about the sound of the word. At least, it was a joy to know that such a place was not the property of the skulking Wilbur.

He went up the driveway, swinging his heels into the crunching gravel. Even that sound comforted him. It made him feel cleaner and more normal. And then he came out from the screen of trees and under the mighty façade of the mansion. It was as huge as he had guessed, with three towering series of bay windows.

# CHAPTER IV

# THE HOLLOW WALL

**THE MAIN ENTRANCE** was small for such a façade. It gave more the effect of one of those strong, stealthy medieval portals. Strains of music came out to Loring as he approached it and he heard a murmur of many voices coming to him through the thick walls like strong light through a velvet curtain—just a hint of sound except when a girl laughed, and that sound was sliver thin, but clear.

There was apparently an entertainment, many people, happy faces—all at once the nightmare thoughts of Loring seemed ludicrously out of place. He felt a sense of shame and a sinking of the heart. After all, what proofs were his that Wilbur was in danger of death? How could he enter those glowing rooms and speak—of what? But his habit was to see things through to the bitter end. His hand faltered, and yet he pressed the bell.

When the door opened, he looked at the portly servant in a new dismay. Was the "Charles" who owned the place a man or a woman?

"I wish to see Mr. Charles," he said boldly, and gave his card. "My business is urgent."

He was bowed into a lofty, paneled hall. At a short distance it widened into a great room, and at the end of the room a double staircase descended with solemnity to the floor. Iron lanterns lighted them on either side, and the steps shimmered away to darkness above. A door opened on a burst of music and merriment and Loring's surety vanished again.

"Mr. Charles," the servant was saying, "is engaged."

At least, his guess at the name had been right. He met the eye of the servant firmly.

"I must see Mr. Charles," he repeated. "Only for a moment. He will not know my card, but you may tell him that my visit is of the most vital nature."

He found the other looking at him intently; the fellow even half turned, but faced him again, shaking his head.

"Mr. Charles is already engaged in an interview of the most vital nature," he parodied. "If you care to wait, however—"

Loring leaped at a passing thought. After all, he had acted so much upon chance impulses this night that he might as well either abandon the whole affair or else continue to try to follow a spider thread through the labyrinth.

"Mr. Charles is engaged at present with Joseph Wilbur," he stated, prepared to see the other shake his head in bewilderment.

Instead, the hand of the servant closed convulsively over the card. It seemed to Loring that the fellow actually changed color.

"I beg your pardon, sir, but are you, by any chance, a friend of Mr. Wilbur?"

"Yes," said Loring boldly. "That's exactly what I am."

A child could have seen that this last speech made by no means a pleasant impression upon the doorkeeper. He actually scowled at Loring and for a moment it seemed that he would dare to be a man, and an angry man at that. Instantly, however, he schooled himself back into the servant with calm features.

"But my business," continued Loring smoothly, watching the face of the man as the pilot watches his guiding star, "is with Mr. Charles alone."

He found that he had buried himself more deeply than ever in the mire. The doorkeeper started to answer and then paused, so that there was only an ugly lifting of the lip. Mysteriously the remarks of Loring seemed to have thrown him into a fighting fury. Loring became aware of shoulders almost as massive as his own thrown forward. It was like the bristling of a trusted and tried watchdog when a stranger steals into the homestead grounds.

"You and Mr. Wilbur," said the doorkeeper, with an odd blending of savagely controlled insolence and hatred, "have no doubt equally important matters to take up with Mr. Charles. But since he is engaged already with Mr. Wilbur I do not see how I can introduce you, sir. The instructions of Mr. Charles were emphatic. He is not to be disturbed."

So saying, he looked past Loring toward the door, as if he recommended strongly an exit at this point in the parley. But retreat was now the last thing in Loring's mind. Somewhere in this house the skull-faced Wilbur was talking with Mr. Charles. Perhaps Charles was himself the inescapable danger to which Wilbur fled as the bird flees to the fabled snake. Or perhaps Wilbur was making to Charles, as to a court of last appeal, a final plea for the money which he failed to win at the gaming house.

No matter how the affair stood, Loring felt reasonably certain that a doom was stealing upon Wilbur in that house and that there would be a death. He knew it as certainly as a man knows that, when he turns the corner before him, he will meet someone he knows. He knew it as certainly as a man knows the influence of an unseen eye behind him. Wilbur was about to die.

Staring at the broad, complacent, stolid face of the door-keeper, Loring for an instant wanted to smash him to the floor and rush down the great, silent hall shouting: "Murder!"

Indeed, a feminine hysteria to which he had hitherto been a stranger was taking his nerves. It seemed to him that the very air was full of warning; everyone must understand a danger coming—everyone except this pompous ass of a doorkeeper.

"I warn you," said Loring solemnly, "that if you keep me from Mr. Charles there will be serious consequences."

The doorkeeper bowed; Loring saw the last vestige of a dis-appearing sneer on his mouth and wanted to drive his muscular fist into those lips. Evidently, the fellow had lost all respect the moment he had heard that Loring was a friend of Wilbur. What reputation could Wilbur have that made even his acquaintances unclean? What was the leprous nature of the man?

"Then," insisted Loring desperately, "I'll see any other person who is near the head of the household. Who is the son?"

"There is no son of Mr. Charles," answered the doorkeeper.

He stood with placid hostility, making no suggestions. The result was that Loring, for the moment, forgot himself. He went one stalking, cat-like step closer to the servant; if one hunts the tiger long enough he becomes a bit tigerish himself, and Loring was a hunter of big game.

"You have a head on your shoulders," said Loring without raising his voice unduly. "Use it. Find me someone with authority in this house."

He had at last impressed the doorkeeper with fear. The latter slipped back as though he were taking his foot from the fleshy, soft back of a snake; and his face was the face of a man who sees a viper.

"Very well," he said shortly, and went off down the hall with his rubber heels padding heavily.

Loring took out his watch and decided to give the man three minutes to produce the requested person. At the end of that time he determined to go on a still hunt himself. In the meantime he walked up and down the hall, examining its treasures. They were many, but assembled with such profusion that Loring profoundly suspected the hand of an interior decorator rather than the taste of the owner.

He paused at one angle, where, out of the shadow, he caught the flash and glimmer of full burnished steel. It was a complete suit of armor; as nearly as he could make out, it was of the period of the fourteenth century, and close to the end of it when chain and plate were intermingled or used separately. He recognized the bassinet, peaked and ridged.

Molded leather covered the studs which fastened the short

camail; over the cunning joints of the elbow and knee plates
there was soft velvet; to one side was the hauberk with flowing
sleeves; and near it the curved bladed bracquemart with a suggestion of the Saracen. Loring gripped the hilt and found it
fitted neatly to his hand.

It was while his hand still rested on the roughened grip of
the hilt that he felt behind him the opening of a door. Suppose
a whisper, unheard and yet somehow known. The opening of
that door was no more real to the brain of Loring. Indeed, he
could not have been sure of it at any other time, but to-night
his senses had become as alert as though he stalked big game
through an African jungle, never knowing what eyes watched
him through the stalks of the giant elephant grass. And as surely
as he stood there, he felt a pair of eyes look out and take hold
on him and survey him with hostile intent from head to heels.

It was a nightmare moment that set the hair prickling on
his head and made the skin of his brow contract with cold. For
an instant his hand closed convulsively on the hilt of the bracquemart; then he forced his fingers to loosen by a strong effort
of the will and made himself turn slowly, drawing his nerves as
hard as drawn iron.

The moment that movement began he was aware that the
door was closing with the faint whispering sound. When he
had completely turned, as he had wholly expected, there was
no sign of a door behind him on the farther side of the big
niche.

The hall was as huge and dim and empty as ever, and the
reassuring mirth from the people in the near-by rooms, and
even the faint slip and whisper of the feet of the dancers came
out to him.

Yet he listened to those sounds with a contracted brow. For
he knew beyond question that a danger had been looking out
at him the moment before. He made sure that no one was near
in the hall and no one approaching. Then he crossed the niche

with two strides and sounded the wall with cautious blows of his knuckles. Low, high, to this side and then to that, he struck.

Then in the center of the circle, and this time he was sure that he had made his discovery. There was an indubitably hollow sound of an echo within the wall. In other words, this was a false panel. Once again, as he stood there, he had that keen apprehensive feeling that someone stood behind him.

He whirled on the impulse and saw that the doorkeeper was in fact a little distance away, looking at him with a smile which he instantly forced from his lips. Beside him stood another man in evening dress.

# CHAPTER V

# FENCING

**IN THE SILENT** approach of the two there seemed to Loring something infinitely malignant. In vain he told himself that there was no reason for them to suspect or to hate him; neither had there been any reason for the door to open at his back. But the fact remained that they had stolen up behind him and for an unknown number of moments they had been watching him rap on the wall.

The silence of their coming was quite adequately explained by their rubber heels and the depth of the heavy rug which stretched on the floor. And yet—when Loring turned he turned with a shudder, and when he met their glances he narrowed his eyes—as a beast will do when it is in danger. Which is as much as to say that there was a good deal of the animal in Loring.

He had been born with a love of danger for its own sake, an animal-like love of it. It had given him the gray hair at his temples; it accounted for the suddenly savage set of his mouth now and then; but also, perhaps, it was the reason behind the boyishness of his smile.

He smiled now, at once.

"Old style of building, this," he said. "That's a heavy wall."

"Exactly," said the newcomer, failing to reply to the smile. "Those walls are so thick that no rat has ever been known to bore a way through them."

There was no denying the ugly meaning behind the level voice and the level eyes of the man. He was a finely made chap, a good inch or more taller than even Loring, the lean-waisted, athletic type, though his face was a little full fleshed by good living.

In spite of that, he was remarkably handsome. Put him in training, thought Loring, and he would have made a noble figure in the ring or on the wrestling mat. Instinctively, as one strong man always feels toward another, Loring wanted to match speed and power with the other.

"My name," went on the man, after a pause of needless length to allow the full import of his first sarcasm to strike home, "is Geoffrey Charles. I understand that you are Mr. Samuel Loring and that you wish to speak with a representative of Mr. Peter Charles. Perhaps I will do."

It was not the sort of introduction to be followed by a handshake. In some elusive way it piled insult upon insult. Loring was tempted bitterly to say some small, nasty thing which would precipitate a climax. Indeed, the whole manner and set of the burly Mr. Geoffrey Charles implied that he was entirely ready for some such climax. Loring controlled himself with a new effort.

"I don't know. Perhaps you'll do. Perhaps you won't. It depends on how close you are to Mr. Charles and his affairs."

He saw the jaw of young Charles thrust out an aggressive trifle under this touch.

"Perhaps I'll be a sufficient judge of that when you tell me your errand. Sit down."

With the same gesture that invited Loring to a seat, he dismissed the doorkeeper. It seemed to Loring that there was an interchange of glances between them in which the doorkeeper asked a question and young Charles assured him that he was quite able to master the situation. The servant retreated with obvious unwillingness.

"I'll talk standing; no time, in fact, for ceremonies, as you seem to have gathered, Mr. Charles," said Loring.

"I hardly understand that."

"I'm sorry. Let me be brief."

"Thank you," said Charles.

He had passed the neutral ground; his manner was openly insulting, but Loring kept his temper behind his teeth though he felt the striking muscles leap into a ridge against his coat sleeves.

"I have followed this evening a man named Wilbur to this house."

"I understand that you're a friend of Wilbur?"

"I never saw him before to-night."

He saw Geoffrey Charles start, and a shade of bewilderment crossed his face. Then he looked again at Loring with all the manner of one who thinks he is hearing a lie, and a bald lie, at that. Never in his life had Loring so yearned to take a man by the throat.

"I never saw him before to-night," repeated Loring, "but what I have seen this evening—I don't wish to alarm you need-lessly, Mr. Charles, but—"

"Of course not. Pardon me."

And Mr. Charles deliberately took out his watch and glanced at it.

"Go right on," he said. "Don't mind me. My nerves are toler-ably strong, and of course one expects to be a little shocked by anything relating to Wilbur, eh?"

"You infernal puppy!" said Loring behind his teeth.

Aloud: "I first met Wilbur in a gaming house."

"Ah?" said Geoffrey Charles with a smile of annoying un-derstanding, as though this admission helped him to place Loring definitely. But the smile was cut short by a contraction of his lips. It seemed to Loring, indeed, that Charles was labor-ing under a strain of excitement; there was something expect-ant behind his eyes.

Not expectant as far as Loring was concerned. The latter, in fact, gathered that nothing he could say would disturb the big-shouldered youth, but Geoffrey persistently looked past him as though he expected a horror to start out of the wall. The very tinge of pink good living at the back of his cheeks was the more pronounced because of the nervous pallor of the rest of his face.

"And in the gaming house?" suggested Charles.

"What happened there is not of importance—"

"Ah, no. Of course not. Then, to proceed?"

"Except that I gathered that Mr. Wilbur was living under a strain."

"He generally does, I believe."

"Kindly let me finish, Mr. Charles. I mean to imply that Mr. Wilbur acted as a man in mortal fear."

"Really? He must have developed a conscience."

"When I say 'mortal,' I mean that word and no other. Wilbur, Mr. Charles, is in fear of death!"

It pleased him immensely to see that he had driven a point past the guarding nonchalance of Geoffrey Charles. The last tinge of color departed from the face of that self-satisfied gentleman. His voice, too, struck a deeper, harsher note.

"What the devil! Do you mean that—"

"That he has fled to this house either for a shelter from danger, or because, sir, the danger is actually under this roof!"

He saw the glance of Geoffrey Charles waver; then it straightened. Obviously the man believed him, but wished to pretend disbelief.

"Mr. Loring, you are a man of imagination, I see! At this moment you may be surprised to learn that Mr. Wilbur is interviewing Mr. Charles himself!"

He said this as a settling point which banished all fears.

"Exactly," said Loring, staying by his guns. "And in that very room, then, there is danger. A danger so inevitable that Wilbur knows he cannot escape. He may have come to the very trap. Perhaps that room is the trap."

"I assume," said Charles heavily, "that you are sane. As a sane man, I ask you if a doomed man would run into the very jaws of danger—I dismiss the absurd supposition that he could possibly find trouble in this house."

"He may have come like the bird to the snake."

"A fable," sneered Geoffrey Charles.

But he was shaken. His interest was no longer outside of Loring. He fastened earnest eyes on the latter.

"I tell you, sir, my profound conviction: that Wilbur will be a dead man before morning—and if he is in this house his death will occur here."

"There is no inconsiderable accusation in that, Mr. Loring. Do you dare to presume that because of past unpleasantnesses between Mr. Charles and Mr. Wilbur, my uncle would for a moment consider—"

"Ah," said Loring eagerly. "Then there *have* been unpleasant relations between them?"

"Unfortunately, yes."

"I knew it," said Loring beneath his breath.

"Geof!" called a girl's voice, the sound muffled to begin with and then coming clear as she came through a door. "Oh, Geof."

Geoffrey Charles turned his head in haste and put out his hand a little way toward Loring. It was as if he wished to conceal the latter.

"I suppose," he said hastily, "that this concludes matters? I assure you that I shall convey your warning to Mr. Charles."

"No, Mr. Charles, I'm not done. I've followed Wilbur for twenty-five miles. I won't drop him now. I want to see him safe and sound when the dawn comes."

"Geof!"

There was a struggle in the face of Geoffrey Charles; at length he appeared to make up his mind. His frown cleared. "Mr. Charles's daughter is coming," he said. "Perhaps you will wish to tell her of your suspicions?"

"Mr. Charles," cried Loring, "it seems to me you're dodging a matter which is obviously for men to handle!"

And then he saw her coming out of the more brightly lighted part of the hall. The lights glowed in her hair; she came into the shadow and walked toward them smiling.

"Louise wants to tell you, Geof—" she began, and stopped short as she saw the stranger.

Geoffrey Charles stepped back. There was an infinite relief and even, it seemed to Loring, an amount of pleasure in his expression.

"I'll go to Louise, Beatrice," he said. "In the meantime I wish you'd stay here just a moment and hear the strange story my friend here has to tell. Perhaps you can make more out of it than I have. Miss Charles, this is Mr. Samuel Loring, who has called with a warning. He'll tell you about it. Will you excuse me?"

# CHAPTER VI

# BEATRICE

"BUT—" PROTESTED BEATRICE CHARLES faintly. However, Geoffrey was already striding away, laughing over his shoulder as though he rejoiced in her dilemma. She turned to Loring and acknowledged his bow graciously enough. He was too angry to see her. His anger stiffened his body and in his face showed a savage impulse to rush after Geoffrey Charles and arrest his flight.

The girl was frankly curious and frankly afraid. It was the latter expression which struck the eye of Loring when his own vision cleared of its rage. He saw that she was by no means beautiful. She had exquisite bronze hair, masses of it, sea-green eyes to match, and a clear complexion such as comes under the skies of England with all that unpaintable transparency of skin.

Nose and mouth were by no means perfect features; the one was decidedly too small and the other too large. But when she smiled she was wholly charming and she smiled now at the anger of Loring.

"I don't quite understand," she said. "Geoffrey said that you are a friend of his and that you have come with a warning?"

"Miss Charles," said Loring heavily, "you misunderstand. I am not the friend of Mr. Geoffrey Charles."

"Oh."

He explained hastily: "I have never seen him before to-night. As for the warning—it is nothing. Nothing I can talk of to a woman. For the rest—Mr. Charles has placed me in an impossible situation. I save us both from embarrassment by saying good-night."

His violence had made her wince, but for some unknown reason a man in a fighting mood is peculiarly attractive to some women—outdoor women. Beatrice Charles by nature loved a hard-headed horse with wicked tricks under the saddle. She wanted to prolong this singular contrast between the gay-voiced dance rooms and this bit of the sterner outer world. Evening clothes, to be sure, were not exactly her element; she rather welcomed the straight-eyed fury of Loring.

"If you insist, Mr. Loring, of course, I have nothing to say. But I'd like to know how Geoffrey has made you so angry."

"I assure you," said Loring, "that Mr. Geoffrey Charles has nothing whatever to do with my coming here."

"But," she insisted, "I'm afraid he has a great deal to do with your leaving."

It implied, perhaps, that Geoffrey Charles had tied his hands, and the thought made Loring glare. To his astonishment she began to laugh, and he started violently.

"Mr. Loring," she said with amazing directness, "please tell me what it's all about. Geoffrey said you might."

And to *her* amazement, Loring laughed in turn. She had already made up her mind that he was a good deal of a boor; she had even rather liked his boorishness. Now she had to adjust herself and meet him on an infinitely higher plane. He was laughing freely; he made a little gesture of abandonment.

"Mr. Geoffrey Charles," he said, as frankly as she had spoken, "has left me to make an ass of myself before a woman. And no man relishes that. What I came to tell him, I simply cannot tell you. Excuse me, again."

"I have an idea, though," said the girl thoughtfully, "that you *will* tell me before you go. At least, sit down, and think it over."

So saying, she took a chair near the wall and settled the green gauze wrap about her shoulders, so that the white of her throat was outlined against an odd-colored cloud. There was nothing that Loring found to do except to obey the gesture of her hand. He sank into the neighboring chair.

"As a matter of fact," she said, "Geoffrey acted as though he really wanted me to hear the story."

"If I tell you," said Loring, "will you promise to suspend judgment on me? In one word, I've acted in a freakish way to-night. I'm usually tolerably level-headed. If you want—yes, I'll tell you the whole thing. I've an idea that you'll be of more help that Mr. Geoffrey Charles."

She smiled faintly at the distaste with which he turned the name on his tongue.

"Upon my word, Mr. Loring, I'm ready to listen seriously."

Casting back, he saw that all his actions had sprung from such intangible beginnings that the story would make him out decidedly a fool. He looked timidly at her. Even a dog hates to be laughed at. But Beatrice Charles knew all about dogs and horses and certain phases of men. She had outridden them and outgamed them, if the truth must be known, on many an occasion; therefore her respect for manly qualities meant something.

The instant Loring blushed she began to like him immensely. She judged him with the same speed she used when she read the points of a horse. From that moment he would have to prove that he was evil or weak.

"It sounds like a page out of the *Arabian Nights*."

"I love them."

"Well—this is the Twentieth Century. At any rate, what would you do if you saw a man acting under the influence of a great fear—fear of death, I mean?"

"If I were man, I'd try to find out what threatened him, I hope."

He sighed with relief.

"Thank the Lord. Then I can tell you. I did try to find out. I'm still trying, and the man I followed came here. That's why

I'm here; and that's why Mr. Geoffrey Charles left me to be laughed at. Go ahead; I'll endure it."

But she had drawn back a little and looked at him with a changed expression.

It was as eloquent as if she had twitched her skirts aside to make sure of clearing him in passing.

"You followed Mr. Wilbur?" she asked slowly.

"For heaven's sake," growled Loring, "what's the matter with Wilbur? I saw that he was unnerved. But is the man's reputation as leprous as all that?"

"You don't know him?"

"Upon my honor! No more than I know Mr. Geoffrey Charles."

"You've followed a complete stranger?"

"You're not playing fair," he said miserably. "You're giving me a Twentieth Century judgment. I admit I've been freakish; play Harun al-Rashid and see if you can look at the thing with my eyes."

"Of course, I believe you," she said. She repeated it, and then, as though the repetition had actually convinced her, she smiled at him. "About Mr. Wilbur, I can't say. Mostly, the women know very little about him; it seems—you really don't know him?— that he's so bad that even men won't talk of him. Once he had some business relations with my father; I understand Dad is talking to him now. But what do you mean by Mr. Wilbur's fear of death?"

"A mortal agony, on my honor. As if a gun were at his head."

"Then he came here for protection."

"Miss Charles, I may seem to talk like a madman, but since I've come here the conviction grows on me that the danger to Wilbur is already under this roof."

She rose slowly from her chair.

"Mr. Loring!"

"It's only a wild fancy. But I can't be rid of it. I would swear, even, that the murderer of Wilbur is at this moment under this roof."

And as he spoke the cold conviction got hold on him. He stood before her, as pale as the girl. Her eyes left him.

"There's father now. Dad!"

She hurried, almost ran down the hall toward a white-headed man who was walking toward the stairs. He did not seem to hear her or heed her until his step was on the lowest of the stairs and her hand had touched his arm. Then he turned on her and Loring, who was fast approaching.

"Dad, there's an odd message—"

"I've no time for messages."

He snapped the words with such violence that the girl's hand fell. She stared at him in amazement and even Loring started. It was a deeply marked face that scowled down on her, framed in white hair worn rather affectedly long, and a close-trimmed white beard. His hand gripped the rail of the balustrade with strange violence; his whole body was shaken with a tremor which had struck him the moment the girl's hand fell on his arm. He was recovering from a shock.

"Why, Dad!"

"My dear—no time for talk—hurry—"

"But this is terribly important. Mr. Loring, this is my father. Mr. Loring has a strange message to give you about Mr. Wilbur, and—"

"You!" cried Peter Charles, gasping the word. And he stared at Loring as though the latter were a nightmare. "You!" he repeated.

It made the blood of Loring run cold. The sunken eyes of Charles blazed with horror and fear.

"Do you know me?" asked Loring firmly.

"I don't want to know you—and yet I shall better than you expect."

He added rapidly: "Loring—or whatever your name is—I

warn you! I understand everything. I am warned and prepared. If you attempt anything, it is at your peril!"

"Good God!" breathed Loring. "What do you mean?"

He was not answered.

"Beatrice," said her father. "Keep this man in conversation. Don't let him get from your eyes. If he attempts to leave call for help. Better still, call Cunningham now. Send away the guests. No, let them stay. Scandal—damnation—what shall I do?"

And striking the back of his hand against his face, he turned and fled up the stairs like a man pursued.

He disappeared into the darkness of the first turn; then they heard his steps hurrying faintly down the upper hall, while the girl and Loring looked at each other. She had drawn back from him a little.

## CHAPTER VII

# THE SHOT

"**I GIVE YOU** my word," said Loring quietly, "that you will not offend me if you call one or more of the servants to watch me."

"Who are you?"

"My name is the one I have given—Samuel Loring. My business—amusement—wandering—in fact, there's no way I can reassure you, except to beg you to take me at face-value. Your father suspects me. It is only proof to me that something connected with Wilbur has made him sorely afraid.

"I tell you, he has seen in Wilbur's face the same thing I saw there. You could see the reflection of it in your father's eyes—fear of death. I can only give you my word of honor that I am here with clean hands and clean intentions. You believe me?"

All at once his heart went out to her in admiration and gratitude. She was colorless with fear, but she was by no means on the verge of hysteria. She looked him straight in the eye.

"I do believe you."

"Then, go one step farther. Let me act."

"What do you want to do?"

"Follow your father."

"Alone? Would you do that?"

"A thousand times. Yes."

"No, no! Let me call Geoffrey. You and he can go together."

"You don't trust me, then?"

40

"How can I—absolutely, after what father has just said. No, if you move to leave me, I give you my word, I shall cry out and alarm the house!"

Loring ground his teeth together.

"Miss Charles, I tell you there is a murder impending in this house!"

She swallowed.

"Nevertheless, you stay here! And—and keep back from me, sir! Dad!"

She called out as her father rushed down the stairs. At the bottom he cast one frantic glance at them, hesitated, and then, throwing up his arm like a man distracted, fled again across the hall. The girl moaned with fear; indeed, even Loring was shaken by the horror-stricken face of Charles as he had paused at the foot of the stairs.

Then, with the opening of a door, a flood of music rushed out at them from the dance rooms and was closed in again.

"We must get help," said the girl faintly. "Call them out of the ballroom. Quick!"

"Let me try alone. There's no time for a crowd—I'm armed—" he touched his pocket.

"Call the others, I say. Quick! Run to that door!"

But he had hardly taken a step forward when he was stopped by a sound which was like the closing of a great door, except that it was neater, more precise, and carried clearly through the great house. It was the unmistakable report of a revolver.

The scream of Beatrice cut into Loring's ear, but he had already halted and twitched around with the speed of a snapping whiplash. There she ran before him, racing as fast as her skirts allowed. Instinctively he knew that she was running toward rather than away from the danger, and he lunged after her in pursuit.

But she had a flying start and she knew the way. Around corners she darted with Loring swinging wide behind her, whipping his short-nosed revolver into his hand as he raced.

The music had stopped in the ballroom. A horrible silence had fallen on the house.

Before him she cast open a door; then her cry again rang back at him. Geoffrey Charles, white of face in the gloomy hall, was hurtling forward from the opposite direction, but Loring reached the door first, and saw the tragedy's aftermath.

Beatrice was on her knees beside the body of Wilbur. The dead man lay on his face, his arms and legs sprawling oddly.

The stunned mind of Loring took in singularly small details—the way one of the trouser-legs was hitched high up above the shoe till the sock showed and the bare flesh above it. Beatrice had caught her hand to her bosom and was looking in mute agony at her father.

And there was Peter Charles as tall and gaunt as the dead man—and looking more dead than alive himself. He stood with his right hand half extended, as though the horror had frozen it in that position. His mouth gaped a little and his eyes were dull, as if the blazing terror which Loring had seen burning in them had burned them out and now left them lifeless.

Then a voice shouted at his ear: "My God, Uncle Peter, you've killed him!"

"No!" screamed Beatrice, and leaping to her feet, she rushed to the inert form of her father and surrounded him with her arms. "No, no, no!"

To the end of his days, Loring would never forget the white anguish of the face that looked back over her shoulder in terror of the hand of the law which would, so soon, take that wretched man.

All of this had filled two seconds. Vaguely he scented the sharp tang of new-burned powder; and vaguely he noted that it was familiar and not unpleasant. Then there was a rush of many feet, many voices down the hall from the ballroom.

"You!" commanded Loring, returning to his senses, and he gripped the thick shoulder of Geoffrey Charles and jerked the big man around.

"Go down there. Meet that mob and turn them away."

Geoffrey Charles seemed too stunned to understand.

He was wailing; "Why did you do it? Uncle Peter, why in the name of God, did you do it?"

"You fool!" snarled Loring. "Shut up or I'll break your head! Do you want the whole crowd to see this? Stop them and turn them back."

He stepped aside and himself stopped the rush of men with outspread arms.

"Go back. No entrance here. An unfortunate accident. Nothing of importance. You must absolutely go back. Tell the ladies that there is nothing for concern. Here, you!"

He caught a fellow who attempted to dodge under his arm and yanked that unfortunate back with a force that nearly snapped the neck vertebrae.

But big Geoffrey Charles stepped to his side and took command, giving smooth directions. In spite of his earlier prejudice against the man, Loring could not but admire his quiet way. The man had nerve and self-control, after the first outbreak of natural grief.

"And when you've herded them out, telephone to the police," said Loring quietly at the ear of Charles. "I'll take care of Wilbur."

Young Charles flashed a glance of understanding and nodded; Loring went back into the library. The dull eyes of Peter Charles lighted with a shadow of the old horror when he saw Loring again.

"You've come back to face us, have you?" he growled. "Beatrice, didn't I tell you to keep him under your eye? But we'll hold him; Geoffrey! Halloo!"

The girl promptly covered his mouth with her hands, gasping. "Dad, I did stay with him. He didn't leave me except to come here. And—he wasn't any friend of Wilbur's. You can trust him. But—don't talk!"

She turned to Loring, still holding one of her father's hands.

"They won't take him?" she pleaded. "You—Geoffrey—you won't let them take him?"

"Whatever can be done, I'm here to serve you. You can be sure of that. I've come like a raven, croaking. Now that the damage is done—I want you to use me."

"I believe you. Mr. Loring, I believe you."

"Let me do one thing first. I'll return at once and take your orders. Will you turn your head, Miss Charles?"

She obeyed with a shudder, and Loring stooped and gathered the dead body in his arms. It was an awkward burden, but strangely light. Long fear seemed to have burned away the body of the man; his soul, no doubt, had been dead before the terror began. Yet, with a certain reverence, Loring carried his grisly burden into the hall and delivered it, with curt directions, to the horrified group of servants who waited there.

He returned, and dragged a corner of the rug over a spot on the floor. He found Charles attempting to talk, and his daughter eagerly, almost fiercely, hushing him.

"But have they searched the premises? Have they—"

"Hush, Dad. You mustn't talk. Not even to me. Not a word. For God's sake not a word!"

All at once the old man pushed her away to arm's length.

"Beatrice!"

"Yes?"

"You don't think—"

"Of course, I don't. But come with me. We'll talk later on. Don't—"

She was handling him as if he had become intellectually a child. And indeed, fear seemed to have crumbled the brain of the man.

"Beatrice!"

His voice had risen almost to the pitch of a scream.

"Look at me!"

She cast at Loring a glance so full of terror, sorrow, and an appeal for help, that the big man winced.

Then she looked at her father.

"Yes, dear."

"Beatrice, you don't think that I did it?"

"No, no! I know you didn't!"

He flung her aside and rushed to Loring. There was a terrible entreaty in his appeal: "And you—you don't think they can touch me? You don't think I did it?"

"Certainly not!"

"Don't say it that way!"

"Mr. Charles. Keep your nerve. Pull yourself together. First, we'll get out of this room."

He met the gratitude of Beatrice's eyes and took the arm of Charles to lead him like a child, but the financier tore himself away.

"You do think it. And you—Beatrice! No, not a step out of the room till I've told you everything!"

Geoffrey Charles had come to the door. He entered and closed it.

"A murderer!" Peter Charles was repeating over and over again in a strangled voice. "A murderer!"

"Geoffrey, my boy, my dear Geoffrey!" He went to the big fellow and clung to him pathetically. It was horrible beyond measure to Loring to see the man cringe so from his fate.

"You don't think I'm guilty, Geoffrey? You don't think I'm guilty?"

"Never in a thousand years. But don't talk now. You mustn't turn us into witnesses. Wait until the lawyers have told you how to—"

"You, too," groaned Charles. He looked about at them as if he were beset by wolves, "Everyone of you! You think I—I—"

He could not speak it, and finished with an eloquent gesture to the place where Wilbur had lain.

"Do you think—I leave it to you as a man of common sense, Mr. Loring—do you think I'd risk my neck to kill such a dog as Wilbur? Is it possible?"

"I close my ears; I refuse to hear you. Mr. Charles, what your nephew has said is the truth. You must wait until your lawyers have advised with you about the plan of your defense."

"I'll not wait. I've got to give you the story while it's hot in my brain."

Geoffrey touched Loring's arm and whispered: "Let him talk. It may quiet him. Besides, maybe he's right."

It was as if Loring were invited into the inner circle of a guilty secret.

"I've got to tell every fact," ran on Peter Charles, still searching every face for a trace of belief. "I've got to tell it before the—the police—"

There was a moan from Beatrice.

"They'll try to trip me up. They'll make me forget. I know their methods. But I'll tell the story to you and the three of you will back me up, eh? You, Loring, you have no interest in defending me. I want you to hear most of all. But first—I've to think!"

He cast himself into a chair and buried his face in his hands; the men exchanged glances; Beatrice dropped to her knees beside her father.

"A drink, Geoffrey," gasped Peter Charles. "My head spins. I can't think."

The other poured a stiff bracer from the decanter and took it to Charles and the latter, still veiling his face with one hand, tossed off the liquor as if it had been so much water.

After that he buried his face in both hands again and became more quiet. The convulsive shudders which had been passing through his body at intervals no longer shook him.

What went on behind the screen of those hands, wondered Loring, as the strong brain of the financier rallied from the shock? How was he mustering the truth of innocence? Or how was he building lies to defend his guilt?

At length Charles raised his head, and Loring saw with infinite relief that the hunted-animal look had gone from the eyes of the man; in its place was a desperate determination. He began to speak, talking to the two men, chiefly; now and then glancing at the brilliant head of his daughter; sometimes taking one of her hands in both of his.

## CHAPTER VIII

# NARRATIVE OF MR. CHARLES

**"CUNNINGHAM CAME TO** me while I was talking in the library with McBride. He had his head as high as ever but he looked as if he had seen a ghost. I saw that there was something wrong and stepped away from McBride and took the card from the tray. I couldn't believe my eyes when I saw the name of Wilbur. Joseph Wilbur, without mistake. He had always affected a printed card in big type.

"It was a shock. When I recovered I looked Cunningham in the eye.

" 'Tell him that it's impossible that I should see him,' I said.

" 'I've already ventured to tell him that,' said Cunningham.

"He was deadly serious.

" 'Tell him the same thing again and see him out of the house.' I was very angry. 'You're big enough to handle him by yourself; but if he shows signs of making a fuss, call a couple of the others and take him by force.'

" 'Is that final, sir?' said Cunningham.

" 'Absolutely!'

"Cunningham turned around slowly. Once, on the way to the door, he stopped as though he wanted to come back and speak to me. I remember that McBride grinned at me when I went back to him.

" 'Ghosts walking?' he said.

"It made me start. 'Very nearly as bad as that,' I answered.

"We fell into our talk again, but my mind kept going back

to Joseph Wilbur. Sure enough, Cunningham returned. He stopped at the door and I went to him at once.

" 'What does this mean?' I asked him. I was furious.

" 'Please don't blame me, sir,' said Cunningham, and indeed the poor fellow was quaking. 'I tried to talk to him and explain, but—I wish you'd just step out and say the final word.'

"I was feeling fairly happy. And I admit that I felt a rather ghoulish pleasure at the thought of seeing the man and marking his pain. Of course, it was impossible to meet him in the open hall where others might stumble on us together. It would have made too many opportunities for talk. I told Cunningham to bring Wilbur in here, to my study, and then I made my excuses to McBride.

"The devil seemed to be in the man. He was jesting, but he hit close to the truth.

" 'Cross yourself before you meet the evil eye,' said McBride, and laughed as he went out the door.

"For some reason that made me thoughtful. I came in here to my study with my mind full of the Wilbur I used to know and how he had used me—and abused me. I remembered what a big, powerful, good-natured chap he had been in spite of his villainy.

"Then the door opened, and just as McBride had prophesied, I saw a ghost with an evil eye!

"A shambling skeleton—no more—that was all that was left of big Joseph Wilbur. Why, the man had been successful in his dirty schemes chiefly because he had such an imposing front of careless benevolence. You would have said that he was too big to be mean and too gentle to hurt a mouse.

"But the Wilbur I saw at the door of my study was another man. Not a man. He was more like a rat. Yellow-skinned, his lips wasted away and fleshless, and he had a nervous trick of compressing his mouth hard at intervals. His eyes were buried in deep purple shadow. Rat, all rat; his inner nature had come up into his face!

"Under that shock, I could not speak until he had slipped through and closed the door behind him in Cunningham's face. For a moment he let his weight lean against the door and gaped at me. Then he fell into one of his acting parts. He straightened, shook back his shoulders, nodded cheerfully to me, and came over in front of the fire, rubbing his hands together.

"You would have thought, from his actions, that he was some rich man bringing Christmas cheer into a hovel. But from his face you have seen a vulture come to destroy happiness.

"Why didn't I throw him out the door again? Why didn't I smash my fist into that rat face there and then and throw his carcass to Cunningham? I felt the temptation. But I wanted to feed myself with the horrible spectacle of the man. I wanted to remember how he had once wronged me, and then see him merely as the skeleton at my feast. Well, I'm punished for it.

"I kept wondering how he could possibly start a conversation with me. But no matter how wasted his body was, his mind was still quick-acting.

" 'I seem to be a capable prophet, Peter,' he said.

"That established the tone of the conversation—on his side friendly familiarity. It took my breath; I could not answer.

" 'You remember when I told you how you would settle down in the country? And here you are, Peter!'

"He rolled the name gently over his tongue as if it were a charm that would give him power over me.

" 'I remember that prophecy,' I growled at him. 'You said I'd wind up in the country with a cow and a hat and stack of straw if I didn't forget some of my nursery rhyme morality.'

"I wondered how he'd take that blow. No one could ever judge Wilbur or outguess him.

"He put back his head and laughed heartily; looking through that sound, as you might say, I saw the ghost of the old Wilbur I had known teetering back and forth before the fire and laughing in his deep, mellow voice.

" 'Did I put it as strongly as that?' he said. 'Yes, I used to

*He hurried on again and slipped through the same door.*

lecture you pretty stiffly now and then. But it was all for your own good—and I see that you've profited by it!'

"You see how that snake had twisted my own words against me?

" 'Profited by your advice?' I echoed.

" 'Why, certainly. You live in a palace, Peter, a veritable palace. And who started you? What were you when I found you?'

" 'What was I when you left me?' I asked him.

"He brushed the question into thin air.

" 'We pay with pain for the greatest lessons,' said the scoundrel. It sickened me to hear him and yet I was amused.

" 'Yes, we pay with pain,' he echoed himself.

"Just then the wind picked up a gust of rain and smashed it against the side of the house, and then went howling over the roof. There was a terrible change in the face of Wilbur.

" 'Not yet!' he gasped. 'Not yet.'

"He winced around and looked at the clock.

" 'That's the right time, isn't it?' he said.

" 'Of course,' I answered.

"He began to breathe more freely, but he had to wipe the sweat from his forehead; I was breathing hard myself.

" 'Well,' said he, 'you see that my nerves are badly shattered. The man of action pays for his activity with blood, and I have always been a man of action. You'll grant me that, Peter?'

"There was a sort of whine in his voice that I noticed for the first time. I never really guessed before how thoroughly beaten he was. I don't deny that it gave me a hot thrill of pleasure to see that dog shudder under the whip. I almost thought, for an instant, that it was his conscience that bothered him. Which only goes to show that I was still deceived.

" 'Well,' he went on, 'we all have our ups and downs, and just now you'd be amused to know how thoroughly down I am.'

"He laughed without mirth.

" 'Yes,' I answered him, 'that would amuse me.'

"He pretended not to let my words sting him.

" 'So far down,' he went on, 'that for the sake of twenty thousand dollars—well, I'd almost mortgage my soul.'

" 'What?' I said. 'Have you saved as much as that? Have you still a soul to mortgage?'

"You would not believe that the astonishing rascal could laugh at that? But he did. He put back his head and his voice rang like a bell.

" 'By heavens, Peter,' he said, 'you have improved immensely with time. I knew that you had millions, but I didn't dream that you had a more priceless thing—a sense of humor. What is a man without a sense of humor? An engine without a governor; a barbarian; a brute.'

" 'Meaning that I was a brute before?'

" 'There you are in your absolute vein again,' he chuckled. 'But I rejoice to find you so developed. You were always that way, though. You went up a step at a time, but you stuck to every gain. And since you now have a sense of humor, of course you'll appreciate the absurdity of my position. Imagine such a man as I in desperate need of twenty thousand dollars?'

"All at once the easy light went out of his eyes and he stared at me like a starved man. What he saw in my face must have given him a hope, for he went on eagerly: 'Of course, the need won't extend over any great length of time—ten days—two weeks, at the most.

" 'And don't you feel like laughing, Peter, to think of Joseph Wilbur in such a corner? Think of what I have done? Of the men and money I have swayed? You remember when Albert T. Gloster forced his way into my office and dropped on his knees and begged me to save him with half a million? And here I am in as bad a case for twenty thousand!'

" 'I think you kicked Gloster out of your office, if I remember correctly.'

" 'What a memory you have,' nodded Wilbur in admiration. 'That's one of the great causes of your success. You never forget.'

" 'Neither the good nor the bad that men do me.'

" 'But to get to the point,' he said hurriedly, 'consider how little, how nothing, it would be for you to sign a check for twenty thousand—or even just a little more? Think how little it would be and yet how much it would mean to no less a person than your old comrade and partner, Joseph Wilbur himself!'

"I was so amazed—though he had been leading up to it gradually enough—that I had to blink and look at him again before I understood. Joseph Wilbur himself had dared not only to come back and face me but to beg for money!"

# CHAPTER IX

# NARRATIVE OF
# MR. CHARLES CONTINUED

**"ALL AT ONCE** I broke into a hearty laugh. It did me an infinite amount of good to laugh in his face. All the spite which I had fed during those years seemed to come out in the sound and when I stopped laughing I had to fight myself to keep from springing at his throat.

" 'Do you remember a night in this same month of April? It was the night of Black Friday, April the thirteenth. Do you remember that night years and years ago?'

" 'I was never so keen a head at remembering as you,' smiled Wilbur, but I saw that he was trembling. 'On the other hand—'

"I cut in: 'That night *I* went to you. That night *I* dropped on my knees before you and begged you to help me. Not with money. But only by clearing me and proving to the world that I had not been dishonest.

" 'You could have freed me with a single word. But instead, you let me be damned. I remembered perfectly. I even remember what you said. The words have been burning into me all these years: 'Peter, you are a charming boy, but you have always been a fool. There is only one class of people in the world that gets no mercy. They are the fools. Get up and get out!'

" 'But I only use one part of what you said: "Wilbur, get out. You pariah! You filthy, leper-handed sneak and thief, get out before I tear your heart out!"'

"And in the face of my rage that devil said: 'Tut, tut! Who would believe that little Peter could not only remember my words but actually improve on them. For I admire emotional acting—yes, I admire it intensely!'

"All at once he cast off his manner.

" 'I see the truth. You have never forgiven me? Ah, Peter, you do not know what had been going on in my soul the night of that Black Friday! You do not know the agony which made me speak so inhumanly to you on that night. But I see that the words have always been whips over your head. I retract them. But I must do more? Yes, and I shall. Far more. You think I am proud? No, Peter, Joseph Wilbur is no longer proud.'

"He gathered himself up with a sad face. I was between laughter and rage, seeing him, still acting, still playing one of his rôles.

" 'Joseph Wilbur has lost his pride. He debases himself before you.'

"And before I could prevent him, he had cast himself on the floor and literally groveled while he hugged my knees against his bony chest.

" 'Peter,' he gasped, 'for God's sake—or the sake of the devil— for the sake of your scorn, or your pity—have mercy on me. Have mercy on me.'

"I spurned him away. I tingled with hatred and a wish to get my hands on him.

"He rose, wiping a thin thread of blood from his mouth. I remember that his handkerchief was a huge, snowy, spotless piece of linen—such a handkerchief as the old Joseph Wilbur always carried.

" 'Is that irrevocable?' he asked me.

"I could only curse him wildly.

" 'Then,' he said, drawing himself up, we are damned and lost together!'

"And I believed him. I cannot tell why it was that his accent passed through me with unspeakable horror and belief. It was as though his skinny hands were pulling me down into one grave with him. As I hope for life, I believed him as I would have believed a voice from the tomb. And yet I knew that he was only acting a rôle. I knew that out of his inexhaustible supply of tricks and false shows he had merely drawn another specimen, trying to influence me with fear where pity had failed.

"He turned and looked at the clock.

" 'You have five—four minutes left in which to act. Peter, will you save me and yourself, or will you allow us both to go to terrible, inescapable ruin?'

"I recoiled from him, and yet I managed to laugh.

" 'Listen, boy, fool!' he said. 'I have always detested you and your mock-religious front. I know you and your black heart. As bad as mine. Worse, because the world has never been in much doubt about me. I have always hated you. And now, I swear I hardly know which I had rather do, live on in the same world with you and your millions, or die and draw you into death with me. Not death alone, but miserable shame and disgrace. You hear?

" 'I have come to your house to-night. I have let myself be seen. The world knows that I do not love you; and the world knows that you hate me. What would public opinion say, Peter, if I died in this room? How far would you have to walk to the gallows? What would your power avail you then, Peter?'

"Every word he spoke sent a thrill of conviction through me, but I only laughed at him.

" 'Nonsense,' I said. 'It would be a pretty thing. Very neat. But you cannot bluff me out of twenty thousand dollars by threatening to kill yourself in my house. Because, Wilbur, among your other loathsome vices, cowardice is the worst. You are afraid to lift your hand against yourself.'

"And I sneered at him.

"He cut short my triumph with a cry that I can hear still.

" 'Idiot!' he moaned. 'Do you think I'm still acting a part? No, no. This is real. Not by my own hand, but by the hand of another. They have pursued me. They are at this moment in your house—my murderers! Where they find me they shall strike me; and where they find me, by the eternal heavens, shall be here, in your study, to damn you with the guilt of my murder!'

"I was terribly moved. Was it possible, I thought, that the twenty thousand dollars was the actual blood price for which he was in danger of death?

"But, no. I knew the scoundrel too well. When I had made out the check he would laugh in my face; and then I *would* be tempted to murder. Yet there was an air of reality—the terror of the man seemed so wonderfully acted that I began to tremble. What if a ghost of truth should be in this? And there I stood, not even armed.

"Then I resolved to go and get my revolver, come back, sit down with Wilbur and quietly wait until his threatened time had elapsed. It would be a marvelous way of exposing his sham. And I knew that he hated worse than death to have the mask torn from his face.

"So I left the study and hurried toward my room. The moment I started to hurry a conviction fell on me that what he had said was true and that he was actually in peril of his life in my house. I began to run.

"On the stairs my daughter stopped me. You, Loring, were behind her. When she mentioned that you had followed Wilbur here, what he had said rushed back upon my mind. I felt, madly enough, that you were the destined murderer, and I called to her to watch you. Then I rushed upstairs to my room and opened the drawer where my revolver—"

**AT THIS** point Beatrice lifted her fallen head and looking her father in the face caught a deep, short breath of agony. He started, and patted her hands anxiously. Then he turned and glanced eagerly into the faces of Loring and Geoffrey.

"The revolver was not there! Perhaps I had mislaid it. I could not tell. I hurried down the stairs again, passed Beatrice in the hall with Loring, and, hardly knowing what I did, except that I must keep the danger from Wilbur, rushed back to the study.

"The moment I entered I found him crouched in the corner

and as soon as I saw the quick glancing rat-eyes I swore to myself that the fellow was indeed acting—over-acting!

" 'Now,' said I, forcing myself to become calm again, 'I want you to see that I am looking facts in the face. You are here alone with me. You say that the time of your life is about to end and that a murderer is about to step into this room and kill you.'

"I chuckled, regaining firmness as I enumerated the facts.

" 'But you see,' I went on, 'that this door opens into a hall where people are continually moving back and forth from the ballroom. Hence, it is impossible for the murderer to enter by that door, and if he should enter he could never escape.

" 'There is no window. This study is never used except at night and is entirely artificially lighted. There a ventilator or two. That is all. Yes, there is that other door opening on the veranda. You see how heavy it is? It is locked. No, but now I lock it with the only key in existence and withdraw the key from the lock.'

"I did as I said, and tossed the key on the floor. When this was done, the blood crept slowly back into the parchment colored face of Wilbur. He rose, and staggered as he reached his feet.

" 'God be praised,' said the hypocrite solemnly. 'And to think that you, Peter, have saved me!'

"I could have laughed in his face.

" 'So you have dodged out of the difficulty?' I said. 'You admit that you are now safe?'

" 'Safe?' he cried. 'You fool, it is only postponed. As surely as if God himself had uttered my doom, I shall be murdered, now, to-morrow, or the day after. No matter when, the blow will fall. But I congratulate you, Peter. My blood will not be on your head. And yet—is it possible that they will not get at me at the hour they threatened?'

" 'Who?' I asked.

" 'Why should I not tell you?' he said, grinning at me in a ghastly way. 'For the moment I tell you, you also are doomed. The moment you have the knowledge one of two things happens. Either you become their tool or their victim. Why not? Isn't that a blacker curse to put on you than the gallows?'

"He stepped closer to me and cupped his hands at his lips to whisper in my ear, but I thrust him away with a shudder of mortal loathing.

"He said something, I hardly know what, for I drowned his voice by cursing him. And before he could speak again I heard a faint sound of metal on metal. Wilbur, also, heard it? He cast at me one glance of agony, and then backed against the wall in that corner, staring at the door.

"I had not located the faint scratching sound before, but now I followed the direction of his glance and knew that it came from the lock of the door which opened on the veranda.

" 'The door,' whispered Wilbur. 'God in heaven, the door!'

"Utterly bewildered, I looked at the floor. There lay the only key for that door, and yet, as certainly as I sit here, I heard the lock turn, click, and then the door was pushed slowly open.

"That was the chief horror of the thing. I could have stood it, I think, if the door had been suddenly cast open, and a masked man, say, had appeared in the opening and fired the shot that killed Wilbur. The door opened slowly, as though the incarnate fiend on the other side knew that his very slowness of movement was paralyzing us and keeping us from action as the eye of the snake is supposed to paralyze the bird.

"It opened. The black slit of the night outside yawned wider.

"There was no face; no sign of the body of the murderer. All of that was swallowed by the blackness. But a hand appeared carrying a shining revolver. I saw the gun jerk up with the explosion; then Wilbur caught his hands to his breast and pitched slowly forward to the floor. It was as if a hand had reached up and lowered him gently.

"When I looked at the door it was closed again. I sprang at it and tried to wrench it open, but as my hand fell on the knob I heard the click of the turned lock. Then I jumped back into the corner. There was a scream farther away in the house, hurrying footfalls, and then the door flew open—you know the rest!

"And I ask you, gentlemen—dear Geoffrey—my friend Loring! Print my words indelibly in your brains. They are my proof of innocence. If the lawyers trip me up, you know the whole tale. You will be able to substantiate me. Promise!"

## CHAPTER X

# THE ARREST

**GEOFFREY WENT TO** the older man with a reassurance, but Loring slipped softly to the door into the hall and cast it suddenly open. Cunningham, the door-keeper, stood there, blinking at the light which flashed from the study into his face. But before Loring could speak the servant announced: "Mr. Charles, the police."

What followed in the study Loring did not see, he deliberately turned his back on that painful scene, and letting the sergeant of detectives know that he would be waiting in the hall for any questions they might wish to ask him, he began to pace up and down impatiently.

He had no desire to be gone. He felt that he had passed through a door that had been locked behind him and he was definitely entered into this affair. Wilbur, Peter Charles, the girl, Geoffrey, all in a few moments had been foisted into his life. He could not simply step into the night and out of their destinies.

Neither did he even wish to abandon the affair. In all his adventurous life he had never come upon so many exciting entanglements and he was determined to see the matter through.

His chief emotion was one of profound sympathy for that clean-eyed girl, dragged into this horrible shame and scandal, sympathy for big, boyish Geoffrey Charles, and even for his uncle. He told himself frankly that he did not like Peter Charles, his whining, his hysteria, his clinging to the hand of Beatrice as he talked for his life. Neither was Loring entirely satisfied by the remarkable story of Wilbur and Charles in the study.

On the other hand, it was almost too strange to be a lie. There were, it seemed to Loring, only two possibilities. Either Peter Charles was absolutely innocent, or else he was a consummately clever villain.

Mustering probabilities, it seemed absurd that such a man as Peter Charles should risk his life in order to take that of such a creature as Wilbur, but Loring knew well enough that logic has little to do with murder. What gave him most pause and pointed the accusing finger most strangely at Peter Charles was that stop in the middle of his smooth story—that stop when Beatrice had looked up sharply at her father, as though she feared what he might say next. Over and over again Loring rehearsed the words and gestures leading to that crisis. Why had Peter Charles stopped at the moment when he said that he opened the drawer to take out his revolver?

At this point in Loring's reflections the door to the study opened; he heard the shrill pitched voice of Charles declaiming rapidly. Then the closing door closed out the sound, and one of the police came toward him down the hall. He had possibly been chosen for the force because of bulk, but he also had a broad, shrewd, Irish face.

"You're Mr. Loring?" he said.

"Yes."

"You were the second in the room after the shooting?"

"I was."

The keen eye went over Loring's clothes.

"You were at the dance?"

"I was not."

"Just dropped in for a call, maybe?"

"No."

"A friend of the family, of course?"

"No."

The policeman took out a pad and a pencil. "I'll get some of this. Mind telling me just what brought you here?"

"Not at all. I followed Wilbur."

"Friend of Wilbur's?"

"No."

Obviously he must not bring the mention of Buttricks into his story.

He went on: "I passed Wilbur in the street. He was acting in a frantic manner, stopping now and then and looking behind him as though he were pursued. As a matter of fact, he was acting so queerly that people stopped to watch him in spite of the rain. I saw him get into a taxicab—I had nothing on my hands to do—and I decided to follow him."

"H-m-m! Don't take much to get you in action, Mr. Loring."

"It doesn't," replied Loring dryly.

"You just saw this Wilbur pass by and made up your mind to follow him?"

"Listen to me, officer; did you ever see a scared youngster?"

"Sure. Why?"

"Was it hard to tell that he was scared?"

"No harder than it is to see a lamp in a window."

"And isn't it a good deal easier to tell when a grown man is in fear of his life? Doesn't it come out at his eyes?"

"There ain't much doubt about that. I've seen 'em wild in the face!"

"Very well. Wilbur was wild in the face. I followed him over a good part of Manhattan and finally he came here. I'd come so far that I couldn't turn back. I entered the house. I tried to get to Mr. Charles to tell him my conviction that a mortal danger threatened Wilbur. Naturally the people in the house were suspicious. I was still trying to convince them that I must see Mr. Charles when the shot was fired. That's all."

"You were waiting all by yourself? Nobody was with you when the shot was fired?"

Loring smiled at the open trap.

"I was talking to Miss Charles. She ran for the study. I followed her."

The policeman sighed. "All right. Just gimme your full name and address."

Loring complied and he had hardly finished dictating when the people came out of the study. Geoffrey, Peter Charles, and Beatrice walked first; the police were behind. In the hall a servant brought the coat and hat of the master of the house. Beatrice was insisting that she accompany her father to the door of the jail, but he would have none of it.

"It's only a nasty mess," said the financier. "Nothing more than a silly mess. A year from now we'll never think of this affair, except when we go into the study, eh, Geoffrey? And now, my dear, don't worry. I'll go by myself, with these gentlemen."

From his voice alone one would have judged him to be perfectly steady of nerve, perfectly cheerful; but his face betrayed him. He had aged years since Loring last looked at him. What hurt Loring most was the forced calm of the girl. From the very beginning he was confident that she had made up her mind about the guilt of her father. When the farewells were over he would have followed the party out of the front door, but Geoffrey Charles stopped him.

"It's quite late, Mr. Loring," he said, "and the night has turned cold. Why don't you stay here and we'll drive you in in the morning."

Loring refused politely; they would not wish to have a stranger on their hands at this time, he was sure. But here Beatrice Charles joined her cousin.

"Father particularly asked us to keep you overnight," she said.

She shook her head at Geoffrey, who had flashed a significant look.

"Why should we be mysterious, Geoffrey? Mr. Loring is not a fool; he knows that we want to have him as a friend. We need him, and we're going to rivet his testimony to our side of the case if we can."

It was sufficient frankness to stagger Loring.

"You may be sure," he said, "that I hope all this matter is smoothed out pleasantly for your father. I am confident it will be."

"There!" cried Beatrice. "That's exactly what we don't want! Don't you see, Mr. Loring? If you leave us now your 'polite' interest is very apt to fade away. The district attorney gets you in his hands and twists your story to fit his own purposes. Have I not heard about lawyer tricks?

"We want you to stay here just overnight—have breakfast with us—find out that we're simply ordinary, kind people, no very great deal different from your own family, or from any other gentlefolk. If we can make you feel that way about us, you'll have more than a 'polite' interest; you'll be on our side. And that's where I want you. Now I've let you peep around the corner and see my position. You'll stay, Mr. Loring?"

Loring saw Geoffrey smiling at the girl's animation and guessed that he had more than a cousinly interest in Beatrice.

"I think you really wish me to," said Loring gravely. "And, of course, if that's the case, I'm delighted to stay."

He was charmed with her. She rang as true as gun-metal. For some reason he kept wishing that she were not the daughter of Peter Charles—he kept trying to visualize the mother of the girl and seeing her as the source of all the qualities of Beatrice, body and mind.

"You'll see that Mr. Loring is comfortable, Geoffrey?" she was saying. "But I forget. You must be hungry, Mr. Loring. Let me have something prepared for you—a cup of coffee, at least."

And all the time, behind her smile, he saw the gloom of her concern. She was eating her heart out for her father. Loring wanted to take her hand and tell her with short, strong words just how much he admired her courage.

He refused the offer, told her good-night, and went up the

stairs with Geoffrey. The latter led the way, half a step in advance, and Loring looked him over in detail. He estimated an advantage of fifteen pounds on the side of Geoffrey, and then he chuckled to himself. Unconsciously he had been considering Geoffrey as an antagonist, but perhaps that was a result of the tone of their first meeting.

Geoffrey opened the door into a big yellow bedroom which even the electric light filled with the warmth of sunshine. Not that there was a single shade of color used throughout. From the ivory walls, touched with the glow and depth of amber, to the rich gold in the rug, all was a continual play on the yellow note and variation from it. Loring was not an artist; he only knew that he was pleased. The room seemed like home; it gave him the effect of something remembered.

Indeed, it brought home to him the value of wealth more sharply than almost any experience in his life. The narrow, heavy folds of the blue curtains made the ceiling seem a prodigious height above him; the house of Peter Charles became greater— Samuel Loring became less.

"I hope you'll sleep well," Geoffrey Charles was saying. "And don't let Beatrice's excitement affect your dreams. She's troubled, but, of course, all this mess will blow over and my uncle will come out clean-handed."

"Of course. As for Miss Charles. I feel that she flattered me, and what she said won't bother me at all."

He felt that Geoffrey was looking him over from the corner of his eye.

"I'm glad of that," he said. "She doesn't lose her head this way very often."

And there was a hidden sting in that remark. Geoffrey took the poison out by adding: "By the way, I was rather ugly when you first came in. I hope you won't remember that."

"My dear Mr. Charles," said Loring hastily, delighted by the boyish embarrassment of Geoffrey, "as a matter of fact I was in an ugly position. No wonder you doubted me."

He said good-night and when the door closed on Geoffrey, Loring walked about the room. It was more the manner of one who takes possession of a permanent residence than that of one who occupies a lodging for the night.

# CHAPTER XI

# LORING WALKS BY NIGHT

**THE END OF** the room was filled by one of the huge bow-windows. When a man is tired, windows are annoying; when his mind is alert they are a pleasant relief with their outlook on the world, be it even the blank wall on the other side of the alley. Loring was wide awake. He took his pipe from its case, packed it firmly for a long smoke, and drawing back each of the three curtains sat down with the windows on three sides. But the soft depths of the chair did not bring him closer to sleep.

So surrounded by glass, he seemed sitting in the open night looking over the grounds of the mansion, after he had turned off the light in the room. The glow of the new-lighted pipe fell away as the ash gathered over the fire. The rising smoke he saw only as an intermittent film which made his prospect dimmer now and again.

Outside, the lines of poplars glimmered faintly away into complete dark. To the right, in the distance, the stars spotted the lake and the solemn balustrade of white stone went like an arm halfway around it. He saw these things as much by imagination as by the use of his eyes. The sky was clear, the wind was dying, and the lawn-terraces sent up a ground-smell of delicate fragrance.

Presently the bow-window to his left flooded with light. A form came to the square nearest him and as she raised her arm to the drawcord, Loring saw the glint on the bronze hair of

68

Beatrice Charles. Then the curtain swept before her and he had only the pale outlining of the window as the light stole around the edges of the velvet. Yet that kept his attention more than the outside night. It drew him back suddenly and strongly to the problem of the murder of that night.

Cunningham was his answer to the mystery.

From the moment he laid eyes on the stalwart fellow at the door, that evening, he had put him down as a man capable of almost anything. Nothing that followed had served to remove this early suspicion, and it became a dark certainty when he discovered Cunningham at the door, where he had evidently been listening to the conversation between Peter Charles and the others in the study. The mystery was that such a man should have any motive for murdering Wilbur, but with motives Loring was not occupied at the present.

He felt chiefly a hungry interest in the crime itself. He had picked up the cause of Wilbur for no ulterior reason, and like all things which a man begins as a whim, he was grimly determined to push it through and make something of the case.

Who killed Joseph Wilbur? That was the question. Why? was another matter and it would answer itself as soon as he found the man.

The light snapped out from around the curtains in the adjoining bow-window. Through his own open window he heard the drawing of the curtains, a faint, faint whisper, and knew that the wind was blowing them in.

There had been sounds in distant parts of the house; now he was aware of utter silence, and that sensation of suspense which always accompanies absolute quiet. He could not understand it. A moment before he had seemed in tune with the surroundings—the house, the ground, the light in the neighboring window. Now the extinguishing of that light tightened his nerves and put a weight upon the beating of his heart. The faint whisperings and tickings in the wall of which silence in a house by night is composed, began to besiege him.

His nerves had grown so taut, indeed, that he rose with a shrug of his shoulders and decided to go to bed. It was when he turned from the window that he heard the first distinct sound. It was, to be sure, rather the sense of a jarring weight than a definite sound. It was such a noise, for instance, as a door makes, when, being slowly and softly closed, the suction of the wind draws it violently out of the fingers and sends it heavily home for the last fraction of an inch.

It was, to the growing excitement of Loring, an ominous touch in the middle of the night. Ordinarily he would have paid no attention whatever to it. Now he was perturbed and suspicious enough to slip with cautious steps over the rug and stand beside his door.

There he listened, and presently he made out a noise, or the ghost of a noise, going down the outside hall. That ghost paused just opposite his door, paused for the space of two hammering, slow heart-beats, and then proceeded. Instinctively Loring reached back and got the reassuring touch of his revolver against his finger tips. That whispering sound in the hall meant to him, definitely, that mischief was still afoot in the house that night.

He was afraid, coldly afraid, as though he were facing supernal things and not flesh and blood. Oddly enough, the picture of Wilbur face downward on the floor came vividly before his eyes again. Where one murder has occurred another follows easily enough. It is as simple and logical as question and answer. Yet, Loring turned the knob of his door with infinite caution and gradually advanced his head through the opening.

He had to steel himself to do it. He had a horrible feeling that the thing which had passed his door had heard the opening of it and had whirled soundlessly to spring on him the moment he was exposed. So, poised to receive an attack from either side, he managed to look up and down the hall.

On the one side it was all empty blackness. On the other there was no hall light, but from the illuminated main hall downstairs enough of a glow rose to make that part of the passage as visible, say, as the gloom of late evening. And in that gloom he saw a pale figure go softly down the stairs, descending gradually out of sight.

He thought of a hundred things during the moment while his hand was freezing on the knob of the door. But the first and last thought was that he must follow the creature, whatever it was. Loring had always separated himself into two parts. The one part was the man known as Samuel Loring, indifferently good, indifferently brave, capable of sneaking and unmanly thoughts and impulses.

The other part was a sense of honor which controlled him as mercilessly as a Juju controls a trembling Negro. That sense of honor told him now with no uncertain voice that he must step into the shadowy hall and pursue the filmy figure he had seen go down the stairs. Perhaps it was one of the maid-servants of the house on some forgotten errand. But no servant would move with such stealth, unless, indeed, it were on some pilfering expedition.

The deep hall carpet received his footfall; the door tugged at his fingers as the wind caught it, but he closed it without noise. Now he strode swiftly through the shadows, lightening his step until his knees sagged and arming his senses with alertness.

He was in time at the first turning of the big staircase to see a flash of white disappear into the hall below him. He hurried down, blessing the solid structure which gave no sign of a creak under his weight. The spacious silence of the hall received him. A window or a door had been carelessly left open somewhere. It gave a ghostly feeling that the house was already preparing in prospect and spirit for the end of human habitation. The sin of the murder was already taking its effect.

Full of these gloomy forebodings, Loring followed the direction of the glimmering fugitive down one of the side corridors and again he was in time to see a door open. For a moment, against the black of night, he made out unmistakably the outlines of a woman's body and a gust of the night air blew back on him.

It gave him pause again. What interest had he in errands which led outside the house? But then, again, the very fact that the fugitive was stealing outside the house had a point.

He hurried on again and slipped through the same door. At once the air of the open night breathed around him like a companion spirit and the sense of ambushment and stealthy danger vanished.

The woman was going down over the terraces, a dim figure, but plain enough to follow. Loring began to run with soft, light footfalls, keeping his weight carefully off thudding heels. He took advantage, too, of an occasional bush which would shelter him from any backward glance. But on the whole there was a steadiness in the progress of the other which seemed to guarantee that she had no fear of pursuit.

Never once did she falter until she reached the steps leading up to the higher terrace with its stone balustrade looping around the verge of the lake. Down this she turned to the left, and across to the farther side so that Loring could only see the white veiling that covered her head.

He redoubled his speed unto he had gained the side of the balustrade himself.

His task was now doubly arduous. He had to keep close to the stone fencing in order to see her at all, and when he was near enough for that he was in constant peril of betraying himself by the very sound of his breathing. Only the open pillars shielded him from any chance backward glance which she might cast.

Presently she paused; at once Loring dropped to his knees upon the wet grass and when he cautiously raised his head and squinted from behind one of the balustrades, he saw that she was peering anxiously around her.

Her survey seemed to have satisfied her that she was alone. She stepped to the edge of the terrace overlooking the lake, fumbled beneath her wrap, and brought out something small and shining which she held in her hand and stared at.

Loring watched with a puckered forehead of bewilderment. Then, as the wind caught at the veiling, the cloth slipped from a head of shining bronze. It was Beatrice Charles, and with that knowledge another thought flashed into the mind of Loring.

Strong of hand and light of foot, he raised himself. He was only a matter of a few feet away and directly behind her, but the faint rushing of the wind apparently covered any sound he made as he climbed over the balustrade and stole upon her.

She whipped back her hand with the glittering metal in it, swung it high behind her head to throw, and at that moment Loring sprang. His hand caught her wrist, and under his crushing grip her fingers relaxed and into his other hand fell the cold weight of an automatic pistol!

# CHAPTER XII

# ENTER KING ALCOHOL

**SHE HAD WHIRLED** at this touch, the mantle dropping from her shoulders, and now she flung herself at him in a sudden and silent ferocity that sent him staggering back. Both her hands were on the automatic. Twice she wrenched at it and had almost torn it from his grip when he regained self-control. With one hand he pushed her gently away; with the other he secured the weapon.

She was instantly quiet, no outcry, no moaning, no lament. She merely stood watching him for a moment and then stooped and picked up the mantle and settled it carefully around her shoulders and over her head.

The weight of the automatic was slight. It was a very small weapon, a miniature, in fact, but it was a burden that lay heavily on the heart of Loring, for he knew that it was the gun which had fired the shot that killed poor Wilbur. It was that automatic which Peter Charles had said he could not find when he went up to his room.

The whole thing was suddenly clear in the eye of Loring. The girl, first in the room, had seen the gun lying on the floor, no doubt. With lightning perception she recognized it as belonging to her father, guessed at all the potentialities which lay in the gun as evidence, and had snatched it up and concealed it in her dress.

That was the explanation of the upward glance when her father came to that part of his story in which he spoke of going to his room and looking for the weapon. That was the meaning of the reassuring pat which he had given to her hand. Pity for the girl, loathing for Peter Charles filled the mind of Loring.

She turned, still without speaking, and went down the terrace, but Loring blocked her way.

"Before you go in," he said gently, "I want to tell you this: that I'm sorry. I'm profoundly sorry. I would give anything in my possession to undo what I have done!"

He saw that she was trembling with emotion. When she spoke he saw that it was chiefly anger.

"Even a snake," she said, "gives some warning. Even a snake hisses before it strikes!"

"I know," said Loring. "I have accepted your hospitality. And now I've turned on my hosts. But I accepted your frankness as well. You asked me to stay here for better or worse. It's turned out worse. I can only ask you to believe that I'm sorry."

"I will believe it," she said, "and I'll bless you forever, if you'll prove that you're in earnest."

"Name any proof."

"Throw that gun where I intended it should go—into the water of the lake!"

"Anything but that."

"Ah, where is there any justice? Do you know why you are doing this?"

"Tell me what's in your mind."

"So that you can have the glory of—hanging—a good man!"

"A guilty man," said Loring steadily.

"Guilty of what? If you kick a dog and the dog dies should you be killed for it? But what if the dog is a treacherous cur? What if the brute is mad and runs amuck a public menace. You're rewarded and thanked for destroying the beast. But what is a mad dog compared to what Joseph Wilbur was? You're his friend; you should know what he was!"

"You are simply bitter. There's one sacred thing on earth, and that's the life of a man. Do you know why I followed Wilbur? God knows it wasn't because I respected him; I knew he was waste material—perhaps a scoundrel, as you say. But he was in fear of death, and when a man is in fear of death every human being owes him what help he can give. And afterward—justice!"

"Justice!" she echoed fiercely. "Justice for a creature like that!"

"I am sorry I have argued. Very sorry. You may pass on, Miss Charles."

He heard a sob catch in her throat, but on the verge of starting for the house, she turned again and was suddenly close to him. He saw her hand outflung, the fingers stiff in her gesture of imploring.

"Mr. Loring, I know that I have wronged you by talking like this. I know that you're a man of honor. But I ask you, will you have the death of a good man on your conscience? Are you going to take him away from us? Are you going to do that?"

The break in her voice went through Loring and unnerved him.

"Listen to me," he said, his voice rough. "I've been a weak-headed fool all my life. I've thrown myself away in the interests of others. I've fought for lost causes simply because they were lost. I've taken long chances for others simply on impulse. What have I got out of it? Gray hair before my time, that's all! Why did I follow Wilbur? Because, like a child, I pitied him. And this is my pay for it.

"And yet there's one thing I've kept—thank God—my honor. And you think that anything in the world could tempt me now to throw *that* away because I pity someone else? I tell you, I have my lesson. I'm through with others. My adventures from this time on are going to deal with my own affairs. I've worn calluses on my hands in the service of other people. I'm going to start now and wear calluses on my miserable soft heart for my own sake."

He paused after the outburst, a little ashamed for having poured such violence on the bowed head of the girl. Some apology was finding its way vaguely to his lips when she looked at him again and even through the darkness he was astonished to see that she was smiling.

And he could not give credence to his ears when he heard her say: "I can only thank God!"

"What do you mean by that?" growled Loring. He felt, somehow, that he had been betrayed and made helpless; he did not know exactly how. He was almost afraid of her.

"Because, don't you see?" said the girl gently. "Being that sort of man you can't turn in the damning evidence against my father. You can't do it!"

Loring became rather absurdly formal; in fact, he was a little angry that such a slip of a girl should dare attempt to read the mind of Samuel Loring, man among men, adventurer, danger-lover.

"My dear Miss Charles," he said heavily, "I give you my solemn assurance that I intend, to-morrow, to go straight to the police and put this weapon in their hands with a succinct explanation of how it came into my possession."

He waited. When she replied he discovered that he had not in the slightest shaken her.

"And I," she answered in the same marvelously tender voice, "give you my solemn assurance that when the time comes you will find that your feet have been converted into lead. You will not be able to take one step toward the police. Because I believe every word you have told me. I know it is true. My father's cause is already almost a lost cause; nothing could induce you to give the final blow to him."

He could not answer. He stood struggling with himself.

"I fear," he managed to say at length, "that I have raised false hopes—"

"You need not say a word," broke in the girl. "No, not a word. Because in spite of the little while I have known you, I think I know you almost better than you do yourself. And—I thank God again that there are such men as you in the world!"

He had no chance to answer or protest again. She had slipped by him and was hurrying down the terrace again toward the house.

Loring looked after her. The wind that tugged at her mantle tugged at his heart also.

When she had gone into the shadow, he looked at the lake and listened to the still lapping of the little waves against the shore; and after that he went slowly, slowly toward the house.

When a man finds himself thinking in a certain profound, still way about a woman, he had best begin whistling a tune, even if his heart is aching. But Loring did not whistle. He was exceedingly unhappy and happy at the same time. He had an empty sensation of loss and a feeling that incredible riches had been poured into his hands. It is impossible to describe just what he felt, but those who have ever taken ten steps in the same direction will understand.

He reached one curious conclusion. When he had talked to her in the house he had found himself seeing not her face, but something beyond and behind her. And when she talked to him in the dark he had seen her face as clearly as though a lamp were shining on her while she spoke.

He shook himself roughly out of this reverie, scowled into the darkness on either hand as though he trembled lest someone should have glanced into his mind unawares, and then strode toward the house.

Accordingly, his face was still in a haze of black thought when he came into the hall and found Beatrice saying good-night to Geoffrey Charles at the foot of the stairs. She waved to him and smiled, and then ran up into the darkness. Geoffrey advanced to him.

"Of course," thought Loring, "she has told him that I'm a soft-headed fool."

"I see you can't sleep," said Geoffrey. "Beatrice says she went out for a stroll and found you walking by the lake. Sorry your nerves are so upset, Mr. Loring."

"Oh, my nerves are well enough," growled Loring, yet admiring the smoothness of the courteous lie.

"However, you'd better follow my example and have a drink with me. I have some Scotch I guarantee will close your eyes."

Above all things Loring wanted to be alone, but he could not very well refuse. They went to the cabinet in the dining room and stood up for their drinks.

"To a better night for you," said Geoffrey.

"How," said Loring.

Somehow, the difference in those toasts summed up the differences between the two men.

They followed the first drink with another. Geoffrey became pleasantly talkative, not about the crime, but about Peter Charles. The latter, it seemed, was not his uncle, but a very distant relation. After the death of his wife, Peter Charles had begun to worry because there was no son to whom he could leave his estate. To have the fortune pass, with the marriage of his daughter, into the hands of a stranger, hurt him. So he had looked through the list of distant relations and had found a young orphan of ten years, hardly more of a relation than in the name Geoffrey Charles.

He had made his plan at once, taken the boy into the heart of his family, and raised him for the express purpose of marrying him to Beatrice.

All of these things Geoffrey did not pour out at once; Loring gathered them by inference chiefly.

"But it isn't because Uncle Peter has been so damned fine to me that I'm cut up," said Geoffrey in conclusion. "It's because he's a bully sort all the way through. You'd see that if you knew him better—as I hope you will come to.

"Have another?"

He was pouring the drinks as he spoke, and Loring took up his glass, but while he held it poised he took note, by chance, that Geoffrey Charles kept his own glass well hidden in his surrounding fingers—and into that glass went only the most meager of trickles.

"Why," said Loring suddenly to himself, "does Geoffrey Charles want to get me drunk?"

## CHAPTER XIII

# THE INTRUDER

**HE LEFT THAT** question in abeyance and without finishing the third drink, he refused to accept Geoffrey's pressing invitation to still more of the excellent Scotch, and retired with the plea that sleepiness had suddenly overcome him. The thought that Geoffrey had had some ulterior motive in pressing liquor upon him at once angered and amused him. It angered him for obvious reasons; it amused him to think that the big, simple fellow should have attempted to work so old a ruse upon no less a world-hardened individual than Samuel Loring.

No matter what the motive of Geoffrey, it caused Loring to carefully lock the door to his room before he went to bed.

The chill of the sheets had worn away and sleep was beginning to come over him when he made out what seemed to him the deft trying of the knob of his door. He sat bolt upright in the bed and then, seeing that it was folly to allow his nerves to get the better of him so childishly, he lay down again and resolutely composed himself for sleep.

He had no sooner closed his eyes than there was a fresher draft blown across his face—such a draft as rushes through a room when a door is opened, say.

He dismissed this alarming thought with the remembrance that he had certainly turned the lock at the door before he got into the bed and closed his eyes again.

This time sleep was coming deeply over him when a certainly prickling sensation at the base of his skull—that singu-

lar and animal warning of unseen fears—made him open his
eyes and lie thoroughly wakened and yet without stirring hand
or foot. Some living thing, he knew, was near him.

Straining his eyes into the darkness, he made out a vague
shadow among the shadows—the form of a man leaning over
his bed. This form straightened and moved away, and Loring
with infinite caution slipped his hand under the pillows, closed
his fingers around the butt of Peter Charles's automatic, and
with equal caution, brought the weapon out in readiness for
use. The gale across the room had freshened. Undoubtedly
someone possessing a skeleton key had opened that door.

His mind leaped back to the curious lie of Peter Charles,
about the mysterious opening of the locked door in the study.
There was no sound to attest the movements of the stranger,
but now Loring's eyes were growing more accustomed to the
dark, and he was able to make out the shadow bending above
his clothes—at length he even heard the rustling of the cloth.

It was too much for Loring. He gathered his legs under him
quietly, made sure of the trigger of the automatic, and leaped
from the bed at the intruder. Mid-leap he was met, not by the
body of the stranger, but by a heavy fist which unerringly found
the point of his chin even in the dark. It was a powerful blow
that flung Loring back. When he staggered away from the wall
and snapped up the automatic for a chance shot he heard the
door close into the hall. With a shout he plunged in pursuit,
wrenched at the door, and found it locked.

Still shouting he turned on the lights, picked the key from
the table where he had left it, and opened his way into the hall.

It already held two frightened people. Beatrice Charles in a
dressing robe cowered at her door. Geoffrey Charles in pyjamas,
his face as white as that of the girl, was running with a mighty
revolver in his hand.

Grinding his teeth, Loring realized that it was too late for
action. The few seconds lost in getting to the lights, then to the

keys, and then the opening of the lock, had given the stranger ample time in which to flee from the house and its precincts.

He reflectively rubbed the lump which was forming on the point of his chin and told them curtly what had happened. Geoffrey Charles was for instantly searching the house. The girl was for staying where they were until the servants had come. And already they heard the servants, with frightened cries, swarming in the third story of the big house. Geoffrey ran into his room for slippers and dressing gown and then put himself at the head of a searching party which he invited Loring to join. But the latter was too disgusted with this ludicrous proceeding to even answer.

As the noisy, trembling group disappeared, with Cunningham at its fore, Loring turned to the girl.

"I have to ask you a most important question, Miss Charles. When I came into the hall a little while ago, why did I find you telling Mr. Charles about what had happened on the terrace over the lake?"

She stared at him in bewilderment.

"*I* tell him? Good heavens, Mr. Loring, I wouldn't dream of it. Tell Geoffrey? He'd go mad, if he thought there was a shadow of danger for—no, no, I wouldn't dream of telling him. But why—"

"Nothing," said Loring curtly. "But this grows more and more a mess. You can be sure of one thing, however, which is that other eyes than our own saw the episode on the terrace. Goodnight."

And he went, rudely enough, back into his bedroom.

Naturally, there was no sleep for him during the brief remainder of that night.

The thing was beginning to haunt him. Two people, he knew well enough, had obvious motives to desire the possession and destruction of that tell-tale automatic with its single discharged bullet. But those two people, Geoffrey and Beatrice, were accounted for. Who else, then, could know of the scene on the terrace? Who was it that had dodged him just as he dodged Beatrice and saw the weapon change hands?

For there was no question in his mind but that the intruder had come for the automatic. Mere burglary was no explanation. Instinctively he connected the weight of the blow which had flung him against the wall with the broad shoulders of Cunningham. There, at least, was a possibility. But why, under the blue heavens, should the door-keeper wish to have the weapon? How could he even dream of its significance? Yes, he might have learned that by listening at the door of the study.

The explanation was so sound that it grew rapidly to a moral certainty in the mind of Loring. And that certainty made it easy enough for him to keep awake until morning. A cold bath washed away all sense of fatigue, and he came down for an early breakfast to find that Geoffrey Charles was already at the table. Beatrice, it developed, was ill with a headache, the natural result of the terrible night, and would not be down. Loring opened the conversation, at once, with Cunningham.

"Your man Cunningham," he said, "how long has he been with the family?"

"Started as a gardener, I believe. Oh, fifteen years ago."

"And what's his character?"

"That of every other domestic in the house of my uncle. He goes over the past of these fellows with a fine-toothed comb, I assure you. There's nothing wrong with Cunningham. Except that he's apt to lose his good manners now and then in a pinch. Why do you ask?"

He looked keenly at Loring.

"Manners have little to do with it," said Loring, rubbing his chin meditatively. "But—may I make a suggestion, Mr. Charles?"

"You've certainly earned a right to make any number of them. I'm terribly sorry about that rotten experience of yours last night."

"Let that go. In these days a man has to be prepared for odd things. But Cunningham—I don't like to give advice on such matters, but if I were you I'd hand the fellow his walking papers. Or if not that, I'd keep an eye on him."

"The devil!" groaned Geoffrey Charles. "What on earth has he done?"

"Nothing I can put my finger on. But I give you my word that imagination doesn't often run away with me, and I have an odd feeling about this Cunningham. Well, let the matter drop."

But Charles was by no means willing to let such a matter drop. He tried in vain during the rest of breakfast to drag information out of Loring. Failing in that, he kept up a running fire on the same topic while they were being driven in to Manhattan a little later.

It was a beautiful beginning for a day—a pale blue sky, cloudless, bright, and the sun gathering warmth as it climbed—but the chauffeur kept the car at a gait that iced the cool wind and made talk of any kind difficult. So Loring fell into a profound silence, with his chin buried in the upturned collar of his coat, and his right hand in the overcoat pocket gripping the automatic of Peter Charles.

He heard the voice of Geoffrey coming from a distance and nodded yes and no to sentences which he only vaguely understood. And in the meantime he turned the question in his mind. Peter Charles was guilty. Of that there might have remained the slightest doubt, had he not seen, when he examined the gun in detail before breakfast, the name of the owner engraved delicately on the butt of the gun. And with that weapon he retained in his possession the evidence which would assuredly damn the murderer in the eyes of the most conservative of juries.

Only one thing held him back, and that was the trust of the girl in his tenderness of heart. He would be worse than a leper in her eyes, of course, if he gave the gun to the police. After all, it might be better that way. It might be far better to know that she had shut him out of her mind even with loathing, for that would help him to forget certain things which persistently crept into his memory. Besides, he had begun this quest for the sake of Joseph Wilbur; for the sake of Joseph Wilbur he would bring the murderer to the full vengeance of the law.

As he reached this point in his convictions, the automobile swung into upper Park Avenue, and as the speed was cut down to agree with the thickening traffic, a man ran from a corner and waved his arm frantically at the driver. The latter brought the car to a grinding stop; two strangers ran up and one of them, opening the door, put in his head and looked from Loring to Geoffrey Charles and back again.

"One of you," he stated, "is Samuel Loring?"

"I," said Loring.

"Very well. Consider yourself arrested. Will you come with me or will you have the car driven to headquarters?"

# CHAPTER XIV

# LORING TRIES LAUGHTER

**IN AN ARREST** there is always a grimness out of proportion with the fact. In spite of his many experiences Samuel Loring winced and he understood when he heard Geoffrey Charles muttering: "Good gad! Good gad!"

In fact, the big, pink-cheeked fellow had changed color so decidedly that Loring smiled at him and regained his assurance.

"It's simply a mistake; or else they've stepped into a blind alley. There is no reason in the wide world that the police should want me."

"Better keep the talk," said the plain-clothes man gruffly. "Now how about it? Come with us or drive us there in your car?"

"In your car," corrected Loring, nodding to Geoffrey. "How about it?"

"I'm entirely at your disposal," said Geoffrey quickly. "Terribly sorry, Mr. Loring, but, of course, you'll have it fixed up in half a dozen words. By all means let's take them into the car."

"Good," said the first detective.

He turned to his companion, and Geoffrey whispered quickly to Loring: "Shall we try to shake them off?"

"Not a word and not a move!" muttered Loring. "They've nothing against me. For heaven's sake don't compromise both of us by being wild!"

"As you say—but it makes me mad—damn 'em!"

All at once Loring found that he was liking his companion

*His hard finger tips probed every inch of Loring's clothes.*

better than he had ever done before. He guessed that Geoffrey was a good deal of a cad and a prig; but he straightway guessed that upbringing and teaching accounted for the disagreeable veneer. Under the surface there was plenty of the mettle of downright manhood.

One of the plain-clothes men left them. The other slipped into the seat beside Loring, leaving Geoffrey Charles to ride backward.

"Sorry," said the detective, who, as soon as he felt the softness of the cushions, seemed to realize for the first time that he was an unwelcome intruder. "I think I can tell you—our business with you won't take long."

"Thanks," nodded Loring, and grinned comfortably at his seat companion.

He could have laughed aloud at the deadly serious face of Geoffrey, who sat with his lips pursed in a fixed, faint smile, steadfastly looking over the heads of those opposite him. He was determined, apparently, to do the right thing, and was not quite sure whether he should maintain his distance or attempt to do Loring a good turn by becoming jovial with the man of the law.

In the meantime Loring was casting far back in his mind. This arrest cast a bright light upon his past. Every little wrongful episode since adolescence flashed across his memory, magnified. But there was nothing of a magnitude to interest the law.

Naturally it must be something connected with the death of Joseph Wilbur. What could it be? Certainly no suspicion could rest on him. If he had pursued the man it had been only to carry a warning to the house of Charles, a warning which, if listened to, would have saved the victim.

What could the law wish of him? Only one thing: evidence tending to prove the guilt of the murderer. What could that proof be? Here, again, there was hardly more than one possibility—that possibility was the automatic pistol of the unfortunate Peter Charles.

The thought staggered Loring, not because of a fear, but because he could not dream how the officers of the law had learned that he possessed the weapon. Yet the more he thought of it the more convinced he became that he had been arrested only to be searched for the gun. If they found it, there would follow the questions as to how he gained possession of it, and out of those questions would come testimony which, beyond question, would hang Peter Charles.

A hot anger began to grow in Loring. He had been firmly determined, in spite of Beatrice and her sureness of him, to go straight to headquarters with the gun and the story of how it came into his hands. But that the law should doubt his honest willingness to bring justice on the murderer made him furious. Of a sudden, he was thrust upon the side of Peter Charles, determined to keep this weapon out of the hands of those who could best use it.

But how could he hide it?

Once he thought of opening the door of the car and hurling the automatic into the street. But that was foolish. The very thing the detective wished, probably.

There was a faint possibility that he might convey the gun to Geoffrey Charles, but that possibility was faint indeed. If the youngster were more alert, if it were possible to convey meaning to him by glances and covert signs, much might have been done, but the stolid face of Geoffrey forbade even an approach to such an attempt. He would be sure to betray excitement to the keen eye of the detective.

Yet what a temptation! To slip the little weapon into the pocket of Geoffrey's overcoat, where the wearer himself no doubt would notice neither the weight of the weapon nor any bulge in the pocket, for the automatic was hardly more bulky than a pipe case.

He discovered that the detective was watching him with a cat's eye; not a chance of conveying anything to Geoffrey under that watchful gaze.

The automobile, under the direction of the detective, drew up before headquarters.

"Now," said the plain-clothes man to Geoffrey, "I'll have to ask you to leave the machine first."

The heart of Loring fell, for this little maneuver completely removed the last chance to put the weapon into the coat of the big man. Geoffrey obeyed.

"Now, if you please," said the detective to Loring.

"Very well."

He started up, leaning to avoid the roof of the machine and at the same time, naturally, bringing the automatic out in the palm of his hand.

Glancing down, he saw the leather-lined pocket of the detective's overcoat—a heavy coat, and the pocket bulging out. The very danger of the experiment tempted Loring, and as he brushed against the detective he allowed the automatic to slip gently out over his finger tips and into the pocket of his neighbor.

He got out of the machine with his heart close behind his teeth. Had that pocket been deep enough and open enough to allow the weapon to fall with a jar that would attract the attention of the plain-clothes man?

On the pavement he turned with a forced smile and looked back. The detective was getting out without a vestige of more than watchful attention for Loring, and as the latter waved farewell to Geoffrey and started into the building, he saw a faint bulge in the pocket of his man.

The detective had become philosophical.

"Most of these birds when you tap 'em on the shoulder and tell 'em to come along, think they're walking straight for Salt Creek. Make you laugh to see 'em. It's sure a pleasure to pinch a gent like you."

And so he brought him into a small room where there were already two policemen in uniform, waiting.

"All right," said the captor. "Have to ask you to take off your overcoat and coat, Mr. Loring. We're going through you. Won't take us a minute to get what we want, and then you're loose."

As he spoke, he took off his own overcoat—for the room was warm—and hung it on a peg. Loring complied with the request patiently.

"Very well," continued the detective. "You take the coat, Joe, and I'll take his overcoat. Simpson, you run over him and take note of everything. One of them things don't take up much room."

Simpson obeyed thoroughly. His hard finger tips probed every inch of Loring's clothes and rolled every seam, as though he feared the thing for which he searched might be hidden in a fold of the cloth.

Before he was through the other two had finished their examination of the coat and overcoat and were looking on anxiously. Who, thought Loring, could have known? Who could have sent them the information? Of course, he thought of the man who had visited his room the night before, but officers of the law were not in the habit of making nocturnal visits at the risk of their lives.

It seemed, on the whole, that both things had been done by a man who was desperately anxious for the conviction of Peter Charles.

Was it Cunningham? The face of that man haunted Loring like a Nemesis.

In the meantime, the search had failed. The three drew apart, watching Loring from the corner of their eyes. They conferred and finally went into another adjoining room. They returned with a stocky little gray-haired man.

"There isn't any question about it," he was saying hotly as he came in. "It's on him. You fellows are blind."

He added, as he surveyed Loring with his keen eyes: "Come on, now. All over again. Here! I haven't forgotten how to go through 'em!"

And in person he began the task of probing Loring.

Then he took the coat and overcoat one by one, examined the contents of each pocket, crumpled the stiff material between his hands, and finally turned with a stifled oath.

"Custer," he said sternly to the detective, "you've slipped!"

"Not I, sir. I watched him like a hawk!" asserted Custer eagerly. "Watched every move of his hand!"

"Nevertheless, you slipped. He left the Charles place with it. I told you this was important!"

The white face of Custer was ample proof that he understood the importance.

For a time the gray-haired man stared at Loring. There was a sort of brutal anger and impatience in his eye, as if he wished that on the spur of the moment he could trump up a charge and put his man behind the bars. However, at length he swallowed.

"Put on your things and get out," he ordered curtly.

Loring held the man's eye for a moment, and then obeyed in silence. He swung into his overcoat, and while he reached for his hat on the higher peg, he dipped his hand into the pocket of Custer's own overcoat.

The finger tips plunged into the softness of a handkerchief, there was no sign of the automatic there!

Little things unnerve a man. Loring had to fight to compose his face as he turned, putting on his hat. And then he realized what a fool he had been. It was the right pocket and not the left into which he had dropped the automatic. But how could he manage to delay long enough to probe that other pocket?

He half turned away, putting his hat in his left hand and bringing his right hand close to Custer's garment.

"Good-day, gentlemen," he said.

And to the gray-haired man: "Above all, sir, I appreciate your courtesy."

"Eh?" snapped the other. "What's that?"

But Loring laughed. He knew well enough that laughter is the oldest mask in the world for deceitful actions. In the midst of his laughter, while his head was back and the sound was ringing into the amazed faces of the detectives and the police, his right hand had slipped into the pocket of Custer's coat, had found and brought out the gun, and had transferred the weapon into his own pocket.

Still laughing, more softly, he went out of the room.

"Custer," said the gray-haired man the moment the door was closed, "I'd like to make a bet with you."

"Well, sir?"

"That that laughing devil has walked out of this office with the automatic on his person."

"Impossible," declared Custer.

# CHAPTER XV

# THE OTHER SIDE
# OF THE STORY

**THERE HAD BEEN** something of wistfulness in the glance with which the gray-haired man followed him out of the office, and it warned Loring that he might be followed again. Accordingly, when he ran down the steps in front of the building and felt a touch at his arm as he turned on to the pavement, he whirled ready to fight. The ferocity of his expression made the boy who had stopped him jump back.

"You're Mr. Loring?" he asked.

"Who told you that?" snapped Loring. "I have a note for you, sir."

And he handed Loring an envelope in which he read:

> DEAR MR. LORING:
> I am instructed by Mr. Peter Charles to get in touch with you as soon as possible. If you can possibly spare me a moment, will you come to my office with the bearer of this note? It is a matter of the most urgent import.
> Very truly yours,
> JACKSON LOWRIE.

Loring had learned from Geoffrey that morning that the lawyer who would handle his uncle's case was Jackson Lowrie. But his mind had reached a state of hair-trigger nervousness. He was prepared to be suspicious of every shadow that crossed his face. So he looked narrowly into the face of the boy; he was a harmless-eyed, clear-faced youngster of sixteen.

"Who put you here?" asked Loring.

"Mr. Lowrie sent me here, sir."

"Have you seen me before?"

"No, sir."

"And yet you know me by sight?"

"Mr. Lowrie described you, sir."

"The devil! A man I've never seen described me to a boy who had never seen me? Come, come, my young friend!"

A twinkle came in the eye of the youngster.

"He even told me you'd come running down the steps," said the boy. "Anyway, it isn't hard to describe you."

And he glanced in open admiration at the broad, ponderous shoulders of Loring. There was something ineradicably whole-some and normal about him; Loring instinctively trusted the boy and those who had sent him.

"I'm going with you," he said, "but I have my eyes open—if that means anything to you."

It apparently did not. Loring was taken to a waiting auto-mobile that bore him uptown to the East Forties, where they stopped before a towering office building, and Loring was guided into the office of Lowrie, Parkhurst & Lowrie.

Doors opened as if by magic at his approach. There was a bustle; he was aware of people looking at him sharply as he passed through, and finally he stepped out of the noise of the outer offices into a cool, gray room, where a thick carpet dead-ened the floor, where the windows looked over smoking roofs to the south, and where a vast, low mahogany desk was the bulwark of Mr. Jackson Lowrie against the world. He rose from behind it, one of those chubby little men about whom it is impossible to tell whether they are plump with muscle or with fat. He came over the silent carpet to Loring taking off his glasses with one hand and extending the other.

"I'm very glad to see you, Mr. Loring," he said. And he put Loring in a chair and took one near-by.

It seemed to Loring that there might be a bit of prearranged stage-play in the fixing of those chairs, for that of the lawyer was so placed that his face was in shadow while a bright light struck against the eyes of his visitor. A professional trick, no doubt. Loring steadied himself and began to throw himself into key with Lowrie.

"I don't wish to seem brusque," he said, "but I'm curious by nature and I don't understand how you could possibly know that I was at headquarters being—"

He stopped.

"Searched?"

"Well, perhaps."

"It does seem omniscient, I imagine. The fact is this. As soon as I completed my interview with Mr. Peter Charles this morning early, I rang up his house and learned among other things that you and Geoffrey had left for the city. My chauffeur knows Geoffrey Charles and the limousine; I sent him out Park Avenue, which is Geoffrey's usual way into the city, and he was about to intercept you when he saw the machine stopped by two men and very wisely assumed that they were detectives.

"At any rate, he followed to headquarters, saw you enter the building, and then drove to the office and reported to me. I couldn't go in person. But Miss Charles had described you and her father had described you also. So I sent the boy, who has a good pair of eyes, to wait for you."

"You even told him that I'd come out in a hurry?"

"People coming out of headquarters generally do."

"Very well," said Loring, not entirely convinced, but feeling that it might be better to appear so; "I think that clears up the mystery."

"Shall I strike into the heart of the matter?"

"Please do."

"Good! Well, when they had taken the gun from you, what questions did they—"

"What gun, Mr. Lowrie?"

"The automatic," said the lawyer, his face hardening a little.

"They took no gun from me."

"Come, come, Mr. Loring! You admit that you left the Charles home this morning with the little automatic?"

"I admit nothing."

"So!"

It was rather a sigh of resignation than an exclamation of anger.

"You were not searched by the police?"

"I was."

"Good! But what they found you will not say?"

"I will say that I left them with everything I had when they searched."

In spite of himself Loring could not keep a note of triumph out of his voice; but the change in Lowrie was instant. He fairly leaped out of his chair.

"By heavens, sir, you still have the weapon?"

"Weapon?" said Loring slowly. "What weapon?"

Lowrie sank back in his chair, flushed, but hopeful.

"I am not forcing you to talk, Mr. Loring. But I am taking the attitude that in some mysterious manner you were able to preserve the gun from the hands of the police. How *they* learned that you carried the weapon is a mystery all by itself, and between you and me I think that when that mystery is solved we will have the man who killed Wilbur."

"Very possibly."

"You don't actually believe, Mr. Loring, that Charles killed Wilbur?"

"That is a question I don't choose to answer, naturally."

"However, it is not difficult to read your mind. You think he is guilty. No wonder. If ever circumstantial evidence were piled up to damn a man, Peter Charles is he. And you have in your possession the final evidence—I talk freely, you see—which would make any jury in the world vote his guilt. I believe I am right in presuming that you will not turn in that evidence, however. I believe you will not put your hand to the work of sending Peter Charles to the chair?"

"I think I had better not understand you, Mr. Lowrie."

"Very well. I am sorry you make it so difficult for me. But I can't blame you. If I read aright, you are balancing between a desire to see the murderer of Joseph Wilbur punished as he deserves and an unwillingness to ruin Peter Charles and his house. It is a delicate matter. Mr. Loring, I am about to tell you a story which I think will go far toward turning the scales."

"I hope that story starts with the point where Peter Charles went to his room for the gun."

"Let it start there. I know what is in your mind, but I assure you that he told the truth. His gun was not there. It had been stolen by the clever fiend who wished to throw the blame for the shooting upon poor Charles himself. Very well. Let me jump, now, to the place where the door opened into the study. You remember?"

"Clearly," said Loring, shrugging the cold out of his blood.

"When the shot was fired, that hand threw the revolver on the floor of the study. Beatrice, entering first, saw the gun and knew to whom it belonged. She snatched it up to shield her father. And you can see that if the gun had remained there the evidence against poor Charles would have been overwhelming.

"Even in his shaken state of nerves he realized that he must alter his story of the killing and leave out the fact that the gun was thrown on the floor. No jury could be brought to believe such a tale. Even as it is we have a hard fight before us. Now, Mr. Loring, I am telling you this in the hope that you will not make our fight any harder. Can you answer that question?"

"You believe the story of Peter Charles?"

"I give you my word of honor, outside my business, and man to man, I believe the story of Peter Charles from beginning to end."

There was a ring of conviction in his voice that half convinced Loring himself.

"I even ask you to go one step further," said the lawyer. "To let Charles have a fighting chance, would you, in case you are put on the witness stand and embarrassing questions were asked, qualify that statement, and leave out all reference to the automatic pistol?"

"That is a great deal to ask."

"I understand it. We all understand it. But we can do nothing except throw the case into your hands."

"I refuse," said Loring, "to accept the trust, and must take no responsibility. At the present time, I tell you frankly, I consider Peter Charles guilty and hope to see him punished for the crime. His story doesn't hold water. Whether it would in the eyes of the jury even without the additional evidence of the automatic, I don't know.

"I know what is in your mind. In case I have the weapon, you wish me to surrender it to you. In case it should ever be regained and I could ever be connected with the gun, the whole story of how I took it from Miss Charles in the act of throwing it into the lake would be sure to come out and Mr. Charles would go to the chair.

"So much is clear. I wish to make it plain to you that I have no wish to have this responsibility in my hands, but since it is resting there, I shall consult my own conscience and no other power on earth as to how I use the evidence."

Mr. Lowrie's forehead was bright with perspiration. For some moments he rested with one elbow on his knee, studying the face of Loring. Then he rose.

"I see that that is a final statement," he said, "and I am glad to say that I feel satisfied by it. Let the matter rest in your hands. Mr. Loring, I trust you!"

# CHAPTER XVI

# LORING SEES A FORTUNE

**TO BE TRUSTED,** particularly in this manner, was the thing which Loring least in the world desired. Behind the manner and method of the lawyer he felt that he could discern the fine influence of Beatrice. Even over the telephone—unless she had stolen a march by slipping into town early that day for an interview—she must have conveyed to Lowrie her trust in the good nature of Loring.

It irritated him, this blind confidence in what he called his own "soft-headedness." That irritation had almost driven him to the officers of the law with the damning testimony. Their own stupid haste and eagerness alone had kept the evidence from their hands, he felt.

He was full of this half gloomy, half sulking emotion, when he left the office building and stepped into the street. The sun was still sufficiently low to leave the crowds on the pavement in the dense, slanting shadow of the skyscrapers, but through the bluish haze of shadow he made out in the crowd on the opposite side of the street a hurrying form which arrested his attention.

It was a big man, walking with such force and haste that the crowd gave way before him like water before the prow of a ship, and he left a wake of angrily turned heads. In one of his collisions the big fellow encountered, however, someone braced for the shock; he was turned halfway 'round, and then Loring understood why his back had been familiar, for he saw the face of

Cunningham, the doorman at the Charles residence in the country.

Loring had never connected that broad face with any good; he frowned now, heavily. For he could not avoid the conclusion that Cunningham had been standing there to mark his exit from the office building.

However, it was useless to pursue him and ask questions. He would be met either with silence or with pointed insolence. Accordingly, Loring took his way moodily down the street in the chill of the shadow. At the corner he selected three or four papers at random, and on his way home in a taxicab, he glanced over the headlines. One broad item was spilled across the top of each front page; and all that liberal use of ink was to inform the public that no less a person than Peter Charles had been jailed on a murder charge.

One thing struck Loring. There was almost no mention of Joseph Wilbur. Who the dead man had been did not matter. The fact that such a man as Peter Charles had committed murder, or was accused of the crime, was alone important. The flaring, incriminating details were placed at the head of each article, with a futile "it is charged" to qualify them and protect the owners of the paper from libel suits.

What did qualifying phrases matter? Loring knew from his own reading experience that a thing put in print is believed. A man accused was, in the eyes of the public, a man condemned.

He felt his first qualm of sympathy for Peter Charles. For Loring, as may be understood, was one of those obstinate people who instinctively take a point of view differing from that of the man on the street.

He wandered through accounts of the life and accomplishments of Peter Charles at the foot of the articles concerning the crime itself. Anyone with a *Who's Who* and a bit of writer's imagination could have written those articles. It seemed to Loring that they were appended not to waken any sympathy for the accused, but simply to make his fall the more spectacular. A ghoulish business, he thought.

In the meantime there remained one important object to take up his attention. How was he to safeguard the automatic which meant so much both to the prosecuting attorney and to poor Peter Charles? Both sides wanted it. He could guess that the prosecuting attorney would leave no stone unturned to secure a conviction in a case so spectacular; and certainly the Charles family would do their utmost to steal the weapon from him.

In his little apartment he looked about for a hiding place. He had read that often the best place to hide an object is the place which is most clearly in view. But certainly that theory was never meant for the concealment of a weapon of polished steel that caught the eye like a jewel.

Sooner or later his apartment would be searched during his absence. Of that he was perfectly certain. Even his own person was not secure, as had been amply demonstrated that very morning. The most obscure places would be examined. He knew something of the methods with which every cushion is probed, every joint of furniture examined, every bit of floor space examined, every wall sounded for false panels.

He might put the gun in a safe deposit vault, but he dared not venture on to the street again. There might be another arrest, another search, and a second time he dared not hope to baffle that keen-eyed, gray-haired man who had looked after him so wistfully.

Indeed he felt that the only way he could beat the searchers would be to baffle their intelligence—outguess them, in short. And then a way occurred to him. To hide the weapon in a secret place was impossible, since to modern methods secret places do not exist. It only remained to hide it in an open, easily accessible place. But that place must not be actually open to the eye.

One thing was sure. Both sides would know that *he* knew

they intended to hunt for the gun. Both sides would expect him to conceal the weapon. And what Loring did was to take the little gun to pieces. Then he went to the closet and into the pockets of the suits which were hanging there he inserted the gun, one fragment in a pocket at a time.

There was hardly a chance in a thousand that they would ever suspect him of concealing the gun in those clothes. And certainly if that suspicion did come to them, they would only tap the garments one by one for the bulk and weight of the gun. But taken piece by piece the weight of each part was negligible. Having finished his work, he went back into his living room with the guilty conscience of one who had outwitted the law.

But he had hardly settled himself into his big chair by the window, with the traffic humming through the side street just below him, when there was a tap at the door and in answer to his call Geoffrey Charles entered the room.

He brought with him an air of luxury which made Loring acutely conscious of poverty. His apartment, indeed, had that combination of partly stuffed and partly threadbare effect which generally goes with furnished rooms. Since his windfall of the night before at Buttrick's he was able to afford far more sumptuous surroundings than these, but he had not yet had the time to put his wish into effect.

Oddly enough, when Geoffrey Charles faced him, Loring felt that it was the eye of Beatrice that looked in upon him and judged him on account of his room.

But Geoffrey at once put him at his ease. One hasty glance had told him everything, and after that he considerately centered his attention on his host alone. He seemed quite oblivious to his surroundings. Of course, Loring understood, but he was nevertheless grateful. He envied Geoffrey both his clothes and his breezy manner; after all, he thought, one is judged by his possessions, and not his manner of attaining them.

Happiness to Geoffrey Charles was the gift of his uncle.

Happiness to Loring was the fruit of a life half desperate, half gay, wholly thoughtless, wholly filled with hard labor of mind and many a time of body. Money came to him in bunches—as it had done the night before—or else not at all. The miracle was that he had kept both hands and mind clean while living such a life.

"I suppose you want to know how I turned out with the police?" suggested Loring.

"That, of course. I would have waited, but, you expressly said good-by—and I had no means of knowing how long you'd be."

That was obvious enough. As for his coming to the lodgings, he had asked Loring for his address and secured it on the way into town that morning.

"They went through me," said Loring, "but they didn't find what they expected."

He smiled. Now that he felt the automatic was securely bestowed, he could smile at ease and mock the world.

"I think I know what it was," nodded Geoffrey Charles, watching Loring with acute interest. "If I'm not mistaken, it's the same thing that brings me here—chiefly."

"You, too?" groaned Loring.

"Has it become an old topic so soon?"

"I recommended you to Mr. Jackson Lowrie. He'll tell you about my position."

"Mr. Jackson Lowrie's ways are the ways of Mr. Jackson Lowrie," smiled Geoffrey. "Mine are different. I have come to make a bald proposition to you, Mr. Loring."

Loring froze.

"I hope I don't understand you," he remarked.

"I'm afraid you do. But let me explain in more detail. I'm a bad hand at business, you know, but I gather this much: that there are bargains of all kinds. Suppose on the stock market a fellow gathers in a few shares that are desperately wanted by a bull on the one side and a bear on the other; or suppose his shares are at the balance and can turn a share-holder into an owner? Well, the lucky chap who has those shares can strike a bargain very much as suits his fancy, eh?

"Now, Mr. Loring, to be entirely frank with you, you hold that position at the balance. The weight of your testimony can destroy poor uncle Peter. No doubt about that—you see how frank I am? Very well, that testimony of yours is the balance. The little automatic is the additional weight which might very well sink the ship. In a word, the price of that automatic is the price you choose to ask for it.

"Don't answer hastily. I see you are about to say something ugly. Please don't do it. By Jove, as I look at it, the amount of time and labor and danger you have put into this thing deserves some recompense. Put false modesty in your pocket, my dear fellow, and talk out man to man. Be frank with me as I am being frank with you.

"Let me go further, and you see that we have laid our cards absolutely on the table before you, for you to play them as you see fit. I have in my pocket a signed check of Uncle Peter's. The amount is not filled in. I shall fill it in with my own hand according to your dictation.

"And why not? You have a thing of value. Don't misunderstand me. I don't mean some petty sum. I mean that at one stroke you can make you and yours financially independent forever. I mean that literally and not as a figure of speech. You probably know that my uncle is rich—very rich. His fortune, as a matter of fact, is one of many millions, and not newspaper millions by any means. Out of that fortune he can well afford to spend a large sum in this crisis.

"To put the position as shortly as possible: without your testimony the law has a strong case against him. With your testimony against him, he is absolutely ruined. Now, sir, name your figure?"

"Are you quite done?" said Loring.

"Come, now. Dignity is all well in its place. Admit that I've tempted you?"

"Tempted me? Of course you have! Why, Charles, I've been between the devil and the deep sea all my life." He laughed. "Tempted me? I tell you, I like pleasant things as well as the next fellow, or even just a little bit more. Tempted me? Tush man, you have tempted me so ably that while you talked I actually received the money and spent it!"

"Which means?" said Geoffrey eagerly.

"Which means that it is now gone and that I am as poor as ever."

He rose and went to Geoffrey Charles and dropped a hand on his shoulder.

"I'm a rotten preacher, Mr. Charles, and I'm not an old man, but I will say that if you were a trifle older you would not have come to me with this proposition."

A profound wonder spread on the face of Geoffrey Charles.

"But you don't understand! My dear Mr. Loring, I am entirely earnest. See! There's Uncle Peter's check!"

"By the Lord," growled Loring, "you shake my own good opinion of you, Mr. Charles. But no—you're a youngster yet, as far as the ways of men go. If you say no more about it, I'll forget that you've already said too much. If you mention the thing again, however, I shall consider that you openly insult me."

There were a darkening and contorting of the face of young Geoffrey. Then he rose slowly to his feet.

"That's final?"

"Do you need to ask? And let me tell you this, you and the rest of 'em: I don't enjoy playing the part of Providence in this rotten affair, but if I have it, I'm going in for it with all my might and to the best of my ability."

Geoffrey Charles was able to raise his head at last.

"We're still friends, then?"

Loring shook hands with him heartily.

"I know that Lowrie put you up to this. Of course we're friends. Good-by, Mr. Charles, and good fortune to you!"

Geoffrey smiled feebly and turned away like a beaten man. And Loring, stepping to his window, watched him go out to the street, still with his head bowed. But just before he stepped into his waiting automobile, two men detached themselves from the crowd on the pavement and stepping up to him, tapped him on the arm. One of the two was a little gray-headed fellow whom Loring recognized, and he was chuckling to himself as the detectives entered the car and drove off with the millionaire's heir.

"By Jove," muttered Loring, "even if he had been able to buy it, they'd have had it away from him inside of three minutes!"

CHAPTER XVII

# THE DANGER LINE

**THE NEWSPAPERS WERE** too keen scented on the trail of a fine yarn to let the Wilbur murder story lag. Not a day passed without its articles. Not a day but some enterprising reporter dug up material suitable for running under a large photograph. While Peter Charles was being duly indicted on the charge of killing Joseph Wilbur, the dailies were running pictures of the great Charles mansion, the architect who built it, and a photograph of the check paid for it, mysteriously obtained. There was a picture of the Charles yacht.

There were pictures of the dead Mrs. Charles in the clothes of her début, and at the time of her marriage, and before her last illness. Loring was disappointed to discover that she was not at all like Beatrice. In fact, she was far more lovely. Then there were pictures of Peter Charles's prize winning chow. And pictures of Geoffrey Charles.

But above all the editors loved to give space to Beatrice side by side with her father. His worn face looked like that of a man already with one foot in the grave, hounded down by a sense of his guilt; and Beatrice, beside him, seemed more fresh and blooming than ever.

Even had he striven, Loring could not have banished the story from his mind; and the editors were seeing to it that he had not a chance to forget Beatrice. That was his chief desire, and he was baffled. It was by no means the first time that he had been attracted by a girl; but he vainly waited for the first happiness to fade away into the commonplace.

He told himself that ordinarily he would hardly have looked at her twice, and that only the unusual situations of that stirring night had brought him so close to her. But to name a fact is not to explain it away. He found that the thought of her had taken root in him, and every time he ruthlessly cut away that thought, it sprang up and blossomed again with threefold luxuriance. He found, in short, that he was helplessly and hopelessly in love. He even began to yearn for the trial when he should meet her again face to face.

There were other things, besides, that kept the Wilbur murder uppermost in his mind. Three distinct times, as he had occasion to know, his apartment had been ransacked from top to bottom, and three distinct times he had gone to his clothes in the closet and had found every part of the automatic in place. The simplicity of his ruse had completely baffled them, whether they were the secret agents of the law on the one hand, or of Peter Charles on the other.

Twice Lowrie sent messages to him, asking for an appointment; twice Geoffrey Charles himself called; once Peter Charles even wrote him a letter, but always Loring returned refusals. As a matter of fact, he felt himself too weak to be exposed to temptation. And then came the note from Beatrice Charles.

It was short, and full of meat, he found. In it she wondered why he had dropped so completely out of sight since that unusual night. She often, of course, remembered that night, and—Loring. She and Mrs. Philip Seagrove, her aunt, would be at her father's town apartment the following day and Miss Charles would be very happy to receive Mr. Loring, it appeared, for tea.

Loring found in the note so much matter, in fact, that he read it again and again. One thing gave him a sharp qualm. The trial was now a matter of a very few days' waiting. What if, having wasted temptations of money upon Loring, they were now descending so low that they wished to use the influence of the girl as a last resort and swing Loring to their side definitely.

Geoffrey and even the lawyer, Lowrie, he felt, would be above suggesting such a maneuver, but he was not sure about Peter Charles. He had gone much into the past life of the millionaire, and he had read unsavory accounts and many ugly surmises between the lines of print. Peter Charles, beginning business as an honorable man with a bold imagination, had twice failed, the second time for a huge amount and in partnership with the notorious Wilbur.

After that he had begun to climb for the third time and he had never paused thereafter or met with a serious setback. He retained his bold imagination and his foresight. He added to these qualities, it seemed, the heartlessness of a sharpster. Black tales were afloat about the business methods of Peter Charles; now that the blow had already fallen upon his reputation, these stories came to the surface and were bruited abroad.

Nevertheless, Loring presented himself for tea.

It was an apartment on Park Avenue. He found Mrs. Philip Seagrove to possess lovely hands and delicately rounded wrists which she was an adept in setting off with her gestures. For the rest, she was rather more faded than she seemed to realize, but Loring was stupid to a degree, and after a few moments Mrs. Philip Seagrove found something to take her out of the room.

Loring turned with immense relief to Beatrice. She had on a dress of some green stuff that suited her hair and eyes marvelously; Loring found that it was necessary to avoid looking directly at her. Not that she was beautiful. He kept telling himself that she was not; he would carefully dissect her features and name over their faults, but in spite of himself, whenever his glance wandered near her he would find his pulse leaping.

We knew that he was being insufferably silent, but she played about him like a child having a game of suppose with a wooden image. She talked of everything and anything, and finally hardly

waited for the answers which came out so haltingly and mean-
inglessly from the tongue of Loring. She even sat down to the
lovely old painted harpsichord which stood in a shadowy corner
of the room and on it she played Mozart. Through the shadow
he watched the glimmer of the white hands, and the sheen of
the bronze hair; and the music of the old instrument was as
frosty clear and sweet as distant sleigh bells over snow.

It drew Loring out of his chair until he was leaning lightly
against the harpsichord and watching her face as she played.
She paused in the middle of a piece where the harmony trailed
away and grew thin. And still she looked down at the keys for
a moment, as though she wished to gather her thoughts before
she faced him. Then she looked up; and once more Loring tried
to look away but could not keep from meeting her glance.

"You like Mozart?" she said. And she went on mercifully, so
that he need not find a complacent answer. "I like him, too;
sometimes he's a bit meager and tinkly, but he's always pleasant.
And you see, he shows off the old harpsichord. Beethoven is a
ghost on it!"

"Mozart is Greek to me," admitted Loring, "but I like the
picture." He was afraid the compliment was too broad and he
hurried on with: "You understand, I have to fight to find the
melody in the old stuff; that's where it puts me out. I don't like
to be puzzled. Never!"

Something about his way of saying that made her stand up
from the music bench.

"I think you've hidden away an innuendo, somewhere in
that," she told him.

"There is. I'll bring it out into the light at the risk of being
boorish. But—why have you been so extraordinarily nice to me
this afternoon."

"That might call for a pat answer," she said, trying to smile
and making a mess of it.

"You see," he went on gently, "I perfectly understand that
there is only one subject in which you're really interested just

now. Good Lord, you wouldn't be human if it were otherwise, but here you've been playing a charming play for me all afternoon. On my honor, I've felt like a spectator looking across the footlights."

She made an odd little gesture, as though she admitted failure.

"What shall I say?"

"This: which of them made you do it? Which of them suggested it to you?"

She watched his face carefully for a moment.

"I knew you were like this," she said quietly, at length. "I'm sorry. Is there any harm done? I told them you were like this and that you would see through poor me. But they insisted. It seems that these affairs have to be staged. The stage is always set for the—jury—you know? And I was to set a stage for you and play a little piece. So that it might help you to remember, when that terrible day comes, that we are human beings—and that we are afraid of you—because you can hurt us all!"

She laughed, and the sound stopped short.

"But I've spoiled everything. I was never any hand at the stage. Now do you want to go?"

"I suppose I ought to. If I stay now you'll talk about—the other thing. And that isn't fair to either of us. All I can say is that I wish you well—I wish you well!"

She caught at the phrase eagerly. She literally seized hope in her extended hand.

"Then it means that you *will* be with us?"

She added: "If it's only to color your words by the tone you give them? Even that might mean everything!"

It was the hardest thing Loring had ever had to say in his life, but he said it.

"I am sorry to say," he answered, "that I haven't made up my mind. And when I do make up my mind it will be because I've decided either that your father is guilty or innocent. And when I've decided—cold-bloodedly, and justly, I hope—I'll give my testimony. I don't even know yet. I won't know, Miss Charles, until I see the face of your father when he sits opposite the jurors!"

She closed her eyes under the blow.

"But finally, I haven't thanked you. You have given me a beautiful afternoon. I shall never forget it. Never!"

Her eyes opened a little, but her face was ash colored. Loring retreated. When he closed the door behind him, with his coat on his arm in the haste of his retirement, he heard a dull, throbbing sound—a pulse of sound—from the apartment. He knew well enough that it was the stifled sobbing of the girl. And he loved her so that he would have mortgaged his soul to give her one moment of happiness.

Accordingly, he put on his coat, settled his hat firmly on his head, and was humming gayly as he went down in the elevator. That was the way of Loring.

CHAPTER XVIII

# THE TRIAL

**IT WAS LIKE** a social event, that famous trial. The business world went to see Peter Charles fight for his life, to see him who had so often directed storms that broke over the Street; the social world went to see Beatrice Charles. As for the commoner orders, they sifted in here and there and filled the few gaps and made up the encircling borders of the press in the big room. They supplied the noise; the elements out of the business world supplied the color.

All eyes, chiefly, looked from Peter Charles, who was intensely calm, if such a thing can be, to the twelve good men and true. There were a carpenter, a baker, an ironworker, a plasterer, a real estate agent, a man of no occupation, a butcher, a goldsmith, an author, a teacher, and two merchants in that jury box. They had the power to say yes or no to the question: "Shall this man live or die?"

Consequently, they avoided looking at the defendant except during cross-examination of a witness, when a strong point was being brought out. At all other times, whenever evidence favored Peter Charles or whenever the questions were of a drab nature, the jury seemed preoccupied and gave only a summary attention, but in a crisis when the prosecution struck heavily at Peter Charles, then twelve pairs of eyes suddenly flashed at the defendant and Loring, watching steadily, sometimes wondered why they did not give voice like twelve bloodhounds.

The twelve ceased to be men of certain walks in life. A great dignity fell upon them; they were the law. The guardians of society, they sat behind their fence and looked soberly over the crowd, and the crowd looked with awe at the twelve, each man thanking heaven that the impersonal gaze of the twelve was not singling him out.

When the jury frowned the crowd trembled and grew excited. When the jury leaned forward the crowd held its breath. When the jury smiled or chuckled the crowd shuddered. It seemed more terrible than words can convey that the twelve awful voices of society should be amused!

Sometimes Loring felt that Peter Charles was a fugitive hare. His defense was dodging here and there, doubling, crossing, stretching off at terrific pace, but always the jurors' calm eyes kept the poor creature in easy distance, ready to spare or destroy as the whim came to them.

If Charles and the jury were the main centers of attention they were not the only ones. Like the voice of a god from a cloud the judge spoke now and then. People hung upon his dry words when he decided on a point. He was always squinting over his glasses, past the heads of the lawyers, past the crowd, through the wall far away at the other end of the room.

One felt that those tired, patient eyes were gazing through the words of witnesses, lawyers, probing constantly to find the truth. His quiet was more awful than the carelessness of the jury. His patient attention was more terrible than a loaded gun. Human sorrow, human joy, human motives, human weaknesses were brushed away.

Besides the judge there was a quiet figure in black with a collar of white lace that kept her from looking pale. That was Beatrice. She was continually looking at her father and smiling at him, though he never paid the slightest attention to her. For the lawyers and the crowd she never had a glance, except now and then a stern lifting of her brows. Only when Jackson Lowrie was talking—then her expression became one of painful interest; what he said always seemed to fall short of her expectations.

As for Jackson Lowrie, he gave an impression of being very busy, even when he was sitting still. Loring felt that he would be more effective if he had been more massive and still and confident. But he was always bouncing up with objections and being bounced down again, but not at all disheartened, by the dry voice of the judge.

What a contrast was William McLane Lorriston, attorney for the State, tooth for the law, eye for the people! He was a man with a perfectly bald head, a perfectly red face; he had a large stomach crossed by an immense gold chain. The expanse of his waistcoat gave an impression of great wealth and stable experience and large knowledge. His eyebrows were brilliant, white and long and thick. When he looked down his eyes were like those of a sleeper.

When he looked up, it was the glance of a fox through a hedge about to pounce out. He seemed quiet, sure of himself, sure of his case.

In reality he was trembling with eagerness, for he knew that reputation was within his grasp. He was a consummate actor. For all his size he could mimic a woman on the witness stand so that he seemed smaller than she. And when he spoke one forgot his face and was conscious only of a voice of tremendous range, capable of all the notes of scorn, honest indignation, scathing rage, mockery, honey-throated sympathy, loud jesting.

When he questioned Peter Charles he barked his questions and looked away as though he were disgusted by an unclean thing and wished to get the dirty job done as soon as possible. When he questioned Beatrice Charles his voice was that of a gentle father drawing a disagreeable truth from a child.

Those were the great forces which played in the courtroom. But all the time Loring knew that the final power was in his hands. He had assembled the automatic the night before and now the weight of it tugged at his pocket. Now and then he caught the eager, doubtful eye of Lowrie upon him. Now and then the fox glance of William McLane Lorriston flared at him, looked through him, found the weapon beneath the cloth. Sooner or later they would have him on the stand for the final version of his story.

Already they had combed his tale with a fine-toothed comb. The theory of Lorriston was simply that Wilbur was not at all in fear of death when Loring saw him, but worried, gravely worried. He brought witnesses on the stand who testified that Wilbur was on the verge of bankruptcy. And Lorriston built a pathetic tale of the bankrupt fleeing to his old associate with an appeal for aid, being cruelly refused; he described how the quarrel must have arisen, the mutual recriminations, until finally Peter Charles went up to his room, took his pistol, and coming down to the library cold-bloodedly shot his old companion. The story of the early association between Wilbur and Charles was mercilessly brought to light.

The counter theory of Lowrie was necessarily built on the assumption that Loring had been right from first to last. That Wilbur was actually fleeing from death. That his appointed time was almost up. That his singular wandering flight through Manhattan had been to see for the last time the scenes with which he was most familiar, and that when this was done, he had gone to make a final appeal to Peter Charles, and if that failed bring the curse of his death and the accusation of murder on the head of his former associate.

It made a tale even more thrilling than that of Lorriston. The jury was charmed. There was a touch of romance to it. People always with their lips deny the truth of romance, but in their hearts they are profoundly convinced of its reality.

The climax came. Peter Charles made an incredibly good witness on his own behalf. For an hour or more he was on the stand, telling the story of how Wilbur came to him; the skillful questioning of Lowrie brought out every point in a clear light. And then Lorriston hammered that story without avail. At only one point could he make an impression.

"You say the pistol was not in the drawer?"

"It was not."

"Describe the drawer, Mr. Charles."

"A small drawer. Plain, unfinished wood. It was absolutely empty. The gun had been stolen by—"

"That will do. Continue about the drawer. It was an ordinary top drawer, perhaps?"

"No, there was a false bottom in the lowest drawer of the dresser, and under this false bottom was the compartment in which I kept the pistol."

"Why was it necessary to maintain this secrecy about the weapon?"

"It was not necessary. But it was an old piece of furniture. I suppose in the old days it may have been used for jewelry. I stumbled on the spring that opened the compartment by accident. Then I naturally wished to use it for something. Of course I wouldn't have put valuables in such a flimsy arrangement. The automatic just fitted the opening and I dropped it in."

"You found the hidden compartment by accident. You put the automatic in it. Of course you immediately told the members of your household what you had discovered and what you had done?"

Peter Charles gripped his hands closely and looked to his lawyer. This was a point on which he had failed to receive instruction. He was at sea and he looked vacantly at Jackson Lowrie. The latter, as was entirely proper, made his face a blank. But Lorriston was on his toes for such an opening. His flash at the jury made them lean forward.

The courtroom was held in breathless silence. Not that anyone guessed what the importance of this obscure question might be, but everyone was prepared to be surprised by the results of the unique cross-examination of William McLane Lorriston.

He repeated, stretching his bulky arm toward Peter Charles: "You told your household of what had happened?"

"No," said Peter Charles slowly—so slowly that it delighted Lorriston. "There was something pleasantly secret about that hidden compartment. I felt, in a way, as if I would be violating a confidence—the confidence of the maker of the drawer, say, if I revealed the little hidden place. So I said nothing to the family about what I had discovered."

"A delightful touch of sentimentality," nodded Lorriston. His smile implied that for the first time the accused had won the sympathy of the prosecuting attorney. "Of course it is easy to understand your process of thought. You kept this little secret entirely to yourself?"

"Entirely," said Peter Charles, smiling with pleasure as he felt that he scored a point on his side. "I told no one."

"But when you came into town the next day you surely told one of your acquaintances of what you had found?"

Peter Charles had found a point in which he could put the prosecuting attorney entirely at fault. He rejoiced in it.

"Not a soul," he insisted stoutly.

Loring looked at Jackson Lowrie and observed that the latter was frowning slightly.

"What!" cried Lorriston, apparently much put out. "You did not tell a single person what you had found?"

"Not a soul," said Peter Charles proudly.

"Surely, your daughter at least?"

The chagrin of Lorriston seemed to be growing.

"I repeat, I did not tell a soul of the hidden drawer in which I had put the automatic."

"And from that day to this you persisted in keeping the matter a secret?"

"A most absolute secret. Not a word passed my lips."

Lorriston drew back and smiled with sinister pleasure.

"Very good," he said, "not a word passed your lips. How strange, then, that the mysterious secret was discovered! What was the last time that you looked at the automatic?"

"That morning I had particularly examined it."

"That morning! But, Mr. Charles, have you any explanation for the peculiar ease with which the man who killed Joseph Wilbur found this secret drawer of which you had never told a soul, and opening it took forth the automatic pistol of which you had never said a word, not even to your family, not even to your business friends?"

For the first time Peter Charles saw the direction in which these questions tended.

He changed color. Vainly he looked at Jackson Lowrie. The twelve pairs of eyes from the jury box saw that look and they followed its result. Jackson Lowrie was blank and Peter Charles became a blank. It was like seeing an actor miss a cue and stepping behind the scenes to see the why and wherefore.

But at this point Lorriston broke off the examination of Peter Charles. He stopped with an air of combined triumph and expectation. People became aware that he had used a point which seemed on behalf of the defense by surprise. He turned, and Loring was astonished to hear him call to the stand no less a person than Harry Cunningham.

# CHAPTER XIX

# LORING TAKES THE STAND

**OUT OF THE** audience came Harry Cunningham as one bewildered. One could see by the manner in which he used his hands and his eyes that he was taken by surprise. And equally taken by surprise were Peter Charles, Jackson Lowrie, Geoffrey Charles, biting his lip, and Beatrice, turning a shade paler. The audience had gathered that something unexpected was about to take place. There was a general leaning forward. The twelve pairs of eyes from the grim jury box were fixed upon the servant as he took the stand, and raising his hand like one dazed took the oath.

The first questions, establishing the presence of Cunningham in the house on the night of the murder and what he did before and preceding the act, were quickly passed over by the attorney for the prosecution. Then Lorriston came down to vital facts. He came to them like an orchestra leader, beating time with his hand.

"You went to bed?"

"Yes."

"And to sleep?"

It seemed that Cunningham was trying to read the mind of the lawyer and guess the direction in which his questions tended. There was no mistaking that Lorriston felt he was approaching an important point in the case. His lion's voice raised.

"And you fell asleep immediately?"

"Yes."

Lorriston stood up. He smiled. There was no mistaking his triumph.

"But a little later, when Mr. Loring found the stranger in his room and when he called the house to his aid, were you not fully dressed?"

One could see Cunningham fumbling desperately to regain self-possession. Loring looked from Lowrie to Peter Charles and said to himself: "Doomed!"

"I don't know," grumbled Cunningham, casting a beaten look at Peter Charles.

"You don't know whether or not you were dressed?"

"I guess I was, maybe," growled Cunningham, becoming sulky. One could see that he hated Lorriston.

"Maybe you were dressed? Come, come, Cunningham. You testify under oath."

The word seemed to pull Cunningham together. He followed the raised hand of Lorriston with widened eyes.

"I was dressed," he gasped.

"But," said Lorriston instantly, "you just told me that you went to bed. Do you generally go to bed with all your clothes on?"

Cunningham was cornered. The whole courtroom could see that he was cornered. They could see, in the shining eyes of Lorriston, that he was approaching his great climax in the case. Lowrie had forgotten to play a part and was leaning forward. Beatrice Charles and her father were bewildered.

"No," admitted Cunningham stupidly.

"You generally undress before you go to bed?"

"Yes," growled Cunningham, setting his jaw as one who would have liked to fight.

"Then, when you heard the clamor that night, you immediately jumped out of bed, but before you would go down to the second story of the house your exquisite delicacy made you dress completely, even to your necktie?"

"Yes," said Cunningham.

Lorriston turned and deliberately looked to the jury to invite them to partake of his mirth and they smiled liberally.

"What!" cried Lorriston, turning back on the witness with extended arm. "Within ten seconds you were out of your bed and down the stairs, fully dressed? Within ten seconds after Mr. Loring cried out?"

Cunningham hung his head and was silent.

"Answer me, and remember that you speak under oath," cried Lorriston.

Still Cunningham was silent.

"How did you happen, then, to be fully dressed when Mr. Loring made the disturbance?"

"I wasn't in bed," said Cunningham.

"You were not in bed?"

"No."

"You were up and dressed?"

"Yes."

"Why were you dressed?"

"I had just been in my room a little while."

"When did you go to your room?"

"Well—quite a while before."

"How long?"

"An hour, maybe."

"What were you doing in your room? What did you first do when you went to your room?"

"I—sat down."

"You sat down. Good. A logical thing to do. You sat down to unlace your shoes?"

"I—yes."

"You unlaced them?"

"No."

"Why not?"

"I began to think."

"About what?"

"About what had happened."

"Which was what?"

"The killing of Wilbur."

"You sat down to unlace your shoes and before you did that you began to think about the killing of Wilbur. I understand." The voice of Lorriston was gentleness itself. "Easy to understand. You were disturbed. Worried. You began to think about the dead man. Then what did you do?"

"I couldn't stay in my room. I began to want to get outside the house. Seemed sort of close in my room."

"Ah! Go on!"

"I got up and went downstairs."

"And then?"

"I went outdoors."

"In the rain?"

"It had stopped raining. It was clear."

"And then?"

"I went for a walk on the terraces."

"Very natural. You went for a walk on the terraces. Did anything happen there?"

"No. After a while I went inside."

All at once Lorriston jumped forward and thrust out his arm at the unwilling witness.

"Did you see nothing while you were walking?"

"Yes," gasped Cunningham.

"Good! What was it?"

"I went down toward the lake."

"You went down the terraces toward the lake. You wanted to see the water, I suppose. Quieting effect when a man is excited. And when you went toward the water what did you see?"

"Nothing—at first. After a while I saw a white figure come down the terrace behind the balustrade."

"Behind the balustrade along the walk over the lake. Am I right?"

"Yes."

"And what did this ghostly figure do? Did you speak to it?"

"I was scared—at first. Then I dodged behind a bush."

"Very natural. You were afraid the ghost would see you. What happened then?"

"The figure came along the walk. Finally it stopped. Then I saw another figure—dark—following on my side of the balustrade. When the white thing stopped the man jumped over the balustrade. I saw the hand of the white figure go back, carrying something that was shining—like metal—steel. The man caught the arm of the white figure. It turned. The veil fell off. I saw that it was Miss Beatrice—"

Every eye in the courtroom was centered on the figure of the girl. But Loring saw that she kept her nerve admirably. In the crisis her head was high. But only once her gaze turned on him and her eyes burned against his face. For his part, he looked to Peter Charles, and saw that the face of the man was terribly white. He knew that his doom was come.

"What happened then?" persisted the voice of Lorriston in the tensely waiting courtroom.

"There was a struggle. Finally they stood and talked for a while."

"Did you recognize the man?"

"Yes."

"Do you see him in this courtroom?"

The glance of Cunningham wandered, rested on Loring.

"Yes."

"Point him out."

The long arm rose, steadied.

"There!"

"That will do!"

Loring had been designated. From one of the audience he had suddenly been transfigured into an actor in the tragedy. Lorriston called him swiftly to the stand, for Lowrie had no cross-questioning of Cunningham and dismissed that danger-ous witness at once.

"And you, Mr. Loring," ran on Lorriston, beating off his points with a fat forefinger in the palm of his other hand, "you did not go to bed at once? I mean, after the tragedy?"

"No, I went downstairs."

"And then?"

"I kept on, and went outdoors."

The strange thing was to Loring that he himself did not know what he would answer when the crisis came.

"What did you do then?"

"I walked down the terraces until I came to about the middle of them."

"Next?"

From the corner of his eye Loring knew that Peter Charles, Beatrice, Geoffrey, Jackson Lowrie were staring at him. Every-thing depended on what he said next.

"I saw a woman with a white mantle walking beside the lake."

"You recognized her?"

"No."

"Very well. What next?"

It was easy to read the disappointment of Lorriston in the answer.

"I went down toward the lake. She paused. I climbed over the balustrade—"

Loring paused; it was a mental pause as well as a stoppage in his speech.

"And I spoke to her," he resumed.

"You spoke to her—and she—"

"She turned quickly."

"Had she raised her hand?"

"Yes, she put her hands behind her head."

"Ah! And was there anything in her hand?"

It was the great climax toward which Lorriston had built his case. The audience realized it as well as Loring and the accused.

And the words came to Loring almost without his own volition.

"There was nothing in her hand. I think—she was yawning and naturally put her hands behind her head."

Lorriston paused with his next question hanging poised on his lips.

"Nothing?" he gasped. "Nothing in her hand?"

"Nothing," said Loring.

# CHAPTER XX

# RECESS

**LORRISTON WAS STUNNED.** There was no other word for it. He glared at Loring and then turned and cast a malignant glance at Lowrie. The latter could not refrain from sending a triumphant smile back at his antagonist, and at this point in the trial the judge called for a recess, for Lorriston had dismissed Loring.

The dullest member of the crowd knew that a crisis in the trial had been passed and that Peter Charles had escaped a dangerous point. Instinctively, as the case developed and things looked blacker and blacker for the defendant, the sympathy of the audience had turned toward the defendant. There is an invincible logic in it. As soon as there seems no way out for the accused, the public feels its imagination called upon and begins to guess at the impossible. Lorriston, bearing down irresistibly toward a damning point, had been checked. And the audience was glad of it.

In the recess Lowrie, Peter Charles, Beatrice, and Geoffrey, drew together. It was natural that they should rejoice in the happy passing of the crisis. The great point had been decided: Loring had thrown himself on their side and the grave danger of his evidence was passed.

"For the first time," said Lowrie, in the little antechamber to which they had withdrawn, "I began to breathe freely. Loring is with us. As long as that is true, anything is possible. Lorriston broke down miserably. The crowd felt it. Chiefly, the jury felt it. I watched them. When the crisis came I noted their expressions and I saw that the testimony told most infernally against Lorriston. He's lost. He feels that he's lost.

"His case is still strong, but the psychology of the mob now favors us. The jury has swung across like a pendulum and from being wholly against us it is now almost wholly for us. Mr. Charles, when they acquit you, I want you to know that the evidence of Mr. Loring is the thing that has turned the balance in your favor."

Geoffrey Charles was dazed. The wonder of the thing seemed to have taken him by the throat.

"I can't understand," he kept saying, with a blank eye. "I can't understand what brought him over. You know what I did. You know that I went to him and practically asked him to name his price."

"The point is this," said Beatrice quietly. "He has no price. You don't seem to realize that that is possible, Geoffrey."

But Geoffrey laughed.

"No price? I tell you, Beatrice, the fellow is a common adventurer. Ask Mr. Lowrie. He looked into Loring and his history at once."

"An adventurer, no doubt," said the lawyer. He seemed a little baffled, but did not wish to appear so. "I looked him up thoroughly, of course, as soon as he entered the case. He has been a wanderer. Picking up a living in random ways—anyway. A man of more muscle than brain, I expect, from what I have learned about him."

"A man of honor at all times," said Beatrice staunchly.

"That's a woman's way of looking at it," chuckled Geoffrey. "Good for you, Beatrice."

"What earthly reason do you think he has for testifying on father's side, then?" asked Beatrice.

"Why, dear," broke in Peter Charles, more cheerful than he had been since the trial began, "that's easily answered. It proves that after all your dad understands men and the ways of men. Who was it told you to invite Loring to tea?"

"I told you the outcome of that," answered the girl hotly. "He saw through me—you. He understood everything, and told me flatly that it was a piece of staging. I was never so ashamed in my life. I—I cried after he left to think how stupid I had been. I was ashamed—and I knew we had lost!"

"Tush!" smiled Peter Charles. "Just when you think that you've lost a man you've always won him. It's that way with Loring. He knows where his bread is buttered."

"Buttered?" cried Beatrice. "Didn't he refuse to accept money?"

"Ah, yes," nodded Peter Charles, and his thin old face wrinkled with uncanny wisdom. "But every man has his price. Except that that price is not always in terms of dollars. You can buy one man with hope of fame; another with coin; another with flattery; another with good fellowship, but each man has his price. Oh, don't I know?

"I'll tell you Loring's price. He wants to play the adventurer— the knight errant. I know him! Neither money nor smiles could buy him. Yet he was bought. Right now he is wondering what we will offer him. He is wondering what you think of him, Beatrice!"

She was silent, but Lowrie and Geoffrey nodded. She looked from one to the other, and then her head sank. There was a great deal of eloquence in that; but no one was watching her closely enough to understand what it might mean.

"And now that the trouble is over," said Peter Charles, "I have something to tell you, Beatrice, my dear. Something to tell you, Geoffrey. No, don't turn away, Lowrie, because I want you to witness what I have to say. After all there's no surprise in it."

He gathered them about him with his glance.

"I've hinted at it a good many times before. Aye, you're blank enough, Geoffrey, but under the surface you know, you fox! And you know, Beatrice, with all your blushes."

He stopped and surveyed them. His pride in big Geoffrey had always been a man's pride in his son.

"Here I am," said Peter Charles, "with more money than a man knows what to do with. Am I to die, one of these days, and pass it on to Beatrice, and she to another man whose name will change the name of my fortune, so that eventually the name of Peter Charles will pass out? Ah, Geoffrey—Beatrice, you've no idea how I've thought of all these things during the last few days. Haven't I talked to you about it, Jack?"

Jackson Lowrie nodded.

"Well, my dears, here's the end of all the preluding: when I brought Geoffrey into the family I always had one thing in mind—his marriage with you, Beatrice."

He paused, stepping back as one who waits for the effect of a statement.

Naturally Geoffrey had flushed, but he could not, as a gentleman, speak before Beatrice had spoken. And she did not speak. Her head remained where it had fallen on her breast.

Her father flushed with anger.

"Come, girl," he cried, "there have been matters of life and death in my head these days. Speak out. Are you happy? Are you content with what your poor father has done for you? None of these babyish blushes. There's Geoffrey Charles, a man's man, God be praised, and a woman's man, too, if a woman has half an eye in her head. There's a man among a thousand—"

"Uncle Peter!" cried Geoffrey.

"Shut up, Geoffrey," snorted Peter Charles. "Let me do the talking for you, since you've fallen dumb. I say, there stands Geoffrey Charles, clean of head and hand. Will you have him, Beatrice, and my blessing? Or will you have another man, and my curse. For that's how the matter stands, I swear, and so it does!"

She had tossed up her head at this. But in the background

she saw Lowrie making wild gestures, trying to pacify her from a distance.

"I seem to be commanded," she said, the color gradually dying out—it had sprung into her cheeks in two bright spots.

"Call it that," growled Peter Charles. "Hasn't a man a right to command his own flesh and blood?"

"Uncle Peter," broke in Geoffrey, who had been in a sort of dumb agony all this time, "for my sake don't say any more to Beatrice. God knows where my heart stands."

He turned to her with a quiet and winning dignity. "I've loved you ever since I came near to manhood, Beatrice. But I wouldn't even dream of influencing you. I want your hand to go where your heart goes—absolutely. If it goes to me, I'm the happiest man on earth. But if it goes otherwise, I'd fight Uncle Peter to make you happy!"

She thanked him with tears in her eyes, smiling.

"Ah, Geoffrey," murmured Peter Charles, "you're a clean-hearted lad. You hear him, Beatrice? That's what he cares for millions. Your good wishes count so much more to him. But there's no use making a mess of things.

"All I ask is this. You see, I've been having plenty of chances to think, and the sum of the thinking is that if the jury turn in a verdict of guilty, I want to know that everything is settled on that day. On that day I want you and Beatrice to take each other's hands and become pledged to be man and wife.

"You hear me, Beatrice? Geoffrey? Will you give me your solemn words that if the jury turns in a verdict of guilty you'll be pledged as man and wife?"

"Why, sir," cried Geoffrey, "you know where my heart stands. But I can't speak—not until Beatrice has spoken!"

"Too much delicacy," growled Peter Charles. "Out with it, Beatrice. Are you my loving daughter? Or are you a false mouthed hypocrite?"

She raised her head at last.

"Yes," she said.

"Ha!" cried Peter Charles. "Kiss her, Geoffrey, and seal the contract."

But his lips only touched her forehead.

"To me," he whispered, "such a promise is a holy thing. If you are in doubt, Beatrice, retract your word while your father is here to listen to it."

"I have given you my promise," she said steadily.

# CHAPTER XXI

# THE COUP D'ÉTAT

**TO LORING THAT** recess had not been free from pain. In the first place the newspaper reporters, to whom he had been first class news from the beginning of the trial, now pressed about him and tried to extract some additional embroidery to his midnight scene with pretty Beatrice Charles. One phrase from his lips could have given any of a dozen specific interpretations to that scene, but the phrase was not forthcoming. The reporters retired.

His persecution did not cease. Lorriston pressed close to him a moment later.

"You have lied like a genius," he said bitterly. "Geniuses generally come to an unhappy end, Mr. Loring."

"I'll take my chance," said Loring coolly.

And he watched the attorney go gloomily back to his table and sort his papers. Clearly his heart was elsewhere. He had led up to the main point in his trial. He had enclosed Peter Charles in a net. Now the net was broken by the testimony of Loring and he was discredited in the eyes of the jury. Aside from wishing Loring in the bottom-most pit of hell, Lorriston was busy visualizing all the prizes of fame which would have been his with the successful termination of the case.

Then Loring saw Peter Charles and Beatrice and Mr. Lowrie come back into the courtroom with the end of the recess. Geoffrey was not with them. He appeared a moment later by a different door.

In the meantime the room was settling down for the remainder of the scene. It was generally felt that the crisis of the trial was passed. The spectators were obviously in the mood of the audience as the curtain rises for a third act whose contents are clearly presupposed by the preceding action. They were ready to see Mr. Jackson Lowrie and Mr. William McLane Lorriston storm and bluster to the jury. But the bulk of the conclusive testimony was apparently in.

At this time a little package was brought to Lorriston and Loring watched him closely. To him, the prosecuting attorney had been the villain of the piece from the first. And now he saw him undo the little packet, discover something that gleamed in the midst of a tissue wrapping, and with a start conceal his present in a coat pocket. Next he shook out a paper which evidently concealed a note and read it hastily—then over and over again.

When this was done, his manner changed.

The bowed shoulders of the beaten man straightened. He looked instantly at Peter Charles and it did not require any great imagination for Loring to realize that he had received damaging testimony against the defense.

Next he took the little note-paper and carefully tore it into small bits, and these he took up one by one, as the clerk was bringing the court to order, and tore again, until there was literally no more than a white paper-dust remaining, which he tossed into a spittoon.

The trial was re-opened.

It began with an examination and cross-examination of Beatrice Charles. Lorriston outdid himself in trying to break her down. He tried dexterously to insinuate his theory of how she entered the room and picked up the automatic which her father had thrown down after shooting Wilbur. He tried to shake her again as he came to her interview with Loring by the side of the lake.

But she was quite cool. Never once did she falter. Taking the

*After one despairing glance at Loring, he crumpled in his chair.*

clew from Loring's testimony, she described the weariness that had overcome her while she was walking—how she had yawned and stretched while she was walking beside the lake—how Loring had appeared behind her, and she had whirled in surprise to face him.

As for the gleam of metal which poor Cunningham said he had seen in her hand, she did not understand to what he could have referred. Perhaps it might have been the bracelet. Perhaps it might have been no more than the white flash of her hand in the starlight.

It was easy to see that the jury was convinced. That jury which had been hounding Peter Charles with its looks from the beginning now faltered. Kinder eyes were turned upon him. They were beginning to see his side of the case, no doubt. They were beginning to remember, as Lowrie had amply proved with many witnesses, that Wilbur had been a much hated man and that there were many who would have been apt to hound him and to kill him if the chance was opened to him. His life had had many a dark chapter, and any one of those chapters might have led up to this dénouement.

And they were remembering, too, that in his position it would have been the sheerest madness to shoot down a man like Wilbur for a remembered offense and thus endanger money, position, life. There was too much at stake. And although there still remained a powerful case in the hands of Lorriston, he was now fighting against the prejudice of the jury, and he knew what that meant.

Yet Loring felt that the attorney for the prosecution was holding something back.

He called Peter Charles to the stand again.

"Let us go back," he said. "I ask you to remember. Give yourself time. Go back to the point of your narrative where you describe the singular manner in which the door opened. Give yourself time. I am going to be silent for an instant so that you may muster all your faculties. Recall every incident. Be sure of the tale which you told before. When you are confident that you have remembered everything exactly as you first told it, I have a few questions to ask you."

Having said this, he sat down and tilted back in his chair, lolling at ease. It was a cunning move. The interest which had been flagging since the recess was gradually keyed up to the breaking point again. The judge himself forgot to stare at the opposite wall and fixed his eyes upon the face of Peter Charles.

As for the audience, it followed the example of the judge. Lowrie, Beatrice, Geoffrey, every item of attention was centered for the moment upon poor Peter Charles, and he bowed under the burden of the many scrutinies as a man bows under a weight. His face became bloodless. The hands which he had interlocked upon his knee grew taut.

He had met many a crisis, and now, unexpectedly, something new was to be sprung upon him. It was almost too much. Besides, the patience of Lorriston, the new and sudden confidence of the man, was almost intolerable.

Suddenly Lorriston rose.

"Have you had time enough, Mr. Charles?"

The latter stirred uneasily.

"Plenty of time, of course. This play-acting—go ahead with your questions."

"All in due time," said Lorriston, smiling, and his white brows went up and down again, like a trap closing upon a victim. "All in due time. I wish to give your nerves a chance to steady themselves."

He walked up and down for a moment, and with his glances he seemed to pick up the attention of the audience and of the jury and of the judge and focus it again upon Peter Charles. His confidence had become terrible. All at once it had become impossible for him to lose the case.

"Begin again," he cried suddenly at Peter Charles, "at the point where the door opened into the room. It opened slowly, you said?"

"Slowly," echoed Charles, swallowing.

"Ah? Slowly? A murderer about to fire a shot, opens a door slowly as he looks in upon his victim. Very good. Now, then, you saw a hand enter?"

"Yes."

"Bearing a gun?"

"Yes."

"What sort of a gun?"

Charles blinked.

"I don't remember. Except that it was a revolver."

"What! A revolver?"

Not a soul in the courtroom but saw Peter Charles change color. Lorriston was grinning a terrible smile.

"Very well. What next?"

"Wilbur sprang back across the room, huddling against the wall. The hand advanced a little."

"You saw no face?"

"No."

"In short, it was conveniently dark?"

"Yes. No—I mean—yes, it was dark."

"You grow confused. Be calm, Mr. Charles. Remember everything carefully."

He went on: "The shot was fired. Wilbur fell, as we have heard, upon his face. Then, in a moment, your daughter entered."

"Yes."

"What did she do?"

"She dropped on her knees beside Wilbur."

"Ah?"

"And then looked at me."

"The first thing she did was to drop on her knees?"

"I have just said so."

"But be careful. Remember. When she entered, did she not see something lying on the floor?"

He had risen, his arm extended, and Charles cowered under the gesture.

"Did she not see something lying there, shining there?" cried Lorriston, all the thunder of his voice coming out like the voice of doom. "Did she not recognize the thing she saw? Did she not lean and sweep it up and conceal it in her dress?

"Did she not try later that night to throw it into the lake? Did she not meet an accident in the very act and was not the thing taken from her by Loring? And has not Loring, changing his mind, determining to see justice done on the guilty, placed the very object in my hand?"

His hand jerked out of his coat pocket. In the palm lay a bright, polished automatic of small size. It was so much the same that Loring hastily felt for the weapon in his own pocket and sighed with relief when he found it there.

"Look!" shouted Lorriston. "Is not this the very weapon with which you shot Joseph Wilbur?"

But Peter Charles was beyond the ability to answer. When he saw the little weapon his hands went up like a drowning man going down for the third time. He grasped helplessly at the thin air, cast one glance of despair at Loring, and crumpled in his chair, rolling heavily to the floor.

CHAPTER XXII

# THE LOST CAUSE

**THE HORROR SWEPT** through the courtroom with a sound like rushing waters. In the tumult of gasping, of rustling dresses, of men catching a short breath, in the scurry of picking up Peter Charles and bringing him back to consciousness, Loring noted that the very judge had started up from his chair and was looking down on the prostrate form of the accused with a face of pity, disdain, and just anger. His face—the face of every man and woman in that courtroom—was clouded with an unspoken word: "Murderer!" He saw Beatrice, rising from her knees beside her father; she, too, believed the man was guilty.

But Loring wanted to shout above the clamor: "You fools! It was all a staged trick! It proves nothing! It proves he has weak nerves—nothing more!"

He set his teeth and slumped hopelessly back into his chair; for he had looked squarely at the twelve good men and true and knew that the fate of Peter Charles was sealed. Yet a great light had burst upon Loring's mind, which always moved by opposites. If Charles's story immediately after the murder were a lie, he said to himself, how was it that the iron nerve which must have invented that cunning lie so swiftly should now buckle under the weight of a trick of staging? How was it that a thing for which he must have been almost prepared had toppled over the mental poise of a man capable of a cold-blooded murder one moment, and a most artistic lie the next moment?

One figure remained calm during the storm; that figure was William McLane Lorriston. He had made up his mind to extract every ounce of glory from the scene. And he succeeded. He remained erect with the fatal little automatic still shining in his hand, and when order was at length restored, when Peter Charles could at last sit in his chair again and lift his head and his wan face, Lorriston smiled faintly and allowed the court to hear him say to Jackson Lowrie:

"It wasn't the real gun, Lowrie. But it served the purpose, eh?"

A murmur of admiration went through the place. How abominably, wonderfully clever on the part of William McLane Lorriston! What a power he was on the side of the law! How dexterous a fencer to have struck the decisive blow at the very moment when the opposition seemed to have sent him reeling with its counter-thrusts.

Indeed, in the moment of defeat Lorriston had found victory; his was his Marengo, and beneath his white brows his sharp eyes wandered across the faces of the reporters and drank of their admiration as from a full cup. This would mean pictures in every paper; this would mean fifty thousand votes buckled to his side like a sword.

But Loring was beating his brain to imagine the man who had sent the gun and the advice to Lorriston. There was the power behind the throne. Was it some clever subordinate watching things from a distance who had conceived the simple and so effective idea? It rather seemed the work of one who wished to see the conviction attained without falling back on this last resort. But when conviction was slipping from the hands of Lorriston, this hidden brain had intervened and saved the day.

Who was it?

Two great convictions were rooted in the mind of Loring that moment. They were to influence all that happened to him thereafter; they were the source of the strangest acts which any man ever performed.

The first conviction was that Peter Charles, in spite of evidence, in spite of his collapse, in spite of his white, guilty face, was innocent. The second conviction was that the murderer was he who had entered his room that night at the Charles place; he who had finally turned the scales by suggesting this last trick that had unmanned Peter Charles. For who would have such interest in fastening the guilt upon Peter Charles as the real criminal?

The remainder of the trial was nothing to Loring. He vaguely noted Geoffrey sitting very close to Beatrice. He vaguely noted that she was still smiling a brave, pale assurance at her father. He heard the voices of Lorriston and Lowrie in their final talks, and then the sober instructions of the judge.

The jury filed out.

In five minutes they returned. Five minutes for such a decision: Guilty!

The judge had placed the fatal cap on his head. They were leading forth Peter Charles, a small, bewildered, oppressed figure before the mighty engine of the law. The courtroom seemed a gigantic theater around him. The judge spoke: Death!

The horrible thing to Loring was the complacency of the audience. A grim complacency, to be sure, and yet a definite satisfaction. The tragedy was over; the chief actor was dead as the curtain fell. The prize fight had not ended by a decision on points, but one of the fighters had been stunned by a decisive blow.

Lorriston was like the conquering pugilist; or like the author of the play, receiving congratulations. He kept his face duly solemn; but one felt that he admitted he was a remarkable man.

Loring passed him on the way out. The great lawyer deigned to notice him.

"You were a hard nut to crack," he said to Loring. "You had me worried; but things turned out all right."

"Listen to me," said Loring savagely, his voice low. "I'm just getting into this thing. I'm not through with the fight. Peter Charles is not going to die."

"My friend," smiled Lorriston, "I admire your attitude—but Peter Charles is as guilty as the devil."

Then the reporters swamped him and drew him away—a willing-unwilling victim of publicity. Fifty thousand votes out of this? No, a hundred thousand. He was a made man!

The evening headlines carried the important fact and a description of Lorriston's coup d'état; the later papers brought out the tale in full with glowing accounts of the attorney. "A man who knew how to take advantage of big moments." "Never beaten until the last blow was struck." "A bulldog fighter." "Inexhaustible resource." These were a few of the encomiums showered upon the head of Lorriston. Loring read them with a peculiar smile of contempt.

In his rooms he began to wait, he hardly knew for what. But the next morning, seeing that nothing had yet happened, he rang up Beatrice Charles at the town apartment of Peter Charles. He had a hard time getting her to the telephone. There was a maid, another woman's voice. Loring insisted; finally she answered him.

She could not see him, she said. She wished to thank him for what he had done. She knew that he had stayed with them to the end, influenced by his own sense of right. She wanted to thank him for all of it and say good-by.

"I haven't rung you up to hear thanks," said Loring. "I want to come to you. I have something of importance which I can't say over the wire."

In the face of such emphasis she gave way, and a moment later he was speeding to her in a taxicab. When he saw her he was astonished. She put on no tragic ways. Her eyes were languid and her voice was low, as though she were tired, but her color was as fresh as ever, and her manner was as simple and direct.

"I'm going to talk to you about painful things for five

minutes," he said at once. "In the first place, is there to be an appeal?"

She did not wince.

"No. Mr. Lowrie and father have talked it over. Father is against it. He can't stand another nervous strain."

"Then my time is shorter than I had hoped. I have come to ask you to help me in a difficult piece of work."

"We owe you a great deal; you can count on me, Mr. Loring."

"It is this. I want you to keep fighting to hold up your father's spirits. In the meantime I am going to find, somehow, proof that he is innocent."

She stared.

"Mr. Loring, what have you found out?"

"Nothing. Not a thing, I imagine, more than you know—that is, not very much of importance. I've only an idea—a guess—but I'm ready to fight on that guess."

"Have you as much faith as that?" she asked sadly, and he knew that the last scruple of her own belief in her father had died in the courtroom when he collapsed.

"Let me tell you in brief," explained Loring. "Fear of money obligations, fear of bankruptcy, could never have put into Wilbur's face the expression I saw in it. Neither was it fear of your father. Mr. Charles is a man of ability and force; but he was never strong enough to make Wilbur tremble."

"I tell you, that man knew he was gathered in an inescapable net. There was a force against which he could not appeal. He wanted money to pay a debt—but it was a blood-debt. What that great force was—what the thing could have been that took blood in place of money—that's what I want to find out."

He was surprised to find her smiling mirthlessly at him.

"I'm afraid this is another one of your lost causes, Mr. Loring."

He made a gesture of impatience.

"Let that be. Perhaps. But if from time to time I have to call upon you, will you help? Of course, you will."

"Of course, to the last bit of my strength."

"And you will gather up a little hope?"

"I shall try to. I—I almost begin to hope again now. You are a builder of new faith, Mr. Loring!"

She came close to him and laid her hand on his arm; and as she looked up he saw more in her face than he had ever seen before.

"What makes you do this?"

"A good old Anglo-Saxon desire to see justice done." Something snapped in him; a new depth came in his voice. And he turned so that the light fell full on her face and he could look a great way into the gray-green eyes and see that unknowable thing which lives in the face of a girl. "Shall I tell you the other reason, and the greater reason?"

Her lips stirred; but no words came. And looking at him, wonder changed her as the gold-leaf and the fair colors of the illuminator change the parchment. For a moment silence flowed over them and carried them along with it so that they understood more than words could have told them. Then the stir in the street below them broke in on Loring. He stepped away, and his eyes fell.

"Good-by," said Loring, and turned to the door.

There he looked back once more. The sunlight through the window brushed strongly over her hair, upon one side of her face, and set her dress shimmering. One hand was at her breast, and she was smiling at him as tenderly and frankly as the sunlight itself.

Loring cast open the door and stumbled into the hall like one who has been blinded.

CHAPTER XXIII

# GEOFFREY CHARLES: GENTLEMAN

**STEPPING FROM THE** elevator into the lower hall he confronted big, rosy-cheeked Geoffrey Charles. His coloring, to be sure, was as high as ever, but he seemed to have aged. The blackness which had fallen upon Peter Charles had left a shadow over Geoffrey and Beatrice. There was a new grimness about the eyes and the mouth of the young fellow, and Loring studied his face with sympathy.

Geoffrey was in the act of passing by, abstractedly, his gaze on the stone floor, but he checked himself in time and turned to Loring. He was so buried in his thoughts that he did not recognize the latter at once. He frowned, and then his face cleared suddenly and that bright smile which seemed a heritage in the Charles family was flashing out at Loring.

"My dear fellow!" cried Geoffrey. "My dear Loring!"

He took the hand of the other in a great pressure, and kept it steadily there while he met Loring's eye. And Loring guessed at many things behind that cordiality. There might be a meaning in it of old friends who had turned cold since the verdict of guilty. There must have been many a known head turned away from him. People who had fawned on him and flattered would have forgotten.

That accounted for the savage set of Geoffrey's jaw. Loring's heart went out to him. The boy of ten days before had become a man. Since the first disagreeable meeting with Geoffrey his liking for the man had steadily increased.

He said while he kept crushing Loring's hand in his grip: "Loring, now's the time to tell you how my heart dropped into my boots when you were on the stand and that devil Lorriston began to probe you with questions after the fool Cunningham had messed things up. And I'll never forget how you came through the ordeal. You were a bracer for all of us. I have another thing to say. I want to apologize humbly for the way I went to you and tried to—"

"Hush," said Loring gently. "Don't remember that."

"As you said then," muttered Geoffrey, "I hadn't grown up. Well, I've grown up in the meantime, I think. And I'm ashamed of that interview. What a cocky, callow ass you must have thought me! Well, Loring, I've had the whip on my shoulders since that day, and I've learned how to appreciate a man!"

"You've started in," said Loring lightly, though he was deeply moved, "by breaking my hand."

He shook his fingers to restore the circulation.

"But I'm not seeing the last of you?" went on Geoffrey.

"I think not. You're going up to see Miss Charles?"

"Yes."

"She'll tell you what I mean. I'm just beginning to be involved in this case. I intend to stay involved for an indefinite period. That is, if you think that I have the right to be."

"You have the right to anything we can do for you; but I'm afraid that all the doing is to be on your side again. However, we're a family with a sharp eye for friends—and enemies; and a long, long memory!"

His face was hard again as he said this. Decidedly he had become a man. Loring promised himself that some of the supercilious who had already begun to turn cold shoulders to Geoffrey Charles would sweat for it sooner or later.

"Good-by, Mr. Charles. And—keep smiling!"

"Eh? Yes. Good advice. Watch me!"

He nodded and stepped into the elevator, where he stood with his head bowed, thinking. When he reached the door of the Charles apartment he paused and with his hand at the bell shrugged and straightened his shoulders, lifted his head, and the brightness came back to his eyes. It was almost like an actor preparing himself for a cheery entrance on a comedy scene—an actor who has just received sad news from home.

Inside, he put up his hat and overcoat and went directly to Beatrice. She set aside her book.

"I've been waiting," she said.

"And Loring has been here?"

"Yes. Did you meet him?"

"In the lower hall. He had fire in his eye. What's he up to now?"

"Something you'd never guess—it seems like a dream to me. Do you know what? He has made up his mind that father is innocent and he's going to devote himself to clearing him."

Geoffrey's fingers closed over his cigarette and crushed it to a flat slip.

"The devil! Is it possible?"

"And he said it in such a way—!"

"But what could have put the idea in his head? God knows that you and I have fought uselessly to keep our belief!"

"Haven't we? I was ashamed to hear him! I'll tell you what put the idea in his head. In the courtroom, when Mr. Lorrison took out the pistol, and when the place was in an uproar, and father had lost—everything—I happened to look toward Mr. Loring in the crisis. He was on his feet. Both his hands were clenched. He looked as if he were about to strike someone.

"And his face—he was on fire. I could have almost guessed the words that were behind his lips. In that moment when everyone turned against poor father—even you and I, Geoffrey—in that very moment Mr. Loring made up his mind that he was innocent! Can you believe it?"

"Hardly—but I can manage to. There are men like that. Facts mean nothing to them. I remember what you said about Loring and his lost causes. Well, this is another one."

"But isn't it glorious, Geoffrey?"

She seemed to take him a little aback with that. He looked at her in a different manner.

"Very fine," he said slowly. "A little foolish, too, perhaps."

"The Crusades were foolish; so was the quest for the Sangreal. But thank God there have always been a few men like that!"

"I suppose so. Yes. Of course. And Loring's a fine fellow. About nine-tenths man, I expect. But he has no more proof than that? Just a wild idea out of thin air?"

"He said he had reasons—a few small ones that weren't worth repeating. Chiefly that he thinks Wilbur was really fleeing from some terrible danger when he came to our house."

"I wonder," muttered Geoffrey thoughtfully. "And—you never can tell what a man like Loring will do. The brain of a mature man; the impulses of a child. Half wise; half fool. Half muscle and half cunning. He might stumble on something surprising!"

"You think so, Geoffrey, soberly? My heart has been in my throat ever since he left. I've tried to be calm; I can't help being excited."

"We'll wait and see. There's another thing."

He paused, and Beatrice became suddenly more quiet.

"Yes," she said faintly. "I know. You've just left father?"

"Just now come from him."

"He still insists?"

"Insists?" cried Geoffrey. He stared at her with wide eyes. Astonishing surmises seemed to be flashing through his brain for the first time. Then he went to her quickly.

"Does it need his insistence, Beatrice?" he said rapidly and softly. "If it weren't for your father's desire that we marry would you be of another mind about it?"

She watched his face with painful interest, interlacing her

fingers and nervously plucking them apart. "I don't know, Geoffrey."

"Yesterday you weren't in this mood. What is it?"

"Are you angry, Geoffrey dear?"

He caught himself up with an effort.

"Of course not. But excited, Beatrice. I thought we'd settled on everything!"

He cried in a hard, low voice: "By the Lord, it's Loring! It's Loring!"

"I don't like the way you say that, Geoffrey."

He struck a hand across his face.

"Tell me if I'm not right. You've been swept off your feet by this fellow and his wild talk!"

She did not answer.

"Tell me!"

"I'm afraid I have been."

"But we don't know anything about him. Have you lost your mind?"

"I know him like a book, Geoffrey. I knew him almost from the first moment. At least, I guessed at what was in him, and liked what I guessed."

"And he's told you that he loves you?"

"He hasn't touched me with a word or with a gesture. He hasn't spoken a syllable. That's true, Geoffrey. And yet I know, I think, what's in his mind. I'm sorry."

It was easy to see that Geoffrey was hard hit. He began to walk up and down the floor. Every now and then he paused and drew himself to his full height with a nervous shudder of tensed muscles. At length he was able to face her.

"If that's the way it stands," he said very quietly, "I want you to know that I agree with everything you wish. I relinquish you from any promises. I'll try to smooth it over with Uncle Peter."

She cried out happily: "Oh, Geoffrey, I'm nearer to really loving you this moment than I've ever been before. I hoped that you'd take it this way. I knew you were a man, generous and strong and without malice! And this is what I want to say. I can't break Dad's heart by telling him my mind has changed. I know he is set on this marriage. It's a lifework of his.

"And it shall go on. I like you a great deal; you know that. I think we could be very happy together, for father's sake and yours and mine. I respect you and esteem you, Geoffrey. And if you wish to go ahead on that basis, perhaps I'll forget this other thing, but I had to tell you, so that there would be no skeletons to discover later on. Shall we go ahead like that?"

He was deadly white and she saw his brow glistening. All her sympathy went out to him.

He said simply: "I'd rather have your liking than the love of any other woman. We'll let it go on like this. And in the meantime if you change your mind, you can rest assured that I'll try to make things easy for you."

"I know you will. And—the marriage, Geoffrey?"

"He wants it—the night before—the end. I'm sorry."

They sat with their heads bowed, a singular picture for an engaged couple.

# CHAPTER XXIV

# THE MAN WITH THE OPAL PHILOSOPHIZES

**AS FOR LORING,** having set himself the goal of finding the true murderer of Joseph Wilbur, in case Peter Charles were not, he found himself up against a stone wall with no method of procedure open to him. It was easy enough to say that he would start fighting for new clews, but where would he find them? The police, he knew, had combed the Charles estate with a fine-toothed comb that had included everything down to the past lives of the servants.

If Peter Charles were not a liar, the murderer was someone who had access to the house, or else he had a confederate who had located the automatic in the secret compartment and had furnished the weapon to the gunman. Loring had too much respect for the police to desire to go over the same ground that they had covered. He must find a new approach to the crime.

For that reason, instead of beating his brain to find clews and novel ideas, he decided to forget all about the work until the next day.

So he went to Buttrick's. He had hardly closed the outer door behind him when he remembered a remark of the man with the opal: "Everyone comes back to Buttrick's." On that day he had firmly decided that he would never pass through the doors again, and yet here he was! He shrugged his shoulders and smiled. Also, he was not a little annoyed as he remembered Nicholas Zanten's calm omniscience.

The man had made him think of a soul sold to the devil for

the sake of luck. Joyless in his winnings, calm in defeat and loss, Loring had admired him and detested him—from a distance. He could get no closer to the fellow than he could to the heart of the sphinx.

And naturally, the first man he met in Buttrick's was that same man with the opal. The very ring was upon his finger. Indeed, the thing that caught Loring's eye again was the dull shimmer of the stone as Nicholas Zanten raised and lowered a cigarette. He saw Loring at the same moment and rose gracefully to meet him. His greeting was a surprise—even a little disconcerting—to the latter.

"Good evening, Mr. Loring, I've been waiting for you."

"You wouldn't have me think that you suspected I'd be here this evening?"

"This very evening. With a wallet full of money and a determination to make your mind a blank. Am I right?"

"The devil!"

"Not quite."

"Pardon me, of course. But do you read the mind, Mr. Zanten?"

"I do."

"H-m-m," muttered Loring. He had not suspected that the man with the opal was a charlatan in any sense of the word. He immediately wished he were elsewhere and decided to shake off his companion as soon as possible.

"I certainly," went on Zanten, "do not pose as a mind-reader, however, if that is what you wish to know."

It was answering Loring's thoughts so closely that he squinted at the other. He had every healthy man's semi-belief in the supernatural. After all, this fitted in well enough with the cold eye of the man with the opal.

"Now you're uncomfortable," chuckled Nicholas Zanten, "and I ought to let you recover by yourself. To be frank, I have often mystified gulls with this sort of thing. But not you, my dear Mr. Loring."

"Is that a compliment?"

"Quite the reverse, if you care to take it that way. I mean, it's too easy to impress you."

"I'm not going to be angry; go ahead."

"I knew you wouldn't be. Only cowards are easily angered, I think. They are afraid that their fear will be discovered. They wear their courage on their shoulders. They dare a thousand dangers, desperately eager to prove their valiance to the world, and half hoping that they may be able to deceive themselves.

"Who is it that leads the forlorn chance? The coward! Who is it that leaps out and stops the running horse? The coward! Who is it that takes the powder-loaded ship into the harbor to blow up the fortifications and flirt with the devil or God? Always the coward."

"Come, come," chuckled Loring. "An aphorism is good for the palate, but this is not before dinner. You'd have me believe that there are no brave men? At least that all heroic actions are the work of cowards?"

"No, no! Not at all! The man who puts on the enemy's uniform and goes to live with them, in constant peril, using his wits. He is the hero. The detective who steps into the gang and dons their manners for a month while he works out their plans and discovers their crimes, he is a hero. The policeman who, with only his monthly pay-check to reward him, goes soberly into a den in full uniform, puts his hand on the shoulder of his man, and then walks out with him and turns his back on twenty knives and guns eager to be at him—he is the hero of all heroes! But these impulsive bursts of courage—cowards all of 'em!"

He smiled. "I've fallen into one of my unpardonable lectures. But I revert to the beginning: you are a man of courage as well as muscle. You don't have to prove yourself to yourself, therefore you are careless of the opinion of the world, and therefore you are not out to take offense easily."

"That is a very fine compliment, Mr. Zanten."

"A very heavy one. I am still lecturing, it seems. It is my fault.

I push a man away at arm's length and squint at him as if he were marble. Well—forgive me."

"Keep on talking. I enjoy it. Among other things, I'd like to know how you were so sure that I'd come here to-night."

"So simple that if I explain it will instantly destroy all faith in me. But to begin: You leave here a long time ago. You embark on a series of startling adventures—"

"What makes you think that?"

"My dear fellow, I occasionally read the papers. I read that you were mixed up in the Wilbur mess. By the way, Buttrick is grateful because you so decently kept his place out of the dailies. At any rate, I say, you have embarked on a set of thrilling adventures. They reached their dénouement the other day with the condemnation of poor Peter Charles.

"I give you one day to think things over. On the following day—which is to-day—your mind reverts to the last thing you were doing before you started on these exciting, disagreeable experiences. In a word, you remember Buttrick's and decide to blur the past by a second visit to this house, the more so since you won on your last jaunt here. I think of these things, and patiently sit down here to wait for you. Is it not simple?"

"Some might call it simple. But I won't. You're infernally clever, Mr. Zanten. However, will you explain why you called Peter Charles 'poor Peter Charles?'"

"Gladly."

"You mean, of course, that you don't think he committed the crime?"

"Not at all! Of course he committed the crime. The police in these matters are almost never wrong, no matter what the foolish fiction writers say. If it comes to that, how could the police fall far short of the truth in the majority of their cases? Think of how many clews a murderer leaves behind him.

"Usually from the motives alone one may work out the identity of the slayer. A woman is at the bottom of two-thirds of the dirty work, and liquor is on the top. If a man is killed, go over his accounts, obtain access to his correspondence, and as a rule you have a dozen valuable clews inside of an hour.

"Of course, where the motive is robbery it is more difficult. But those who kill for money are a small class, on the whole. No, sir, the odds are nine to two that Peter Charles is the man."

While Zanten talked the heart of Loring dropped into his boots. In the presence of this white-faced man he felt more childish than ever and more impotent.

"Yet you call him 'poor Charles?'"

"For a tolerably good reason. I always shudder when I hear of some weakling, some fool, some drunken knave, some coward, some dirty-handed robber, who has aspired to the greatest of the works of man—murder!"

"Tush! This is too much to go down, Mr. Zanten! Murder glorious?"

"Of course. Under different names, perhaps. What made the stupid, unimaginative Brutus great? Because he dared to strike one of twenty-three wounds into the body of Caesar. What made the Corday divine? Because she stabbed a dirty, diseased madman in his bath.

"There are more celebrated murderers. We make statues of them. That was because they worked on a larger scale. Your Alexander and Hannibal, who nearly destroyed beautiful Italy. Who weeps for the eighty thousand Romans of Cannes? No one! But who will not weep for the wretched end of great Hannibal?

"But divorce yourself from prejudice, Mr. Loring. Make an effort—a muscular effort of the mind. What could be more divine than at a stroke to turn a living, breathing, loving, hating, aspiring human being into so many pounds of fertilizer? What, I say, is more glorious than murder? To take out a life on the point of your knife, or on your rapier end in the days when men still were not afraid to be happy; even to blow a bullet into the head of an enemy and know that his soul has been knocked out of his body a thousand times more swiftly than your bullet entered it?

"Now, sir, will you not be prepared to say a word on behalf of murder? And do you not shrink and wince when you think of such a pitiful driveling ass as Peter Charles actually putting his gun to the breast of a human life and taking it? It is putting the lightning bolt in the hands of the starveling. Brrr!"

He shivered daintily, and Loring smiled a rather cold appreciation.

"I see that you are a philosopher, Mr. Zanten."

"Good heavens, sir, that is the last of insults! I a philosopher? No, no! I am contented to live on what meets the eye and the ear; I don't have to turn a mountain into a cloud or a man into a dream of a man in order to read new meanings into 'em."

"Very well. But in the meantime you've chilled me to the bone with your ideas. Let's have a drink."

"I'll be glad to go with you. But I shall not drink. I never drink except between eleven and one."

"You keep your head clear, then? Don't like the stuff?"

"Not at all. To be drunk, properly, is divine. To see the colors of the world and of life brightened and sweetened, to gain sudden belief in the goodness of man, the beauty of woman, the rightness of fatherhood and of marriage, the justice of laws, the benevolence of government, the perfection of art—why, sir, to deny one's self the rite of drunkenness is to deliberately close the gate of heaven—perhaps the only heaven there is."

"Such a thinker," smiled Loring. "And yet not an atheist?"

"Not so great a fool as that! Lock out of my mind the delightful possibility of an intelligent first cause? No, no! I shudder at the thought! Abandon the hope of that exquisite dialogue which shall ensue when I face the Maker and justify my sins to Him?

"Tush! I spend hours framing the sentences for that occasion, polishing my periods, strengthening my verbs, diminishing my adjectives, adjusting my voice, composing my features and my gestures. What a moment! And—we shall have so much to talk about!"

They reached a small dining room, paneled in ivory-painted wood. There were Italian landscapes in long, narrow murals, breaking out of the walls toward a garden pool, or through a row of poplars, or down a windy lane. To their little table the waiter brought Loring's Scotch.

"You have touched one subject in which I am vitally interested," said Loring.

"And that?"

"Murder."

"Good! A theme of which I delight to talk. I could ramble on forever concerning its intricacies. I am filled with anecdotes on that charming subject. Only tell me where I am to begin?"

# CHAPTER XXV

# "MURDER"

**"I HAVE AN** excellent starting point. The last time I talked with you—and the first time—you said that on an occasion I held the price of a man's life in my hand."

"I remember it nicely. The very expression on your face when I made the remark."

"Very well. Will you develop that remark?"

"In what way?"

"Tell me how it is possible to buy a life."

"Willingly. There is in this city a Murder Company."

"A what!"

"A Murder Company. Does that surprise you?"

Loring sipped his drink and composed himself.

"I have heard of such atrocious things—in fiction, I think."

"Fiction is drab stuff. Turn to life. Do you want humor, pathos, tragedy? Any ten men make a crowd, any crowd will furnish you with all these things. A Murder Company? Why not?"

"Men gathered for the sole purpose of destroying other men for a price?"

"I repeat: why not? How wanting our civilization would be without such a convenience! No, I thank God that we are still not entirely degenerated. Why, sir, Egypt, Greece, Rome, all had their Murder Companies. That of the Medici in France was a crude organization—but effective in a crude century.

"There have always been such organizations. They meet a primitive need. There are peoples with whom murder is a religious rite. There are head-hunters who hang up their trophies."

"Barbarians! Yes, I can understand that."

"Tush! What difference between the Indian who took a scalp and the Western gunman—now, alas, too few—who chipped a notch on his gun? Different skins—the same vigorous, joyous, manly hearts beneath the skin! Open your eyes to the world, my dear fellow.

"At this very moment, in Central Africa, the spearman hurls his leaf-bladed spear across the corn and strikes down the bought victim; the little brown man in India peeps over the fallen trunk and blows his poisoned arrow into the back of the bought victim; and the hired gunfighter in Manhattan slips through the back entrance and sends his daintily placed bullet into the brain of his bought victim. And yet you shudder at the thought of a Murder Company? My friend, you bring me close to laughter!"

"At least," said Loring, "you are stimulating, if not quite credible."

"It is true," nodded the man with the opal, "that my mind is not limited by the absurd bonds of truth. I thank God that He made me enough of a poet to tell a round, sounding lie with grace and unction. But what is false or unique in the idea of a Murder Company?

"What would you think of a civilization which crowds the thought of the world into your bookshelves, the music of the world upon a series of little wax disks, the art of the world at least shadowed forth in a pile of pictures at a penny a piece? What would you think of such a civilization, I say, if after having heated you without smoke, and lighted you without flame, and annihilated for you space and time, and for you read the stars of heaven like the pages of a book—what would you think of such a civilization if having accomplished all these things for your delectation it stops miserably short and refuses to grant you a thing so disgustingly cheap, so common, so tawdry as a human life? Would it not be a makeshift world without that convenience?"

"You are charming in your theories," smiled Loring. "Please continue. You press a button and the man is dead?"

"Nearly so."

"Then there must be many companies competing. That, no doubt, keeps the price down to a moderate level."

"No, not many companies."

"The murder experts destroy each other?"

"Not at all. Of course there are small organizations who will kill your man on the street, brutally, cheaply, without finesse, and perhaps bring the danger of the killing to your door. But there is only room for one great, perfect, neatly elaborated Murder Company, adequate in all its parts to the solemn offices it must perform."

"You made it out a simple thing a moment ago. Now you pile up the difficulties."

"Not the difficulties of execution. The approach is everything. The salesmanship is the thing!"

"Ah?"

"Consider what polished agents the Murder Company must possess—all capable of seeing in murder an art and not a crime. But how various, how differing one from the other! There must be the soft-faced, blue-eyed youth of gentle speech and appealing manners to come to the lovely girl who has been foisted into the hands of a husband horribly old and gloriously wealthy.

"He must win her confidence; he must paint for her the charming picture of what her life could be, freed from the incubus of her dotard helpmate. He must show her that she is an exquisite jewel in a base setting, and having filled her with horror for her life as it is, he must suddenly open to her dazzled eyes the hope of freedom. He must have such address that she will be sufficiently frightened to rule her tongue; and sufficiently enchanted to pay a high price."

"But what if she denies the price after the death of the husband? Or does the Murder Company work only on a cash basis?"

"Not at all. But there is this peculiarity. The Murder Company always is able to collect. Failing in that, it names a definite date. If the money is not forthcoming, the ingrate dies. No excuses are accepted. No promises pass. Death is the penalty—a death for a death. What could be more appropriate?"

"What indeed," murmured Loring. The horrible tale was fascinating him.

"And consider, too," ran on the narrator of this thrilling fact or marvelous fiction, whatever it might be, "how different a man must be sent to the husband who is tired of his wife and wishes a change without the disgusting scandal of the law courts. Perhaps he is a man of much feeling, a delicate soul, trembling away from disagreeable things. He must be approached with nice distinctions. And the lady must die without pain, simply, naturally, breathing her last in the arms of the husband who has bought her ruin and whose tears fall upon her face. How touching the scene; my eyes moisten to think of it!

"And then, in a decent interval, into the place of the wife who has died so beautifully comes the new wife, the loved wife, and the home becomes a place of happiness—all of this caused by the Murder Company. Confess, Mr. Loring, that you begin to be charmed by my account?"

"I am, at least, interested."

"But so many angles from which the work of the Company should be viewed! Consider, again, what type of agent they must have in order that they may approach the king of finance in the midst of a great raid which shakes Wall Street to its deep foundations! How brusque, how swift of tongue, how sure of detail, how convincing, how grim, how bland he must be, all in a breath, to open the eyes of the king of finance, and show him how the one vital enemy who threatens the plan with destruction and loss may be removed as a gentle wind removes the dead leaf from the tree!

"What men this Murder Company must have! What exquisite statesmanship, what faces bold and grave and fierce and gentle and beautiful all looking toward one end. How dexterous must be the financiers at the head of it who can estimate the price which each of the patrons should pay! How deft the craftsmen who plan the murders in detail! How various the artists who build the scheme!

"Having said all this, Mr. Loring, surely you realize why there cannot be more than one great Murder Company, taking on its hands great killings and small, big and little, weak and strong? One all-powerful company which reaches across the seas, which puts the skinny hand of death on the shoulder of the king, and whispers in the ear of the miser, and strikes down the man of violence! What deftness to reach the most hidden; what might to reach through numbers at the victim; what cunning to walk on tar and sand and leave no traces!"

"And you mean to say that all the crimes are committed with impunity?"

"Of course not. What would be the pleasure in a work devoid of dangers? No, the agents must have human weaknesses. They must from time to time fail."

"And when they are caught they never reveal the secrets?"

"Never! The Ku Klux existed in thousands, and for years, and a secret was never betrayed. Is not that true? And how far more terrible is the control which the Murder Company must exercise over its agents! No, when there is a shadow of doubt, when it is feared that the agent may weaken, the Company takes no chances. With its own grim hand it reaches to the caught agent and slays him before he can confess and incriminate his masters."

Loring brushed a hand across his forehead.

"And now," said the man with the opal, fixing his singular eyes upon the face of Loring, "what is your hidden motive in all these questions?"

"A simple one."

"Have I guessed it?"

"Yes. Mr. Zanten, there is a man who must die!"

"Tush! No whispers! The walls have ears for whispers; for a normal voice there is no listening spy. There is a man who must die. Good! I am glad to see that you have a soul strong enough to use the great engine of which I have been speaking."

He nodded, smiling down at his interlaced fingers.

"And how shall I meet an agent?" asked Loring.

"I shall relieve you of that difficult thing. Place the name of the man in an envelope; put with it the requisite sum of money, and I shall see that the envelope reaches the proper destination. There must be a date with the name."

"The date of the murder?"

"To be sure."

"And what sum of money is necessary?"

"That depends, of course. It depends on the wealth you possess and the difficulty of the task you impose."

"As for my wealth, I have most of it with me."

"I presumed that. And now, for the gentleman whose existence you wish to terminate. Is he a man of many friends?"

"Almost none. Acquaintances, yes, but no friends, I think I may say."

"Is he surrounded by servants in a house difficult of access?"

"No. A public lodging house."

"A simple matter. Now, as to the nature of this man. Is he capable of action?"

"I should say that he is, decidedly."

"A dangerous man in a pinch, perhaps?"

"He has been considered dangerous."

"I believe it. From the glint in your eye I should say he is a man worthy of much consideration. He is wary, steady of nerve, strong handed, a fighter with weapons, eh?"

"All of those things, to a certain extent, I think I may say he is."

"In that case, I think I may say that the Murder Company will do your work for—say, five thousand dollars. I will not hide from you that I am fortunate enough to be highly esteemed by those who are powerful in the councils of this organization, and I shall see that part of your money is refunded if the work is simpler than you expect it to be."

"Five thousand is a good deal. My man would be flattered, I suspect, by such a price. Five hundred for a good horse, but five thousand for a man! Well, well!"

He counted the money from his wallet, wrote down name and address and date on a piece of paper, and enclosed the whole in an envelope which the waiter brought. Then he rose and said farewell to Nicholas Zanten. The latter was surprised by the abrupt departure.

"You see," said Loring, "I am anxious that you should set the machinery in order to work as soon as possible."

And so saying, he left Buttrick's.

# CHAPTER XXVI

# THE GREATER POWER

**THE MOMENT LORING** was gone, Nicholas Zanten went
to a telephone in Buttrick's, and having spoken for a moment
to his party, returned to his table and sat down to wait. He was
one of those rare men who can wait calmly whether for a train
or an assignation. Half a dozen passing through the dining
room for a drink or supper, stopped to speak to the famous
gambler. But each one of those who stopped had been picked
up by the eyes of the gambler, and after a word a slight coldness
in his face dismissed them.

And finally his man came.

He was in formal evening dress, and he was in a great hurry.
He drew off only his right glove to shake hands with Nicholas
Zanten and sit down to smoke a cigarette. He was a broad-faced
man, with high, healthy color and a tuft of shining black mustache across his lip. He was a man who spoke carefully, relish-
ing his words.

"I have two minutes—no more. So hurry, my dear Zanten."

There were two things which displeased the gambler in this
speech. The first was the mention of time; the second was the
familiar phrase of address.

"The time is not enough."

"Very well. Then ever so little longer."

" 'Ever so little longer' is not enough."

"Good gad, Zanten, I am bound for a party I wouldn't miss
for worlds!"

"Then by all means "don't miss it, Mr. Kane. Good evening, and a happy time to you."

"But the commission?"

"I can find another for it. Besides, it is only a small sum, and no doubt you will not be interested."

Kane stopped in the act of rising.

"You know that the work is the thing and the business is nothing."

"So I hoped. However, you are busy, Mr. Kane. I'm sorry I interrupted you. By all means run along to your party."

"But tell me in ten words."

"I rarely confine myself to ten words; a thing done in a hurry is a thing spoiled."

Kane writhed with impatience.

"Shall I call off my engagement?"

"Not at all. I hope I have not implied that. No, no! I shall find another."

"Mr. Zanten," said Kane soberly, "I have been honored by a direct call from you. Tell me what I must do. Shall I break off my engagement?"

"That is a matter in your discretion."

For a moment Kane struggled with himself. Then, sighing, he went to the telephone. When he returned: "I am at your service for the evening," he said.

"Good," nodded Nicholas Zanten. "You begin to know me better."

There was a dying flash of impatience on the face of Kane. Then he settled back in his chair, attentive.

"You are aware," said Zanten, "that at various times I have been of service to the Company?"

"Naturally. All of those within the inner circle understand, Mr. Zanten."

"Then you will perceive a sharp point when I say that I am about to ask a benefit from the Company."

"By all means. I am not rash in stating that the entire re-sources of the Company are instantly at your disposal."

"I am deeply sensible." Zanten bowed. "As a matter of fact, the service is not directly to me. It is to a friend."

He added hastily: "A friend whom I esteem so highly that work done for him is more than work done for me."

"I understand."

"But be sure that you understand entirely. My friend is one of those rare men who unite in one nature the strength of a bold nature and the heart of a child, a terrible simplicity, tem-pered by the saving grace—a sense of humor. Summon such a man into your mind's eye."

"I am doing it as well as I may. This is the nature of the person who wishes us to execute a commission?"

"Are you smiling?"

"Certainly not. I only suggest that you qualify your remark about the 'heart of a child.'"

"Mr. Kane, I never qualify my remarks. They are, in the incep-tion, as accurate as I can make them."

Kane swallowed, accepted the lesson humbly, and bowed.

"Very good, Mr. Zanten."

"This rare man, I say," went on Zanten, "this heart of gold, this unique and generous spirit, has honored me by placing a trust in my hands. That trust I am about to convey to you. It is a solemn moment to me; I am not accustomed to giving the affairs of my few friends into the hands of others—even to the Company. You realize, Mr. Kane, that this is unusual?"

"I do, sir."

It was easy to see that Kane was entirely subdued by the dominating personality of this man.

"Then take this envelope."

He passed it across the table, and Kane accepted it with a frown. He was very serious.

"It is a personal commission for me?"

"For you?" cried Zanten. "God above! No! You are a capable man, Mr. Kane. I know it; I admit it; I admit it with pleasure. But in a matter which I have carried in person to the Company, I expect that its fullest resources shall be brought to bear on my behalf.

"There is no strength of hand, cunning in conception, skill in execution, polish of detail, which I do not expect to be lavished upon this matter. The price is five thousand dollars. If that price is not sufficient I shall be glad to make up the deficit from my own purse."

Mr. Kane bowed profoundly.

"Between you and the Company, sir," he said gracefully, "permit me to say that money is not a consideration."

"Tush! Permit me to say that in the twentieth century money is always a consideration."

"Sir, I can only answer that definite instructions have been given me concerning you and your wishes; those instructions came from the highest authority that I acknowledge."

It was impossible to exaggerate the depth of Zanten's gratification. It was marked by a flush and the sparkle of his eyes.

"Then—open the envelope, Mr. Kane."

The latter obeyed.

"The date?" said Zanten.

"The eighth of this month."

"Ah, he is liberal in time to the Company. It shows that he has forethought. Or perhaps he wishes to make sure—he esteems this man a dangerous fellow."

"Now, the name of the man he wishes removed? Or perhaps it is a woman? No, the last would be impossible!"

"It is a man, sir."

"Good! His name?"

"Samuel Loring."

"What?"

Zanten rose.

"I asked for the name of the man who is to be killed, the price of whose death was enclosed in that envelope! No jesting!"

Kane was pale and troubled. He extended the paper with a shaking hand.

"Upon my honor, sir, that is what I find written here."

Zanten glanced down at the writing. There, written in a bold, firm hand, he found that Loring had indeed inscribed his own name. The gambler sank into his chair as though borne down by a weight.

"Is it possible!" he gasped.

He drew himself together with an effort, with such a fury in his face that Kane blanched again.

"I have said that he has a sense of humor," said Zanten, "this friend of mine?"

"You do not mean that his name is that name I have here! The proscribed man?"

"Do I not mean it? Boy, idiot, do you dictate to me what I think? What I dare to think? I tell you, it is the same! He has dared to treat me, Nicholas Zanten, lightly. He has made a jest at my expense. By the thunder of God, he shall die for it! You have heard me speak before? Now write all that I have said down in red! The man shall die!"

Kane was overwhelmed.

"It shall be done, sir."

"Shall it be done?" said Zanten, repeating the trembling tone with terrible mockery. "It shall! Go to the highest power in the Company. Give him my message. Not as a request. Tell him that I, Nicholas Zanten, command that it be done. That no stone be left unturned!"

He sank back in his chair, exhausted by his passion, and glancing here and there as though he sought an object on which he could wreak his wrath.

"And if the Company fails—and I warn you that they will find a difficult task—tell your masters that a greater power than the Company will then take the matter up."

"I beg your pardon, sir," said the shaken Kane. "Did you say a greater power than the Company?"

"I said it and I repeat it. A greater power than the Company. For if you fail, I, sir, I myself shall kill Samuel Loring. Now, begone!"

He had no need to repeat the order. Kane shrank away from the table like a whipped puppy. He left Zanten standing erect, again, behind the table, with his tall form quivering and his eyes blazing into the blank wall before him. A group, entering the room, saw that imposing figure and of one accord shrank out of the dining room. The word hummed through the tapestry softened rooms of Buttrick's—Nicholas Zanten, for the first time in history, was palpably enraged.

# CHAPTER XXVII

# THE LIVING CLEW

**IT HAD BEEN** sheer despair on the part of Loring. He knew well enough that he had neither the experience nor the practical wit to actually pick up the traces of the crime and follow them back to the criminal—always providing that that criminal were other than poor Peter Charles. What remained? If he could not go to the crime, might there not be the only other possibility? That he could make the crime come to him?

From the first he had said to himself: "If I had been in the shoes of Joseph Wilbur, I should not have submitted meekly. I should have struck back and struck hard and taken a fair fighting chance with the man who hounded me."

But all the actions of Wilbur presupposed that he was fighting against an overwhelming power. And as Nicholas Zanten developed the remarks about the Murder Company, the conviction grew in Loring that that gruesome body and no other had been at the basis of Wilbur's fear. That was the inescapable net in the toils of which he had labored. What Loring had seen, as he heard the words of the man with the opal, had not been that bloodless face, but Beatrice Charles, her color gone, her eyes abased—the branded daughter of a murderer!

Loring proceeded with grim logic, shuddering as he approached the conclusion. If that which had destroyed Joseph Wilbur was the Murder Company, the way to make the murdering power known to the law was to take some member of it red-handed, force a confession from him by heartless torture, if necessary, and exposing the entire organization, discover the truth about Joseph Wilbur.

In a word, Loring determined to do what he had often wished to do. He would step into the shoes of Joseph Wilbur, upon his head he would draw the full force of that terror which had wrecked the dead man, and using all his cunning, all his courage, all his strength, he would try to parry the blows of the Murder Company, and at last, knocking the weapon out of its hands, secure it, and with it the clew to the death of Wilbur.

To a calm-minded man this wild conclusion would have been impossible. Loring was not calm-minded. He was worked up to a pitch of frantic enthusiasm, and the stimulant had been the last interview with Beatrice. He knew of her engagement to Geoffrey Charles, but in spite of that when he remembered how she had stood smiling toward him, with the sunlight about her, he began to hope foolishly, wildly.

When he left the man with the opal he was already a victim of the Murder Company. Walking down the street he stared earnestly at the buildings he passed. He stopped and listened with wonder to the gay laughter of a crowd in an automobile. His own time for laughter had ceased. Perhaps, already the man with the opal had transmitted the commission and had set the bloodhounds on his trail.

For all he knew, Zanten himself might be the ringleader of the Murder Company. Yet something told Loring that the man with the opal was tied to no partners, even partners as grim as the Murder Company. The man must, by his nature, operate alone.

To return to his rooms Loring had no heart. Once he entered them the end would approach. He would sit, conscious of every window as of a watching eye, trembling at each sound in the hall, shaken by every whisper of the wind, shuddering when a hand knocked at the door.

He would not return to that place, already become a place

of death in his imagination. Instead, he went to the park and
began to walk rapidly.

But his thoughts kept pace with him and circled around him
in Seven League boots. How could he tell? Perhaps, as he left
the room Zanten had placed the envelope in the hands of the
emissary of the Murder Company. Perhaps that man had followed, had watched the course he took, and was even now
dogging his footsteps!

Loring turned abruptly and looked back over the crowd. He
had never looked into faces as he looked now, with the horrible
question: Which is my murderer?

He sat down on a bench beside the path and let the crowd
drift past him. What faces! Fat, pinched, young, old, yellow,
white, flushed, dark, man, woman—any one of these might be
the agent. Perhaps the old woman huddled in her shawl. It must
be part of the technique of the Murder Company to use every
element of surprise.

The few men he knew might be corrupted by the hand of
the Murder Company. And this very bench on which he sat
with the crowd drifting before him—how could he tell that he
was safe here?

He jumped up. Behind him a wave of shrubbery rolled close
to the bench. An ideal covert. Through those green mazes, how
simple to stalk up to that bench, to fire the five thousand dollar
shot, and then disappear while the stupid crowd swerved and
gathered around the dead body and the murderer slipped away
in the opposite direction—nay, even came out and joined the
crowd and pretended to be horrified, and looked into the dead
face of his victim, and took a foremost hand in summoning the
police. How simple!

Loring started on hastily, feeling that he had already gone
through one death. He felt that now, indeed, he was walking
in the shoes of dead Joseph Wilbur. His glances roved and
rested on every face which passed him, just as the glances of
Wilbur roved.

*"You feel that pressure in the small of your back?"*

He had neglected one obvious thing, like a fool. To remedy that neglect he turned back toward his house and on the way he stopped at an electrician's shop and bought the articles which he needed. He had some knowledge of electricity picked up here and there, and he must use all his knowledge to make his room as safe as possible.

It was already the gloom of evening as he approached the place. Tired laborers, businessmen, clerks, girls, were going slowly home, all happy, all with inert faces from which the work of the day was slowly passing. They were happy. It was the pleasant and relaxed time of the day. But to Loring alone of all that crowd the coming darkness was terrible. It was putting a mask over the people he passed. It was turning every corner into a lurking place.

When he opened the front door the blackness of the hall struck at him like a hand. A dozen men might be hiding there! No, they would not choose such a place. They would have entered his room and hidden there!

The thought turned him cold with his hand on the knob of his own door. He turned it, cast the door open, and stepped deftly to one side.

Silence met him, a listening silence and utter dark. No, through the window of the living room the light streamed faintly, paler than moonlight. Behind every chair a danger might be crouched. Gathering his nerve power, he stepped into the room and slammed the door behind him. The impact shook him to the heart, but with his teeth set, he switched on the lights and thereby made himself a target!

Hurriedly he made his examination. Under every couch, behind every chair or bed, among the clothes in the closets. He missed nothing that might shelter the bulk of a man.

Then he sank down in a chair to think. These agents of the Murder Company were experts trained in the finest details of their horrible business. They had mastered all the methods of famous criminals; they were adepts in that science upon which so much human thought and mental labor have been expend-ed—the science of taking life certainly and securely.

"To kill is nothing," the man with the opal often said. "To kill with immunity—that is to rival God."

If so, the men of the Murder Company must be godlike. Although Loring had searched his little apartment from one end to the other, he was not satisfied. He remembered how he himself had managed to deceive the experts by hiding the parts of the automatic. How vastly easier for them to deceive him?

He turned his head—then started up with a low cry. The window—the open, gaping window was behind him and op-posite the window was a naked roof. Loring shuddered. It was a very old house, gas-lighted, and the windows guarded with ponderous shutters. He blessed the antiquity of the place for the first time, now, as he drew the shutters and locked them.

So much was done. But still the entrances were not watched. He could not be in both the living room and the bedroom at the same time For that reason he had brought the electric ap-pliances. He arranged them carefully, spending the entire evening in the work. When he finished the tiny wires had been buried, leading from the doors and the windows to a bell, and, when he closed the switch connecting the batteries, no one could budge door or window without giving a noisy alarm.

But having accomplished this work, he did not breathe the more freely.

His position was the more terrible in that he could not flee from the danger or hide himself from it. His whole aim was to expose himself, in appearance, as recklessly as possible, and trust to his speed of hand and eye to strike before the striker.

Growing thirsty with the fever which was getting hold on him, he drew a glass of water at the tap. With the glass at his lips his fingers opened. The glass crashed on the floor and the water drenched his feet.

That was a close call! Might they not, with their devilish cunning, have poisoned his tap? Would not that be a neat device, to enter his room in his absence, put the poison in the faucet, and without danger, without effort, secure the death of the fool who had drawn all this upon his own head?

Loring had some faint memory of such things being done. He had heard rumors of poisons so terrible that a quantity no larger than the head of a pin put on the tongue of a horse would kill the great beast instantly. Poisons so horrible that a breath of the gas would kill; poisons so concentrated that in the hollow of his hand the murderer might hold the lives of an army!

Feeling suddenly weak, Loring picked up the broken fragments of the glass. Then he took the table lamp and the length of the cord enabled him to examine the faucet. He saw nothing amiss in it. But what of that? Were there not poisons which were both colorless and odorless?

He was thirsty; he was ravenously hungry. But did he dare to venture into the hideously black night for food? He made up his mind that this was a craven shrinking from inevitable things. He settled his hat firmly on his head, took out his neat automatic, looked well to the parts, and then left the house.

At every step he wanted to halt and swing about suddenly

to see who pursued. For the sense of the pursuit was never from him.

He went to the restaurant around the corner where he often ate breakfast, and he sat down at his corner table. Fritz, the waiter who always served him, came at once, smiling, and paused over the order to gossip a moment. Loring drew him out. It was heaven to have that honest, smiling face leaning so close to him. And when Fritz left, boldly he drained the glass of water. Must he not take infinitely greater chances than this?

Finally the food came. But with his fork in his hand he was stopped.

It was as though someone had jogged his elbow. Fool! fool! fool! What would the Murder Company's agents have done first of all? They would have inquired into the habits of their destined victim. They would learn where he lived and slept first, and next, where he ate. Certainly that would be their procedure. And first of all they would learn about the little restaurant around the corner.

With that point established, how simple was all the rest? The cooks they would leave alone, but what of Fritz? Was the servile affection of Fritz, purchased at the rate of a ten or fifteen cent tip each time he ate, proof against a five thousand dollar bribe?

All at once he looked down and saw the ragged edge of the waiter's trousers, frayed at the heel. Loring rose in haste and went to the desk, where he paid his bill and stepped into the night. His forehead was wet. Another narrow escape!

If he would eat, he must go to an unexpected place. Accordingly, he got on the subway, rode for half an hour, got off at a random station.

He made his mind a blank about the place. For if he dared to think they might be able to guess his thoughts. Had not the devilish Nicholas Zanten done a more difficult thing than that, and done it simply, surely? He left the subway, entered the first lunch-counter he came to, and ordered a meal.

But when it came his appetite was gone. With a shaking hand he broke the bread. The meat was tasteless. He could only force himself to swallow a few morsels, and then betook himself back to the subway? No! Surely he was not fool enough to return the same way he came!

He hurried around the block, walked for ten minutes down-town, then doubled back, took a surface car, and in this manner arrived at the lodging house.

But he was weak, now, from the steady strain and the lack of food. And entering the house there was the same ordeal to go through again—the black hall—the horror of entering his room—the hasty search through every inch of his apartment—the examination of his electric apparatus to make sure that it had not been tampered with.

And at length, he lay down on his bed.

And this was only part of the first day! There remained six days—six eternities—six hells before him!

CHAPTER XXVIII

# THE FIRST ATTEMPT

**FOR SOME TIME** he was awake. It was an old house, as had been said, and old houses are haunted. There is no doubt about that. For every light-footed girl who has lived in an old house; for every ponderous man who has thumped up and down the halls; for every feeble, halting crone; for all these people there remain ghost-sounds.

And when the wind blows one who lies awake will hear the swift patter of the girl as she flies lightly up the stairs once more to recover the vanity case which she has forgotten on the eve of going off with her lover; and again there is a dull and regular sound as the heavy man treads solemnly on his way; and sometimes, more awful still, the ancient woman comes halting up the stairs, with irregular steps, pausing with loud creaks on the landings, and then going up step by step, step by step, in this second infancy of mind and body.

Loring listened while those phantoms climbed the stairs and stole down the hall and hearkened at his door. Once or twice he was absolutely certain that a hand was trying the lock of the door. And he steadied his nerves against the clangor of the alarm.

He had hardly settled back in bed after the breathless tenseness of one of these alarms, when sleep swept over him, numbed his brain, and to the last he was conscious of fighting against an invincible enemy.

He slept. Into his dream there came nightmares of doors

which opened without visible agencies. He was continually finding himself seated in his room, and looking up to discover that mysteriously someone had stepped through the solid wall and stood with arms folded, looking down at him, mocking him with a smile. Usually the features of these phantoms resembled the features of Nicholas Zanten.

At length the dreams altered to a more pleasant character. He was riding in the country. It was the joyous time of the year. The fields were wakening. A fresh scent of the wild flowers was in his face.

That fragrance persisted, grew heavier.

The scene changed to a funeral. On all sides were the banks and masses of the flowers. The scent was terrible, stifling, for the church was warm. Thick drifts of incense smoke clouded the air. The crowd was dimmed. A bright light shone over the coffin only. He approached the coffin, looked in, and beheld his own features locked in the rigidity of death smiling the cold, last smile which mocks the living.

A reeling faintness overcame him—and he wakened. At first he was conscious of only the heaviness of head, the reality of the vision, and a slight hissing sound, as though someone were warning him to lie down again.

And then he caught the thick, sweetish scent of gas. He managed to reach the jet. It was turned on and the warning hiss was the sound of the escaping gas. Then he stumbled to the window, flung open the shutters, and let life blow back into his face. Gradually he came out of the dream, and into throbbing, painful life.

There was a knock at the door. The fumes of the gas were now fairly well cleared from the room. He closed the shutters in spite of the impatient repetition of the knock, turned back the switch of the electric alarm, and opened the door upon the haggard face of his landlady in her bathrobe, with wisps of thick gray hair hanging about her face.

"What in the world, Mr. Loring!" she snarled at him. "The smell of gas is something awful in the halls. You ain't been—"

She stepped back a little as though to view him more clearly; as though there were more in his face than she could read at one glance.

"I'm all right," he answered roughly. "Nothing wrong here. Try one of the other rooms."

She remained watching him for a moment, nodding her head with an unpleasant wisdom, as though she had read his mind to her own satisfaction.

"It ain't for me to give no young man advice," she declared. "Them that ain't come to fifty ain't able to understand sense."

With that mysterious declaration, she turned on her heel and left him without further greeting. Loring closed the door, connected the alarm again, and went to bed.

But there was no sleep.

Until day he lay studying the night noises, and wondering. Certainly no human being had entered that room since he returned. And yet some hand had reached to the gas jet and turned it on. The mystery was more awful to him than the peril which he had so closely escaped.

He did a foolish thing in the morning. He went to a shooting gallery and practiced with the automatic. It was a needless precaution. The skill which a lifetime of familiarity with firearms had given him had not been perceptibly dulled by his late inaction. His hand was as true and as steady as ever, and his eye almost as sure. He made the bell sing a tune, smashed an entire circle of spinning clay ducks, and then went out into the street.

He had been a double fool, he felt. Beyond question they would know what he had done, and after that exhibition they would be asinine indeed if they ventured to match the skill of one of their gunmen against his quick trigger finger. He had simply removed his one good chance of facing the murderer and beating him at his own game, for hereafter that game would not be played with his own weapons.

They had tried gas. Next they would try what? A bomb? Poison? Poison gas? The ways were illimitable.

During the day he felt comparatively safe. The night would be the time of peril, and against the night he must guard himself. But how? With a sudden thrill of hope he thought of the police. Why not go to them, lay his cards on the table, declare his purpose and his danger, and invite their protection.

But he decided quickly enough that this was not an available way out. In the first place they would undoubtedly think him mad. In the second place, to convince them that he might be right, he would have to tell a story inculpating Nicholas Zanten. In the third place, if he put himself in the hands of the police, might he not be putting himself in the hands of the Murder Company itself? It was more than probable. How simple for them to approach one of his guardians and corrupt the man! For Nicholas Zanten had shown him how cheap lives are bought.

The defense of his life must rest in his own hands. The apprehension of the agent of the Murder Company must rest in his own hands. And in the meantime he had one dire enemy in himself—that enemy was sleep. No sleep for six days was impossible. But he must never do more than nap, with one eye open, and in the dog-watches of the nights he must protect himself with a stimulant.

He went to a doctor whom he had visited before. He told him a simple enough story, and the doctor after a careful examination of Loring's heart, prescribed strychnine and instructed him in the use of it. With that drug purchased, Loring was ready to fight the one inner foe.

It took such a burden from his shoulders that he went for a long walk, heedless of the fact that physical exertion was a certain means of wooing sleepiness. His way carried him through the park and across to Park Avenue; and there he was surprised by a hail in a woman's voice from an automobile that stopped a little way ahead of him. He saw Beatrice Charles looking back at him. And he went to her with his hat in his hand.

She was frankly glad to see him, and asked him to lunch, and Loring accepted because there was nothing else to do. What he wondered at was her cheerfulness; what he wondered at most of all was that she carefully avoided all reference to the affairs of her father, except when he bluntly and a little brutally asked questions.

Then she told him that the last stone had been turned in vain. The governor had been approached; he had definitely refused to grant a pardon. He had even refused with gusto. In vain they had attempted to apply political leverage. The men who had once been proud to call themselves friends of Peter Charles now scorned to remember his name and when they were approached declared that they hoped he would be visited with the full penalty of the law. As for an appeal to another court, Lowrie himself had now discountenanced it.

She recited these terrible facts which removed hope from her father with a steady voice. It was almost as if her concern for her father were swallowed by some other and new worry, and Loring noted that her eyes were marked with shadows and pinched at the corners from want of sleep. He knew those symptoms all too well!

As he was leaving, the cause for her concern—at least in part—appeared. She stopped him as he was turning to the door.

"I've tried not to speak of it," she said in her low voice. "But I can't help it. Mr. Loring, what's wrong?"

"Nothing that I know of—if you refer to me."

She brushed his evasion aside.

"You are no more like the man you were the other day than you are like the man in the moon. What has happened?"

"Late hours. Do you mean that?"

"Sleeplessness may make a person heavy-eyed. But it isn't sleeplessness."

"How do you diagnose it, then?"

"Shall I tell you frankly?"

"Of course!"

"When I called to you in the street, you jerked up your head and whirled as though you had been struck. First you looked behind you. Then you saw me and your face straightened. It was set, up to that time."

"A start—that was all. I was thinking of something else."

"All the time you ate lunch you've been thinking of something else, then. When I offered you a chair at the table you asked to sit on the other side on account of the light. The other side was close to the wall. Why did you wish to sit there? So that no one could pass behind you? When the door opened suddenly you started—violently. When I spoke to you, I always had to repeat my question."

"I've been inexcusably rude, I admit," he said stiffly.

"Do you think I'd tell you all these peculiar things if I attributed it to rudeness?"

"And to what do you attribute it?"

"I hardly dare to tell you."

"Please do."

"Very well. You've already described it to me. It is what you saw in Joseph Wilbur—fear!"

She added hastily as he drew back: "I don't mean that you're a coward, but I mean—an odd, horrible suspicion has come over me—that the thing which hounded Joseph Wilbur is now hounding you!"

"My dear Miss Charles—you are imaginative! What possible connection is there between me and Joseph Wilbur, and his ilk?"

"There is one connection: his death, and the part you've played since in the affair. There's one connection: you're fighting now to take the blame from my father and place it on another man. And doing that, I have a feeling that tells me you've thrown yourself into a grim peril. Is it true?"

"Of course not. Why on earth should I?"

She did not answer for a time, but kept looking at him quietly.

"Mr. Loring," she said, "I am going to talk as I have never talked to another man. From the moment I met you I have trusted you. For what you have done, for the manner in which you have done it, for what you are, as I know you and for what I guess you to be, I admire you and respect you with all my heart!"

With what a voice she said that! And with her head high and her eyes shining on him.

"And now I beg you to step out of this trouble and have nothing to do with it again. I beg you for your own sake, and because I am going to be tortured with fear for you. Mr. Loring, will you give me your word that whatever you are trying to do for us now, you will drop it this instant? At least, sit down, and let me try to persuade you!"

"I'm afraid to stay," said Loring huskily. "All sorts of queer things are boiling up in my brain. I have a great deal that I want to say to you, but I mustn't do it. Why should I pretend that I can act out the part when I know that you are looking through and through me? Everything that is in me I know that you see. It's in my eyes, what I want to say, and I know you see it there. When you speak your voice takes hold of me—like a hand, you see?"

His big hand made a clutching gesture. He went on slowly: "When you smile, it's like music to me. There isn't a part of you, a gesture, a glance that I'd change. Do you see? You fit into my mind and fill it. Well, why shouldn't I tell you these things? There's no stain. If you were the wife of another man, to be loved as I love you could only make you purer and more beautiful in spirit.

"And let me tell one last thing. I was weakening under a strain. I was giving up. But since I've been with you to-day I've been drinking courage like wine out of a cup. And now nothing you can say will dissuade me. Good-by!"

She whispered her answer; he saw the tears welling up in her eyes; and he fled before they fell.

# CHAPTER XXIX

# THE SECOND TRIAL

**HE WENT OUT** glorified if ever a man was. He went out treading air and unafraid of the devil. There followed the only hours of relaxation which he knew during the six days. He went to a matinée, let the first dull act slip half by, and then slept sweetly and unafraid until the usher tapped him on the shoulder after the final curtain.

"I don't blame you," she said, smiling and whispering.

He tipped her generously and went out with his heart more at peace than ever. The sleep had refreshed him; his brain was crystal-clear; and he knew that he would be able to get through at least that one night without the use of a stimulant to pry his eyes open.

He went straight back to the lodging house after the theater, glad to get there before the dusk began. It removed the grim entry through the blackness of the hall, though even in midday that gloomy hall was dark enough to serve as a lurking place.

After that, he went out to dine. His nerves were still under the steadying influence and hope which had flowed into him during his time with Beatrice. He looked from the front door up and down the street with the eye of one who commands and fears nothing. Then he hailed a passing taxicab, ran down to it, and gave the name of a downtown restaurant.

The warmth and lights of that old eating place closed around him like the security of an armed guard. And while he waited for his order he took up again his new and ceaseless study—the examination of faces. Just why the human face had become so fascinating to him he could not tell, except that in every mature human being he saw he felt that he was seeing his possible destroyer.

But his study revealed other things to him. He read a life's history into the way a dark-skinned fellow shrugged his shoulders and sneered as he talked to his woman companion. There was another life's history in the apologetic smile with which a fat man dared complain to a waiter about an underdone steak. And yet another history in the all-possessing gesture of the very young youth with the diamonds as he talked to a girl not quite so young—and without jewels. But wherever the gaze of Loring fell, and rested for a moment, it seemed to him that he saw damning weaknesses, open breaches through which the tempter could enter.

It was while he was letting his gaze wander in this manner that he saw a face which he seemed to remember, one of those vague, dream-like things about which one cannot tell whether it is a man met in a drawing room, or seen in a street car—a half-forgotten schoolboy chum or a clerk who has served one in a store. It was a very commonplace face, the bulldog type so often seen in prize rings. The body of an athlete went with it; he was built close to the ground with thickset shoulders and a neck that bulged against his collar when he turned his head.

In the meantime, Loring's spirits were steadily rising. The battle against the Murder Company was no longer such a deadly affair. It was becoming something of a desperate lark, with death, perhaps, to give point to the jest and sting to the adventure. But after all, he kept telling himself, the Murder Company was composed of human beings, who were not omniscient. Being human they must humanly fail. Why should not he, Samuel Loring, prove one of the exceptions?

The argument led to great cheer of mind. Loring kept at it, and by the time he had paid his check, he was in a mood to fall into step with the music as he walked out of the restaurant.

Only when he reached the street outside did he think, gloomily, of his room.

He paused on the edge of the pavement and looked up and down. To flee from his room in search of diversion, he felt, was fleeing from the inevitable dénouement of the whole adventure. For he had one of those strong preconceptions which will seize even the most hard-headed men that the adventure of the Murder Company would come to an end in the dingy living room of his apartment.

He turned with a sigh, and looking back regretfully at the entrance of the restaurant, through which the music was still coming faintly—a pulse rather than a sound—he saw at that moment the bull-throated individual whom he had particularly noticed now coming forth.

He had been some time behind Loring in beginning his meal; but that was a type of man who was apt to eat with speedy precision. The stranger went up the street, and Loring sauntered down it in the general direction of his lodging house.

He was not foolish enough to risk a long walk by night, but he intended to stretch his legs in that direction for a short time. At the first corner an attractive headline caught his eye. He bought the paper, squinted across the main news heads, and lowering his hand as he brushed through a group, the paper was knocked from his hand.

Loring bent to pick it up; the wind slid it away from his reaching fingers. He bent again, and looking back as his fingers caught the fugitive paper, he saw the man with the bulldog face. The latter had halted a few windows back and was intently studying a display of hardware.

Loring straightened and walked on briskly.

There was no question that he was followed. He made sure of it in the next block. First he paused under a street light and spent a full three minutes reading the news item. But when he went on, he found that in the next block the stocky stranger was an equal distance behind him.

Even the sagging weight of the automatic was not a great comfort to Loring. To be on a man-trail is exciting enough, to be leaving such a trail curdles the blood.

But when a moment of reflection remained to him, he began to rejoice. After all, what did he want more than a chance to see the enemy approaching? And here, with unhoped for clumsiness, was an agent of the Murder Company trailing him! The hunted became the hunter. Loring cut across the street, whistling gayly, turned down an alley—and abruptly stepped back into a sunken doorway, black as night. Before him rose the barred, black windows of a factory; down the alley a street lamp peered weakly at him; an excellent place for a murder, thought Loring.

He did not actually expect that the pursuer would follow him into this blind. At least, the sudden change of Loring's direction must have made him suspicious. And suspicious he certainly was. Loring saw him come almost instantly into the light of the street lamp, glance down the alley, and then turn squarely and peer into it.

He did not appear to like that alley, with its many black doorways, but at length he shrugged his heavy shoulders and began a cat-like advance, putting his feet down deftly, toe first, and yet coming along at a brisk enough gait. And all the time his head jerked from side to side as his glances swept every opening he passed.

Loring pressed in close to the left wall of the crevice where he stood. Something told him that the man on the trail would not waste time in questions. As Loring had himself observed, this was a stage already set for a fine murder. What more could the gunman ask?

But Loring kept his own gun in his pocket. He determined to decide this matter with his fists. For a shot would sweep both him and his victim into the arms of the law; and the arms of the law most undoubtedly would mean the arms of the Murder Company.

He waited, not daring to look out, drawn back as far as he could squeeze against the concrete; yet it was a shock when the other swung into view, a bulky, ponderous man, with the springy step of an athlete. On the verge of disaster he saw the form of Loring and reached for his gun.

That was his mistake. If he had jumped back instead of standing for a shot he would probably have come clear. As it was, Loring lunged and crowded his weight behind a stiff left arm. The blow landed with a brutal force that jarred the nerves to his shoulders; and the man on the trail went down without a sound.

Over him Loring leaned with the tenderness and the joy of a finder of gold. He, Samuel Loring, single-handed, unaided, had beaten the Murder Company and brought their agent helpless in his hands! Now for the questions.

He examined the motionless bulk of the fellow carefully. He had fallen on his face, cleanly knocked out, and at first Loring feared the fall might have fractured the skull, but when he turned his man on his face he discovered that one pillowing arm had kept him from injury on the pavement; there was only a discolored swelling near the point of the jaw to tell where the blow had landed. Loring took the other's gun.

Presently he opened his eyes, and Loring shoved the nose of the weapon into his throat beneath the chin.

"Wait a minute," he advised sternly. "Wait till your head clears."

"He hit me behind the head," muttered the fellow.

Loring grinned.

"Steady," he said, "and keep your voice down."

The other suddenly attempted to sit down, but the throttling pressure of the muzzle of the revolver sent him back, gurgling.

"Another move like that," cautioned Loring, "and I'll blow your spinal cord in two—and everything that lies on this side of it."

He found that his victim lay now with eyes perfectly clear,

his face pale and set. His senses had entirely returned and he watched Loring with rat-like eagerness.

"All right," he murmured. "You got me."

"Sit up."

He obeyed.

"Get on your feet and come back here in the shadow. No use reaching for it. I have your gun, and I'll feed you with your own lead, my friend, if you make one move I don't like. You understand all that?"

"I can read a book," snarled the victim. "What does all this mean?"

"You'll find out in a moment," chuckled Loring. "Don't come at me like that. Turn around. I like your back better. Now here you are. Keep coming. Good! You feel that pressure in the small of your back? It's the muzzle of your gun. Listen! Your life is no more to me than salt on meat. Now, my boy, will you talk?"

"About what?"

"About the ones who sent you."

"What ones?"

"I know part of it already, I warn you. The first lie and I'll trip up your feet. The whole point is this. You may know something that'll be worth your rotten life. It all rests with you. Now do you talk?"

He heard his man breathing hard.

"Do you talk?"

"Not a word!"

"Then pray, you fool; your time's short."

He jabbed the muzzle into the yielding flesh. His victim winced.

"Boss," said the trailer, "I'll tell you what."

"That's right. Talk hearty, now!"

"I'll bring you to him that got me for this."

"You'll bring me to him?" murmured Loring, his heart leaping. For it was more than he had dared to hope. There would be danger, but that danger would be more than neutralized by striking at the Murder Company by surprise at headquarters.

He explained briefly: "I'm going to get a taxi. You can come and show the way. In the meantime I put your gun in my pocket. You walk a little ahead of me, and if you try to break and run for it, I drill you. Is that all clear?"

# CHAPTER XXX

# GEOFFREY TALKS TURKEY

**IT WAS DONE** as Loring directed. His companion was amazingly calm in the pinch. No doubt he relied implicitly on his superiors to clear him from trouble. At any rate, he readily muttered to the taxicab driver an address which Loring did not catch, and they started out with Loring in the back seat and the captured trailer on one of the front stools. Never once did he take his eyes from the face of Loring; never once did he speak; and several times he touched the bruise on his chin gingerly.

Loring was not surprised that they did not strike into the slums. The directing minds of such a corporation as the Murder Company might be expected to live like gentlemen in the neighborhood of gentlefolk. But his astonishment was great when the machine paused before the apartment house in which Peter Charles kept his own place.

The irony of it made Loring smile. In the very building where the victim dwelt was the headquarters of the horrible organization which had victimized him!

"You're sure this is right?" he asked.

"Am I sure I'm alive?" growled his companion.

Loring paid the taxi driver. On the way up in the elevator he kept a wary eye on his companion, but the gunman's expression was sullen and set—as of one who is reckless for himself and eager to bring mischief to others. And straight to the door of the Charles apartment he led the way. It was cold water dashed into the face of Loring. A hundred wild surmises jumped into his brain; and then everything cleared. Cunningham! He had been a fool from the first not to connect the placid-faced doorman with the Murder Company.

But when the door was opened by no less a person than Cunningham himself, Loring was doubtly astonished that his guide pointed no finger.

Cunningham had bowed to Loring and greeted him as a familiar guest of the house, holding the door wide. And Loring entered on the heels of the trailer. Straight down the hall went the stocky man, heedless of being announced, and cast open the door.

It was as if he had looked through the walls, knew what was waiting for him, and had gone straight to it. For on the far side of the living room Geoffrey Charles started up from his chair. The color passed from his face, and the pink of his jowls was the brighter by contrast.

"There!" cried the trailer. "There he is—the gent that hired me. And here's the bird that you wanted me to find, Mr. Charles."

"Good Gad!" muttered Geoffrey.

Loring closed the door and turned the key in the lock. He had recovered quickly from the first shock and now his nerves were steady. Why not Geoffrey Charles? Why not any man? Since his talk with Nicholas Zanten his faith in the human race had vanished.

"Mr. Charles," he said coldly, "you may have an explanation. I doubt it like the devil. But whatever you have to say, I want to hear you out. Therefore, kindly step to that other door and turn the key. Mind you, no odd motions."

He brought his hand out of his pocket, and in the palm of it lay the burden of the captured revolver. It was a ponderous forty-five, and it lay easily in Loring's palm. This was the sort of weapon he loved. At sight of the gun Geoffrey did not, as

Loring half expected, spring back with a cry. He actually stepped forward, frowning.

"What the devil does this mean, Loring?" he asked gruffly. "Has this business got on your nerves? Have you lost your senses?"

"Keep a comfortable distance," said Loring through his teeth. "It's got on my nerves, I admit. But my hand is still steady. You observe? Now go over and lock that door!"

For a moment Geoffrey stared at him with a cloudy face and then turned on his heel and obeyed. He threw the key on the floor and faced Loring.

"Afterward," he said fiercely, "you and I will have an explanation of this outrage, Loring!"

"There may not be an afterward, Charles," replied the man with the gun. "For I'll tell you what's in my mind—that you're a murdering hound in spite of your open face and your pleasant voice, my friend, and if it's my job to send you to Kingdom Come I'm going to do it."

"Mad," said Geoffrey, and sank into a chair, watching Loring with bright eyes.

He was ten times more of a man than Loring had ever guessed. His eye now was clear and never once did he wince when the gun turned directly on him.

"You," said Loring to his first companion, "take that chair beside Charles. I want you both under my eye. That's better. To begin with, my friends, I may as well tell you that I have often passed as an expert pistol shot. And I'm ready to work. Keep your hands well away from your clothes. Don't make sudden motions, and you will be perfectly safe. But at the first suspicious movement, I give you my solemn word of honor I shall see how quickly I can get off two shots into two different targets."

"I understand you perfectly," said Geoffrey quietly. "Now, what does this lead to?"

"It leads to a thing that may surprise you, Charles," said

Loring, leaning forward. "It leads to the murder of Joseph Wilbur!"

Geoffrey turned gray; his right hand closed convulsively, but presently he said: "Very good. Go ahead. How does it lead there?"

"You pretend to humor me?" answered Loring. "I begin to guess that you're a consummately clever devil, Charles. But cleverness doesn't amount to much under the muzzle of a gun. However, I give you your chance. Explain how this fellow was set on my trail."

"Willingly. He is Mr. Gregg of the Waite Detective Agency."

The perfect smoothness staggered Loring, but he kept his face stern.

"When you left Beatrice the other day, her nerves were in rags. You see, she's very fond of you—"

"Never mind, if you please!" cut in Loring.

"I didn't intend to dwell on it," said Geoffrey coldly. "Her fondness for you made her mightily concerned because you came in looking like a ghost, as she said, and acting like—well, not quite so mad as you're acting now.

"At any rate, she came to me and told me that she was seriously alarmed. I tried to pacify her. I don't like to mix into the secret affairs of other men. But the point of what she told me was that she thought you were on the verge of burning your fingers because of a gratuitous interest which you have taken in our affairs. She said she wanted to find out exactly what you were doing so that we could both work to stop you. Is that clear?"

"Very clear," said Loring, shaken, but still determined. "Please go on."

"I asked her to let you alone but she insisted and I finally agreed to do what I could. Naturally I couldn't go to you and ask you to tell me a thing which you had already refused to tell Beatrice. There was nothing for it. Very reluctantly I decided to have you shadowed. I applied to the Waite Agency. They replied to my call by sending me Mr. Gregg. Mr. Gregg, suppose you take up the narrative and tell Mr. Loring exactly what I said to you?"

Loring centered his attention on the detective and it seemed to him that the glance of the stocky man wavered uneasily toward the face of his employer and then back to the floor. But he could not be sure of the impression of hesitation.

"Sure," said Gregg. "I'll tell you. Mr. Charles says: 'Mr. Gregg, I got a very dear friend about whom I am anxious. I think he is in trouble and I want you to get the dope on him. Start in to-day—start in the next half hour and begin shadowing him.' Well, he gives me your address. I go there and stick around until dark, and then you come out of your place.

"I follow you down to a chuck house and watch you eat. You slide out while I ain't half through with my chow. I follow along down the street. Then you duck across and beat it down an alley. Dark place. I figure: 'Here's where I get some dope on this bird.' I soft-foot it after you. All at once you jump out of a doorway and slow me with a straight left."

He flashed a glance of anger at Geoffrey Charles.

"You didn't tell me this gent was a prize fighter!"

Geoffrey Charles laughed heartily.

"My dear Mr. Loring," he said gently, when he could speak, "you see what an infernal mess Beatrice's insistence has led me into? There's always trouble when a man mixes unasked into the affairs of others; I knew it would be disagreeable if I stepped in on you. I'm terribly sorry; that's all I can say.

"I understand, of course. You noted that Gregg was following you, thought that he was a yegg, and planted yourself for him. Eh?"

"A perfect explanation in every respect," said Loring dryly, and he fastened his keen eyes on the face of Geoffrey Charles. "But will you explain why your agent, when I jumped at him, reached for a gun? This very gun that I now hold in my hand?"

Geoffrey Charles gasped. Then he whirled on Gregg.

"My God, man, you didn't reach for a revolver? You didn't do that!"

Gregg sank his head between his thick shoulders.

"How could I help it?" he growled. "I see this gent jump at me out of a shadow like a wildcat. I didn't have no time to think, did I? It threw a scare into me. I go for the gat just as natural as a cat sticks out its claws. Anyway, they wasn't no harm done. None except to my jaw!"

He grinned, half sheepish, half sullen, and touched the bruised jaw.

"Is that satisfactory?" asked Geoffrey.

Loring carried the revolver to Gregg, but instinctively, as he handed the gun to the man he slipped his right hand over the butt of his automatic and held it in readiness in his coat pocket.

"I suppose it's satisfactory," he muttered, eyeing Gregg and Geoffrey in turn. "But you admit that I had reason to be suspicious. Even of you, Mr. Charles."

"I hardly follow you there."

"Suppose you dismiss Mr. Gregg and I'll tell you."

He complied and Loring, turning to follow Gregg with his eyes to the door, then faced his host.

"Because," he said to Geoffrey Charles, "in the business in which I am at present mixing a man cannot be sure of his best friends. In fact, he ceases to have friends. But I'll say that I'm profoundly sorry. I can only explain how I've acted to you to-night by telling you that as Miss Charles noted, my nerves have been worked to a sharp edge."

"Not another word," said Geoffrey, with hearty good nature.

An ordinary man, Loring knew, would have held a grudge in spite of explanation. It is not exactly pleasant to have to stare down the muzzle of a forty-five for indefinite periods. But there was a broad-shouldered manliness about Geoffrey. He shook off big troubles; it was the little things that irritated him.

"I've already meddled too much," he said gently to Loring. "I wish I knew you well enough to meddle some more and give you my heartfelt advice that you ought to get out of the entanglement you're in, whatever it is."

"Impossible."

"Then, if you ever need a friend to give you a hand, will you come to me, Mr. Loring?"

"I thank you—and if I can use help, I'll remember you."

He left, rather hot under the collar with his ridiculous failure. He was thinking of how absurd a figure he would make when Geoffrey told the story to Beatrice when, stepping out into the street, a burly figure skulked up to him.

"You rat!" snarled Mr. Gregg, "I'm going to get you if it takes me a hundred years!"

And then he whirled and was gone down the street with a peculiar scuffling walk.

# CHAPTER XXXI

# LORING LOOKS FOR HELP

**SHAME IS AN** emotion so vitally moving that even fear cannot overshadow it. The hair prickled on Loring's head and heat swept over his face in waves when he thought of the part he had played with Mr. Gregg. And he could hear the laughter of Beatrice as accurately as if she were walking by his side.

But when Loring came again to the unlucky lodging house of Mrs. Mercer his shame was forgotten. For the conviction held steadily in him that in the end he would feel the hand of the Murder Company in this very house. It was not hard to explain the thought. This was the address which he had given them; this was the place where they would naturally come to strike him down.

He entered his room with the same thrill, the same leap of the heart; he searched through the apartment as before. The moment his door was closed, the moment the shutters were secured, a sense of siege sat down around his rooms. But what he feared more than the fear itself was the illusion of security which from time to time came over him. The familiar chairs, books, lamps wooed him into a mood of carelessness, and such a mood he knew was deadly.

The second day had ended, and since the turning of the gas there had been no attempt on him. As for the gas, he had cut off that means of attack by plugging the jets with wax. The house was wired for electricity, also; the gas lights were simply a relic of the past left up because no one wished to bear the expense of taking them down.

It seemed to Loring that a steady attack would have been preferable. He foisted himself into the minds of his assailants. They might very well have said to themselves: "He has met the first feeble attempt. Now for a time he will be strenuously on guard. But at the end of a day or so he will grow accustomed to the danger, his attention will relax, and then we can easily strike past his guard." That would be a logical attitude for them.

The sword hung over him.

He was tired, now, grimly tired, but, of course, he dared not sleep. However, rest he must have. He sat in a chair with its back to the wall. About the thumb of his right hand he made a string fast and tied to the other end of the string a heavy little paper-weight. Then he closed the paper-weight in his hand and composed himself to rest.

Almost instantly the darkness of slumber passed over his mind, his muscles were unknit, and as he was on the verge of oblivion his fingers relaxed, the paper-weight fell, and the tug of the string woke him with a start, his heart beating.

It was a harsh penalty for one instant of near-sleep. But it was all that he could have. Water a drop at a time is better to the starved man than no water at all. Once more Loring composed himself, grasped the paper-weight, and let his eyes close. He concentrated on keeping that right hand closed as long as possible; sleep moved over him; for a moment there was a blissful oblivion, and then again the tug of the dropping weight.

Half the night he spent in this happy torture, always on the verge of rest, but like Tantalus never quite attaining it. It was torture, but it brought him an indubitable reward. At length he was sufficiently rested so that the threat of the falling weight kept him from closing his eyes. When he reached this point he removed the string, sat up, and looked at his watch. It was only one in the morning.

Loring's heart fell. Long hours before the blessed daylight

would come. Long hours to listen with a thumping heart to the ticking sounds that ran through the house, or stole breathlessly up and down the hall and listened at his door! He fought out part of the interim with a book until the print blurred before his aching eyes. How could he read when in the middle of every line his glance jerked up at the door, or his attention reached out to listen to the breathing near the window?

Finally he took the first dose of strychnine and felt the reaction at once. He was steadier; yet in his heart there was a great sense of failure, for he had leaned upon a false ally, he well knew. And the drug was eaten up by his quaking, broken nerves. In the gray of the dawn he was as badly off as ever, and by that gray light he saw himself in the mirror, the hair straggling across his eyes, the eyes themselves deep in shadows, his cheeks fallen, and an air at once desperate and criminal upon his face.

It was not Samuel Loring; it was the ghost of Joseph Wilbur. Under that blow Loring almost crumbled and broke down; and when the morning came he knew that he could not endure the strain much longer. Even one more day of this agony was like eternity to him.

He waited until the morning was nearly spent; then he went to Buttrick's. Zanten was not there. Loring swallowed hard. What if he were unable to call off the hounds which he himself had loosed on his trail? He inquired of the waiter who usually took care of the great gambler.

"You are Mr. Loring?" said the fellow at once.

"Yes."

"Mr. Zanten rang up a little time ago and said that you would call for him. He left this address to be given to you."

Loring was past surprise at any foresight on the part of Nicholas Zanten. In fact, if Zanten expected him, the gambler probably knew exactly what would bring Loring to him. In that case everything would be smoothed down.

He was at the door of the gaming house before the other alternative struck him. What if this note had been left by some agent of the Murder Company? What if they were inviting the fly into the net of the spider?

But he had reached a point at which great chances appeared small to him. He went to Zanten's address with all the speed that a taxicab could make. When he got out and had sent the driver away, he looked about him in amazement and distrust. This for Zanten the exquisite! A spawn of dirty children yelled and raced in the street, weaving incredibly through the traffic of trucks and delivery wagons. The house itself was flat-fronted, six stories tall, narrow, filthy, unpainted since its erection, it seemed.

Loring for the first time was really taken aback. As well look for a crowned king in such a tenement as for the dainty-minded Nicholas Zanten.

He rang the bell. What hope had he if not in Zanten? As well take the chance that this was the trap it seemed. A woman of vast girth opened the door a few inches, peered at him, then swung it wide. She was unspeakably unclean.

"You are Mr. Loring?" she said in a foreign accent. "Mr. Zanten waits."

He drew back from her, mastering his disgust. Then he looked down on the noise of the street and up to the sky. It might be his last look at it. How keenly now he appreciated the actions of Joseph Wilbur when that hounded man wandered over Manhattan in the taxicab for his last look at the places he best knew!

Then he entered the building. He was led by the fat crone up a long stairway. It was now gray with dirt, but once it must have been a spacious, pleasant architectural feature of the old house. He noted, going up, that the ceilings were lofty. And so he climbed to the fifth floor.

"Here," she said, pointing to a door as grimy as any they had passed, and retreated down the stairs. But only to the point where her body was covered by the line of the hall. She loitered there keeping him in view as if she were curious to mark his reception. Loring gathered the automatic in his hand, tipped up the muzzle so that he could fire through the coat pocket if necessary, and then tapped at the door.

It was opened at once. And the moment Loring glanced into the interior his hand came away from the automatic. He knew that this was indeed the residence of Nicholas Zanten. A Negro in white clothes, carefully tailored, opened the door to him. And beyond the servant Loring saw a cool, big interior—a sage green floor, and a color scheme built up to great splashes of yellow and blue in vases and flowers. There were tall green plants.

The atmosphere, with the white clothes of the Negro, made up a suggestion of the tropics. The very air was warmer than was necessary. It made Loring relax as he stepped into the room. It was a room of profusion—careful profusion even Loring could see.

He noted at once the silence. The rattle from the rest of the house was gone. The street noises disappeared. Yet it was not silence. Somewhere birds were singing as though they were pouring forth their hearts in the prime of a summer morning. Nicholas Zanten and birds!

"You are Mr. Loring?"

"Yes."

"If you please, sir."

And he was led straightway through two inner rooms and into a library where Nicholas Zanten sat. He sat in a large chair in a brilliant dressing gown; he was in the act of laying aside a great tome—Loring caught the flash of illuminations as the vellum sheets were closed. Then his hand was in the cold grip of Zanten, and the keen, black eyes were glittering against his face.

"Another case of mind reading," said Loring, wishing to smile but finding it impossible.

"In what way?"

"You had them prepared at Buttrick's. They sent me to you

at once. Even the woman who opened the door downstairs knew that I was coming."

"Mind reading if you will," said Zanten carelessly. He looked over the chairs, found one that suited him, and had Loring take it.

"First of all," he said, "I have to apologize. I always do when a guest comes here for the first time. I have to defend myself from the charge of being a charlatan in the first place and a poseur in the second."

"Not at all."

"Be frank, Mr. Loring. That is your cue, I think. You were disgusted by the dirt and the noise, you were wearied by the walk up the stairs."

"Being here, I'm repaid. A good background for such a place."

"There you have found me out. I love contrast. I live on contrast. I could not exist in the filth and the noise and the jangle of the world; but I could not exist without it. It is my great weakness. If I wish to listen to Bach for an evening I will have them play the moderns first—the noisy idiots who see 'color' in music. After that—Bach—perfection!

"It is the same with my house. I set my unique jewel in lead." Out of the raucous alleys of this new Baghdad I step at a stride into the caliph's palace. You see? If I live uptown I am simply a freak where everything else is calm harmony. I am out of joint. But in this section I am a delightful change.

"Do you know what is my greatest treasure? It is the street below me. In the dull time of the morning when my mind is drab, I go to the balcony and I look down on the street and listen to the voices. In all that squalor I see the joy. I return to my rooms. They are doubly pleasant.

"Or if I have sinned the day before and my mind is ill at ease—if I have plucked the last penny from some foolish bankrupt millionaire and the picture of his agony remains with me, I may descend to the street like God. Like God I shower my benefactions. I have studied my neighborhood. I know where a dollar is a ray of sunshine that will brighten a house all day.

"Sometimes I am whimsical. The beggar at the corner who has a bank account of a hundred thousand, at least—perhaps I stand beside him for a moment and give him a five-dollar bill and listen while he moans and groans and tells me a tale of woe. I enjoy him. He is not a polished liar; he is rather a diamond in the rough, and he carries conviction.

"I return from my errand of mercy. The women bless me as I pass. The little children are too awe-stricken to even beg for pennies. The men bow to me. The fat old devil who owns this house is watching and waiting so that she may open the door as I come up the steps. I return from my errand. My heart is at peace, my vanity has been tickled, I feel my power, and when I enter my rooms I come truly as the caliph."

Zanten laughed.

"You see how I expose my weaknesses and vanities?"

"I understand," said Loring.

"No, no! Not that, I hope. To be understood is terrible. But now let us speak of you, my dear Loring."

## CHAPTER XXXII

# PRIDE

SO SAYING, HIS brilliant eyes were fastened suddenly on the face of Loring. The latter blinked and then steadied himself. "Before we talk," said Loring, "suppose I ask you just what you know. That will make it simpler. Tell me first how you knew that I would come to you this morning."

"Mind-reading, you know."

"The truth, please."

"Nothing so uninteresting as the truth, I hope. But let me see. I know the name you wrote on the paper. Does that explain?"

"You know that I wrote my own name?"

"Yes. You thought it was a pleasant jest. You went away. That night something happened. You began to perceive that it might not be jest after all. You began to be tormented by anxiety. You suffer the tortures of the damned. You cannot sleep. 'Too much!' you say at last. 'The game must end.' And you come to me to call off the hounds. I presume that I am nearly right in my guesses?"

"In your guesses," said Loring, "you are profoundly right. It has to end, Zanten. I'm at the last of my rope. My nerve is gone!"

"A solemn confession!"

"And solemnly confessed."

"You believe that after all there may have been something in what I told you? You find there is an air of reality in the little jest?"

"Jest? I never, for a moment, doubted the reality of the things you told me."

Zanten smiled.

"You don't doubt them now. But in the beginning? Come! You will not have me believe that you did not feel it to be a jest then? You thought it was a sham fire. You decided to play with it? And I assure you, Loring, that you have played with a thing that will destroy you. You have not more than three days to live. In that space you will, most assuredly, be killed.

"Bear in mind that the Company is not invincible. It is composed of human agents. They are frail. If one of them should be cornered he might confess. And one confession will destroy at a stroke all the labor of the many brilliant minds who have given their genius to the making of this powerful organization. Think, therefore, of all that you may do and prepare yourself for a great exertion!"

He seemed enraptured with the picture as he drew it.

"Does it seem a fair fight to you?" asked Loring.

"It seems one which you have yourself invited. But I must warn you. If in the remaining three days you do not destroy the Company, then at the end of that time a greater power than the Company will undertake your destruction. If at the end of that time you have still baffled them, a power which, I believe I may say, is well nigh omnipotent, will then start toward you. Bear this in mind!"

"And what power can that be?"

"One which I cannot name. Something which is always greater than a crowd—a single man! But gather courage, Loring. The crisis is not yet. You have much before you. The jest has turned to earnest; retain your smile and fight!"

Loring frowned, bewildered.

"You don't understand," he said heavily. "What odd theory of me you have composed I can't tell, but it is wrong. There was never any question of a jest. I'm not a complete fool."

"You were in earnest," murmured Zanten, with an approach to a smile, "when you put the Company on your trail?"

"Absolutely! Let me be frank; why should I not be? It is my firm conviction that the power which destroyed Wilbur is this Company. I believed it when I heard you talk; I still believe it more strongly. I determined, if I could, to put myself in his shoes, draw on my head the same power which had killed him, beat it if I could, reveal its action regarding Wilbur, and free Peter Charles, an innocent man!"

He was bewildered to see that Zanten was staring at him as at a ghost. It was, indeed, a great effect. It was easier to move mountains, Loring felt, than to actually surprise Nicholas Zanten. There was no question as to the reality of the cynic's emotion. He looked at Loring with the eagerness of a blind man, almost seeing a great light. His long, lean fingers were wrapped forcefully around the arm of the chair; had it not been for a muscular exertion it seemed that he would be trembling from head to foot.

"By heavens!" cried Zanten softly, at length. "Is it possible?"

He answered his own question. He rose from his chair and stood with his arms tightly folded, his head back, thrusting his gaze into the face of Loring as if he pushed with a rapier to get past the guard of an antagonist.

"It is true," said Zanten hoarsely. "Merciful God, it is true!"

He sank into his chair, as though suddenly become weak, suddenly relaxed and inert. His face he supported in one of the pale hands.

"Tell me," he said in a faint voice. "Tell me in what manner you arrived at the decision to immolate yourself in the service of this man?"

"A simple thing," answered Loring, growing worried. He felt that it was hardly permissible to watch such emotion in such a man. "When you told me of the Company and its working I was convinced. The face of Wilbur, I tell you, reflected just such a devilish organization."

"True."

Then Zanten raised his head quickly. A light as of hope was in his face.

"But there is some great and hidden motive in your devotion to Peter Charles, is there not? He is your benefactor. He has often supplied you with at least the sinews of life?"

"Peter Charles? Never! I take charity from no man, Mr. Zanten."

"Not charity. No. But he has been at least a munificent employer?"

"I have never worked for him. What are you driving at?"

"Not charity? Not even pay for work?" said Zanten, his face clouding again. "Then there is another thing. I have been a fool not to think of it before. Inquiring into the life of this financier since he has been accused of the crime, or since he was condemned to death, you have discovered secret chapters, unknown to the public as a whole.

"You have heard of gentle and generous acts on his part. You have traced him in the commission of many faults of charity, I am sure. You have found him succoring the poor, relieving the distressed, subscribing largely to unpublished subscription lists. This is what you have learned about Peter Charles, eh?"

Loring laughed faintly, the description was so entirely out of keeping with what he knew of Peter Charles.

"Not at all. Far be it from me to say that Charles hasn't done any of these fine things or all of them. But so far as I have been able to find out, Peter Charles is sublimely selfish. He started out well enough, but his association with Joseph Wilbur poisoned his life and his character, I gathered. He really became like the man he hated.

"He is great only in his sublime selfishness. He is one of those rare men who have no life outside the gathering of property. His only interest outside himself is to see that his possessions pass on to another man of his own name. No, of all the men I have ever known, there is none who so completely fails to win my sympathy, to say nothing of my admiration."

"And the reason for this sacrifice on your part?" muttered Zanten.

"I have explained before, I think. I started to get at the bottom of Wilbur's mystery. I determined to follow the thing through. So I did the rash thing. I signed my own name. But it's too much to ask. I can't go through with it. After all, who is Peter Charles? What is he to me? Is he worth the sacrifice?"

"True," nodded Zanten. "What is he worth? Surely not so much as this." His bright eyes glittered at Loring. "Give up the matter. Confess yourself beaten and I shall call off the Company!"

But Loring paused. There was something in the eagerness of Zanten that disturbed him. It seemed that Zanten was pleading for himself.

"Confess myself beaten?" he said slowly. "No. Not entirely. The day may come when I'll go back on this trail. But they have a number; I am alone. I should want to have men I could trust about me before I tackle them."

"A foolish idea," said Zanten. "You see that I cannot ask them to relinquish a task when their relinquishment may mean a future danger to them. Come. Be sensible. Give up this quixotic quest. Surrender unconditionally to a power greater than your own!"

Loring bowed his head and studied the pattern of the Chinese rug.

"When I came here," he said, "I was willing to do anything. But to confess that I surrender! To give up like a beaten dog! I think of poor Wilbur!"

"A snake—a cur—not worthy of a thought!"

Loring raised his head.

"A human being, Zanten, whom I undertook to save."

"We won't argue the point. The question is: do you confess failure?"

"I cannot," said Loring through his teeth.

"Then you have come here for nothing? You leave this house hopelessly condemned to death?"

"Not hopelessly. You have yourself said that there is a hope."

"A desperate one," said Zanten eagerly as ever. "Be reasonable!"

"I wish to God that I could be. But—my mind is made up. I'm not going to cringe. I'm glad I came here, Zanten, because it makes me determined to go through with the thing at any cost."

"But why in the name of heaven, man?"

"I don't know—perhaps because I don't wish to be shamed in your eyes. Perhaps that's the reason. Besides, Peter Charles is an innocent man, and by the Eternal, I'll prove it!"

"Then there is no use in prolonging the conversation. Mr. Loring, I bid you good-day. You have thought for the last time on the matter?"

"For the last time!"

Zanten touched a button and consigned Loring to the guidance of the servant who appeared.

Loring had hardly disappeared when a door opened and Kane entered the room.

"You heard?" asked Zanten, who lay in his chair with his eyes closed, as if he were exhausted.

"A queer chap," nodded Kane.

"More than queer! Kane, he has no motive. It is complete giving!"

"Really? I have already told you that there is a girl."

"Nonsense. She is engaged to Geoffrey Charles."

"That's true. But what's the point of it all. You bring him here to draw him out, hoping that he'll cringe to you. He doesn't do that. He leaves you looking like a beaten man, Mr. Zanten."

"And I am beaten. Thoroughly and soundly beaten for the first time in my life. I thought he was a careless, clean-minded adventurer. I find him, instead, a unique man, a man without parallel—I find him, in short, a man without self. The only human being I have ever known who gave without a hope of a reward!"

Zanten shook his head. He muttered faintly: "Have I been wrong all these years? Is such a thing possible? My creed falls. It is shattered at the base. It leaves me—nothing. It makes me—a cold-headed scoundrel—a villain; in place of which I thought myself—"

He finished the sentence with a shuddering gesture.

All this time, Kane stared at Zanten with a peculiar interest; as though he saw the great man losing his grip, his strength, disintegrating into the commonplace under his very eyes.

"And the result is," he suggested, "that you will have us withdraw from him? You invited him here so that we could gracefully remove him from the world. You will end by forbidding us to harm a hair of his head?"

Zanten opened his eyes.

"Folly must have been both natural and acquired with you, Kane," he said coldly. "Save him? Bah! If he needs saving he's not worth it. I have found him as true-hearted as an Arabian horse. If in addition to that I find that he has the mind of a man and the strength of a man, I shall buckle him to me; I shall adopt him as a blood-brother; I shall accept him as the first and last friend of Nicholas Zanten.

"But if he has not the strength, let him go. Let him go with all his generous nature and his noble mind. That alone does not fit him to be admitted as my equal."

"And what's the test of his strength, then?"

"The test? Why, simpleton, the test is the test of the Company. Go ahead with him, Kane. Let the Company do its best. If it destroys him—let him go. I shall never waste a single regret on the weakling. But if he succeeds—if he lives past the sixth day—then touch him at your peril! For in touching him you will touch Nicholas Zanten! In the meantime, do your best—or your worst!"

# CHAPTER XXXIII

# THE TRAIL

**LORING HAD GONE** back to the torment of waiting.

It was the third day of the suspense, and it passed as a long nightmare. What sustained him was the speech of Zanten. It was true in every respect. The Company was human, made up of human parts, and one of them might fail. For the time of that failure Loring must wait, always on guard. But it was like waiting blindfold to meet the attack of a man possessed of both sight and weapons.

His meals that day were a silly pretense. And the terror of the day was nothing to the night. Once more he was back in the lodging house. He had bought a sealed bottle of water from a drug store in a distant part of the great city. That alone he could be sure was free from poison. He made coffee with that water, black, bitter, strong coffee, and put the dose of strychnine in it. In that way he passed the time of darkness and reached the day again.

He left the lodging house again when it was full sunshine. That day was spent in ceaseless wandering. At only one point did his vigilance break down. He entered a subway at Chambers Street, and falling asleep, did not waken until he reached Two-Hundred and Forty-Second Street. He started up with a feeling that he had been betrayed. Gradually he realized that all was well. But he shuddered at what might have happened. One more break like that and it would be the end, he was well aware. In the meantime, he had been fortified by a blessed sleep.

It was now close to the time of darkness at which the open streets ceased to be a refuge and became more deadly to him than the horrible silence of the lodging house itself. He started back toward it straightway.

It had become a trick to always approach the house from a new direction, twisting in toward it through an alley, sometimes walking down the opposite side of the street and crossing over at an angle. But this time he chose the adjoining alley. It was one which he had avoided before. A new building was being constructed there and behind the piles of lumber and material along the pavement there were a score of convenient places to lurk, while the skeleton of the building itself would give an enemy ample time to shake off the beginnings of pursuit.

Stepping into the alley, he first proceeded slowly, and scanned the building from top to bottom. But there was no stir of life about it. The workers had left. It was only a gaunt skeleton, very black where the upper beams went across the sky. When he had ascertained that there was no sign of activity on it, he continued with a more confident step. He was halfway past the structure when it happened.

The only warning was a slight deepening of the shadow in which he walked. He glanced up and saw that a great scaffolding was rushing down at him. There was only time for one leap, and fear gave him the strength to make it a prodigious one. At that it was not more than barely enough. A flying timber struck him with crushing force on one shoulder, and whirled him. He fell flat on his back and the platform crashed with thunder against the pavement.

Instantly voices began; there was a sound of running steps, but Loring was too bewildered by the joy of the delivery to rise instantly. He lay prone, moveless, almost entirely covered by several projecting planks, and as he looked blankly up at the top of the building, for his head was clear of the wreckage, he saw a head come over the top of the structure—a cautiously moving head which peered down at him.

*She bowed her head, and before she had raised it Loring had fled.*

If there had been a doubt in his mind, it was instantly removed. The hand of the Company was in this!

The first rush of rescuers and the curious reached him; the scantling and boards were torn from above him, and there was a faint cheer when Loring rose, unscathed, and began to brush the dust from his clothes. Some of the officious would have taken him straightway to a hospital, but he laughed them away. He was quite unhurt, he assured them, and leaving them to gossip about the cause of the near-disaster, he slipped away around the corner.

He knew instantly where his best chance would lie of coming in touch with the agent of the Company. He had been able to make out the cap on the head of the man, and he thought that he had caught the glint of a red necktie in the distance. On these clews he would work. Certainly the man would expect no pursuit, for from the top of the building Loring must have seemed entirely buried under the mass of débris.

Once around the corner and out of sight of the group at the fallen platform, Loring raced at full speed, dipped into the back alley, and reached the building in time to see a man in a cap come out of the new structure and hurry ahead of him to the opposite street.

Loring cut down his pace to a walk for fear of the noise he must make in running. Even at that pace his long legs would probably enable him to come up with the stranger. But as he stepped out of the alley into the street, a throng from a moving picture house poured upon him. When he had extricated himself from the jam the fugitive was half a block away and walking with a rapid step.

A surface car stopped providentially for the man in the cap; and as he turned to board it, Loring caught the glimmer of a red necktie. There was no doubt about it. This was his man!

He followed the car in a taxicab which he found on the corner, keeping it a full half block behind the street car to remove any suspicion from the mind of the man with the cap. The way led downtown. Twice at least the car was emptied and filled again with crowds of varying natures and still the man with the cap did not dismount from it.

Loring began to fear that his quarry might have had dexterity enough to discover the trailing taxicab and to change his cap for a hat in the car. It might easily enough have been done, and the simple ruse would have effectively taken him past the eye of the pursuer.

But there was nothing for it except to stay with the car. They had passed the uptown business section, they dropped below tawdry Fourteenth Street—and here the fugitive dismounted.

It was only to take a crosstown car, which he left again at Fourth Avenue and continued south. In the heart of the Bowery, with the Elevated roaring overhead, he finally left the street car and turned into the crowd on the pavement. Loving instantly paid his driver and was on his man's heels.

It was no easy thing to squirm through the crowd. A Bowery crowd is accustomed to jostling and generally jostles back. The result was that Loring found himself swimming against the tide, so to speak.

Much buffeted, he managed to round a corner in time to trace the fugitive with his eye. Halfway down the block, the man with the cap turned sharply to the right and ran up a flight of steps. At the top he halted, and facing around, looked down the street.

As for Loring, he knew afterward that he should have paused and pretended to be loitering, but instead, he could only obey his first impulse and flatten himself against the wall of the saloon which he was passing. It gave him an excellent opportunity to scan the face of his assailant for the first time. He saw a broad face, high cheekbones, a slanting forehead, a massive jaw. All the marks of the beast were in that face, and it seemed that the active little animal eyes were looking straight at Loring.

Then the man with the cap went on into the house, cuffing his way through a mass of children which at that moment tumbled out of the door. It left Loring in an unpleasant predicament. There was every chance that he had been discovered and in that case he would very shortly be the hunted hunter. In any case, it was impossible for him to enter the house; certainly it would be absurd to attempt to trail his man in clothes which the fugitive must know as well as he knew his own.

Loring stepped into one of those secondhand clothing stores which are earmarks of the Bowery. In thirty seconds he paid double their value for a ragged old gray hat and a reddish-brown coat, two sizes too large for him. It had one great advantage. The ragged hat brim flapped down over his eyes, and since the evening was turning chill, with a drizzle of rain, he could turn the coat collar up around his ears. It was a weak disguise to one who knew his face as the man with the cap must, but it was the best Loring could do.

Coming up from the cellar store to the street he examined carefully the house into which his man had disappeared. It was in no respect different from the tenements on either side of it. He rounded the block and examined it from the rear. There was still no difference. Even if he should enter, how could he possibly locate the man with the cap?

He crossed the street, and sitting at the window table of a little restaurant, kept his eyes fixed on the porch of the tall building while he ate a bowl of stew. Half an hour passed in this manner. He finished the stew, drank the unspeakable coffee, ate some of the bread which was piled on a great plate in the center of the table, served without limit or butter.

And then his quarry came into sight again, but how changed! The ragged clothes of the laborer had given place to a pearl-gray suit of Broadway pattern, much fitted, and the fellow looked first up and down the street like the monarch of all he surveyed before he descended the steps jauntily, carrying a suitcase.

Loring was out of the restaurant instantly and on the trail. It led uptown, this time. Perhaps there would be a party to celebrate the completion of the job. Loring smiled mirthlessly at the thought. But at Forty-Second Street the man in gray turned down to the Grand Central.

On the upper level he entered the line to a ticket window, and Loring stepped into line two places back. He had no excuse for keeping his collar turned up in the warm station. He rolled it down again, but he kept his hat drawn low and persistently looked at the floor. Once the man in gray turned abruptly and through a rent in the hat brim Loring saw that the other was staring straight at him, but eventually the quarry turned again. This time he began to whistle a tune.

As he reached the window, Loring crowded forward against the man preceding him, and in this manner came close enough to catch the name of the town to which the man in gray bought his ticket. In his own turn he purchased a ticket for the same place.

Ordinarily, he would have chosen to let the fugitive escape from his sight until the town was reached, but he was uneasy. It might very well be that the other had recognized his would-be victim at any time, during the pursuit. It was quite possible that he would ride on past the station named or get off on this side of it.

So Loring still kept close to his man at the gate, pressed after him toward one of the forward coaches, and entering the same car, picked out a seat near the door. There he composed himself for sleep, with his head bowed, and through the lucky rent in the hat brim he kept steady watch on his man.

It proved a needless risk. Once the man in gray came back through the car; but he returned after a moment on the platform to his seat. And when the train pulled into the station, he got off. Loring passed down the length of the car behind and followed his example.

# CHAPTER XXXIV

# THE TRAIL'S END

**IT WAS A** little Connecticut city on an incutting arm of the sea; one of those drab towns over which the smoke is always a grimy veil, settling toward the ground, blackening the houses, and giving the skin a greased feeling. Through the streets Loring followed his man.

It was easier work now. Either the man in gray had discovered Loring and was leading him to a trap, or else he had definitely decided that he was past all fear of danger. He took a car that brought him past the heart of the city, and Loring, not daring to board the same car, took the next one. He had to stand with his face pressed against the glass of the front platform and at every stop watch with painful intentness to see if the man in gray dismounted in the light of the street lamps.

But they went on to the very end of the line, where the houses were broken into scattering groups. Here the quarry descended. Loring was out at the same stop and took after him across an open lot.

At the next street—it was really more of a country road—the fugitive turned out toward the open. It was, of course, pitch dark, and Loring's work had again become difficult. He had to keep close enough to see the glimmer of the uncertain figure through the black of the night. But he dared not come close enough for the sound of his footsteps to attract the attention of the quarry.

He was glad when his man cut to the right—it was now

entirely open country—and headed for a little shack, whose window was yellow with lamplight. Loring stopped his pursuit, and waiting only until the door opened and admitted the fugitive, he ran in a wide semicircle to come up on the house from the other side. There were two reasons for this. One was that if his pursuit had been noticed the stranger would unquestionably scan the fields from the window. The other was that the man might attempt to get out by a back door.

But when he came in line with the rear of the house, there was nothing to be seen. In another moment Loring was nestled, gun in hand, close to the wall of the shack.

"Beside," a surly voice was saying as he came in earshot, "how d'you expect me to live on beans? Think I'm a dog the way you serve up chuck for me!"

"Look here, Pete," answered another man's voice, high pitched and nasal, "all I ask you is this: why didn't you bring home something for me to cook for you? That's all I want to know!"

"Because I ain't no woman to go marketing," snapped Pete. "And I ain't no cripple like you, neither. What do I keep you for, sitting around and doing nothing? What do I keep you for if it ain't to have chuck on hand for me? Eh? You're too lazy to suit me, Charlie. Here I been keeping you off the fat of the land out of charity; this is the way you treat me!"

"Fat of the land!" snorted Charlie. He seemed to choke. "I've been your drudge. That's what!"

"What I want to know is, are you going to step out and get me some food a dog could eat? Or ain't you? And if you ain't, I tell you short and sweet I pitch you out the door and you stay out!"

"Aw, Pete," answered Charlie, softening. "Is that a way to talk?"

"You get me riled, that's all. Now get a move on."

There was a stir in the shack, and the stumping of a wooden leg across the floor.

"It's a rotten rainy night to go out in," grumbled Charlie.

"How was I to know you was coming back to-night? I ain't no mind-reader!"

"Cut out the chatter and show me some action."

"I'm going, ain't I? How was things on Broadway?"

"Fair enough."

"Thought you wouldn't come back inside six days."

"Told you I mightn't come back before then. Didn't say for sure."

"What was the job, Pete?"

"Something big. That's all."

"Hard?"

"Easy. Easy as taking a bottle from a baby. They wasn't nothing to it."

"What'd you do?"

"Nothing but—" The voice of Pete rose to a whine of rage. "Blast your heart, you pretty near got it out of me that time! Now look here, you one-legged sneak, if you ever talk around me so's I tell you something, you know what's going to happen?"

"Aw, Pete, I wasn't trying to peeve you none!"

"I ask you, do you know what's going to happen to you if you ever get me to say something?"

"I dunno, Pete."

"As soon as I see what I've done I'll bean you, Charlie. That's straight. If I ever tell you something I'd oughtn't to, I'll just up and bust your good-for-nothing head ag'in' the wall. That's straight. You see me look you in the eye while I talk!"

"My God," murmured Charlie, "is it as bad as that?"

"Get out!" roared Pete.

"Back inside of ten minutes," said the cripple.

The door banged behind him, and Loring heard him go down the path, muttering.

"He talks too much," Pete was growling inside the shack.

Loring waited until the cripple faded into the night. Then he stood up at the window. It was useless to peer through it. A light shutter completely shut out his view of the room. He could only look up at the ceiling, through the slits. He stepped to the door and knocked lightly.

"Who's there?" called Pete.

In place of answering, Loring knocked again.

"Who is it?" cried Pete, and a chair scraped back.

He was already alarmed—that was apparent. Loring cast open the door and stepped in with his automatic in hand, and the hand of Pete, reaching for his own weapon, was frozen midway of the gesture. He dropped upon his knees and spread his hands before his face.

"God!" screamed Pete. "It's after me!"

"I'm not a ghost," said Loring quietly. "Get up!"

The terror of Pete changed. He looked up, lowering his protecting fingers by jerks. In place of horror his face was now filled with an oddly disagreeable mixture of panic and cunning.

"You!" he said. "You!"

He stumbled to his feet.

"Well, who are you?"

"Do you ask that?" asked Loring, curious to see how far he would try to stretch the clumsy bluff.

"Sure I ask it. What d'you want? Money? I ain't got it!"

"I don't want money."

"Well, what is it?"

"First, put up your hands. Up, I say!"

As the muzzle of his weapon jerked up the unwilling hands of Pete rose, struggled mutely for a moment as they reached the level of his shoulders, and then went on up to the region of helplessness.

"Now turn your back."

"My God!"

"I'm not going to shoot you—if you keep your head and don't try a quick move. Everything gently, my friend. Good!"

He touched his gun against Pete's back, and then removed the latter's weapon. He stood back.

"Now you can face me again, and bring your hands down. But no sudden gestures. They make me nervous, and all my nerves are in my trigger finger. You know what that means."

Pete turned slowly toward him. He seemed as unwilling to take his hands down as he had been to put them up. His face was a dirty gray; his mouth, even, was pale, and he moistened the dry lips repeatedly with the tip of his tongue.

"Stand over here in the middle of the room."

Pete obeyed. And Loring stepped back in the corner. The power of the Company, he felt, was omniscient. Every entrance into that room was like a gun pointed at his head, even while he stood in that lonely shack. His position was beside the window, pressed against the wall, and with Pete in line with the door.

"Now, Pete," he said, "I may as well begin by saying that I know what you did, and, of course, that's what brought me here. I saw you stick your head over the top of the building while I was lying half covered by the platform!"

Pete blinked.

"I knew they'd tie me up with that!" he whined. "The minute I seen that scaffold go I says to myself: 'Here's where they get a chance to hang something on poor old Pete.' That's why I beat it home."

"What were you doing on the building?"

"What was I doing? Working, of course. Ain't I an iron-worker by trade?"

"The rest of the men were gone. What were you doing there?"

"I was finishing up a little job."

"Are you a union man?"

"Yes. Sure I ain't no scab."

"Then what were you doing, working after hours?"

It was a small thing, but it baffled Pete for a moment.

"I got a right to make a thing the way it ought to be."

"You lie," said Loring calmly. "Why did you run afterward?"

"To get home. I told you that!"

"How long have you been working in New York?"

"About a month."

"Three days, Pete. Only three days."

The eyes of Pete widened; and Loring saw him cast a frantic glance over his shoulder. Pete knew that he was cornered. The rat in his nature came into his face and he looked at Loring with small, wicked, crafty eyes.

"What would I be doing working three days?" he asked.

"Waiting to kill me, Pete," said Loring.

The blow may have been expected. It did not keep Pete from wincing.

"Why should I want to do that?" he asked.

"Because you're paid for it."

Pete shook his head.

"Who'd pay me?"

"Shall I tell you?"

"Sure, if you can."

"The Company," said Loring.

He added: "Sit down and take this easy. I'm not going to be hard on you. Pete."

"What company?" Pete was asking. But he accepted the suggestion and sat down as though he dared not trust to his trembling legs.

"Do you want me to tell you more about it? Do you want me to name names?"

"No, no!" gasped Pete. He looked in terror at the window and then at the door behind him. "For God's sake, talk soft!"

"Why? Aren't we alone?"

"Alone? Me? I ain't been alone for a year and a half. Never once! They're with me—always!"

"Who?"

"Them!"

"They'll never bother you after to-night, Pete. Because, either you tell me their names, where they can be found, and a little about what they've done, so that I can smash 'em—or else you and yourself part company. Is that plain?"

"You mean—" breathed Pete.

"I mean exactly that. You came within an ace of getting me, Pete. I'm going to try to come a little nearer to getting you in case you won't talk. You hear? The chance is good.

"Tell me what you know. Make it brief. Boil it down to a dozen words. When those dozen words are spoken, you can come back to New York under my protection—and twenty-four hours later you'll be in no fear of the Company because the Company won't exist. Will you talk?"

"Not one word," snarled Pete.

CHAPTER XXXV

# THE COMPANY
# STRETCHES ITS ARM

**IN THE PAST** four days Loring had learned to know fear as he had never known it before; but never had the thought of the Company seemed so terrible to him as it did now. Never had it seemed so omnipotent as now, when its invisible presence was more commanding to the poor wretch in front of him than the leveled gun.

"Think twice before you say it," said Loring. "Consider my position. It's either you or me. If I kill you now, Pete, I have one obstacle out of my path. If I let you live I turn loose another dog on my trail. I'll never reach New York alive. Either you talk and put yourself in the same boat with me, or else you die. I'm not bluffing. Look at me, if you doubt it."

And Pete followed the suggestion. What he saw in Loring's face turned him green with terror. Yet he shook his head.

"I can't," he said. "I—I can't talk!"

"Look!" said Loring.

He raised the gun. He raised it until Pete was looking fairly into the muzzle of the weapon.

"It means the end of everything," he said, brutally helping that sluggish imagination. "It means a sleep from which there would be no waking. One long sleep."

"They'd—they'd hang you—sure!"

"Hang me? Of course not! There isn't a policeman within miles. Besides, I'll be back in New York to-night and who on earth would ever connect me with you, Pete? Who on earth?

229

No, I can kill you as safely as if I were shooting from a cloud at you. Don't worry on my account. Think of yourself."

Pete grinned in his agony, but he shook his head still, his bright little eyes shifting helplessly from side to side.

"Count to ten for yourself," said Loring. "Because when you reach ten you die. Start!"

He steadied his hand and raised the gun.

There was a queer tightening of Pete's features. He flashed a look of bewilderment at Loring, as if to make sure that the thing were possible, and then his muscles sagged. He closed his eyes. Doubtless to him the next second of waiting was an eternity. Loring stamped on the floor. There was a cry of pain from Pete. He stumbled to his knees.

"No!" he screamed. "I'll—I'll talk!"

"Quick and short. First, the name of the man who hired you for this particular job?"

"His name—God help me!—his name was K—"

There was a wrenching sound of splintering wood, the shutter was torn from the window, and a shot boomed heavily in the little room. The gun at the window turned and a second shot ripped its way across the breast of Loring's coat as he stood flattened against the wall. He whipped up his own weapon and fired at the flash. Outside, there was a heavy curse, and then silence.

It had all happened—those three reports—in the split part of a second. In the sudden silence, Loring saw Pete reach his feet with both hands crushed against his face—saw him take one long, dragging step, and then sag to the floor, dead before he struck it.

That was the end. That trail had proven blind. But it was not the end for Loring. He who had fired the first shot had been struck, if the curse told anything, by Loring's return fire. But there was not one chance in ten that he had been fatally injured. If not, he was even now waiting for Loring to leave. And leave he must within the next few seconds. The cripple must be coming back toward the shack by this time. And above all things, it was necessary to Loring to keep his face from being seen.

But how should he get out? Unquestionably, after firing through the window the assailant would now have drawn back to watch the door, and aside from these two openings there was no escape from the house. Yet Loring was not paralyzed with fear. He was suddenly calm. The dead man on the floor was nothing. The gunman outside was a triviality. No fact had any terror for him compared with the awful waiting of the past four days.

Out of the very position which the assailant must have assumed, Loring saw a chance open to him. After firing through the window, that was the last place through which he would expect an attempt to escape. He would trust to the danger which had been there before to guard that exit now.

With that hope, Loring hurled open the shutters, and acting on the impulse, leaped into the night. There was a deep, muffled curse; two black figures seemed to rise to his right out of the black ground. Two guns barked at him, and with the sing of the bullets still in his ear he turned the corner of the house.

He did not stay to fight back. The odds were two to one, and more might be coming, how many more he could not guess. He kept on, trending to the left and racing as he had never run before.

There was no more firing. The assailants had had to circle the corner of the house to get in another shot. By that time Loring was a dwindling figure, half melted into the night.

He started a long detour, for he had no wish to enter the town from the same direction by which he had left it. A brisk walk of a mile or more carried him to another scrambled mass of outlying houses, and among these he headed downtown to the first car-line. He had been on the very verge of success, he knew. A single second more and he would have had at least one name—one name beginning with "K" or "C."

And he was not downhearted. To have even come within hailing distance of an agent of the Company, to have come within the verge of making one of them speak was a triumph.

For it showed that, powerful as it was, dreaded as it was, the agents of the Company did actually fear death more than they feared its revenge. He had no pity for Pete. A hired murderer, surely only justice had been done to him. Only one more thing he regretted, and that was that he had passed through the third test against the Company without securing the information he needed.

It had developed into a running battle, each side exchanging shots at random. And in the meantime the days hurried on for Peter Charles. Loring had purposely matched the time of his duel with the Company with the date set for the execution of Peter Charles. Two days after the six were gone, Peter Charles was to die at the hands of the law.

He was lucky in finding a train at the station as he reached it; two minutes later the local was roaring away toward Manhattan and Loring was sitting as one asleep in a rear seat of a car. That train, he knew, was beyond peradventure watched by the agents of the Murder Company. Of the very men who sat in the car having entered after he did, any one or more of them might be among the men he wanted.

Through the torn brim of his hat he studied them, watched their backs with painful interest, waited for side glimpses of their faces. And then he had to tell himself, in the end, that he was on a fool's hunt. It would need a Nicholas Zanten to extricate any information in such a tangle as this.

It was still well before midnight when the train pulled into the Grand Central; and the taxicab that whirled Loring homeward passed through the middle of the after-theater rush of traffic, that maddening press of machines that chokes Broadway with the stinging odor of gasoline and with stifling clouds of burnt oil. Across Broadway, then up town.

The sleep which the excitement of the long adventure had

kept away from Loring's head was now brought back to it by the caressing, trundling motion of the big taxi. When he reached the lodging house there was a haze before his eyes. He paid the driver and turned up the gloomy front stairs.

It seemed brutally unfair to rob him of sleep. If he could have fought the Company and all its power for a definite period every day—but to be dogged day and night was unfair. A hot anger swept up in Loring as he opened the front door. He strode down the hall fearless of the blackness which had made him shudder on each of the three preceding nights. But halfway to his door he was stopped as by a blow in the face.

Out of his own room, as surely as he possessed ears, he had heard a sound. He paused for a moment with his heart beating at such a rate that he had to gasp for air. There was silence now. But certainly just the instant before he had heard a noise. It had been like a sound of running water, but no matter what its nature, the fact that there had been movement in his room indicated that a human being was in it; and no human being could be there except an agent of the Company.

He revolved these facts in his mind, made sure that there could be no other explanation, and then stole toward the door slowly, with unbelievable gentleness.

He heard it again; and again it was like the sound of water— water running from a bottle, say.

Under his finger tips he turned the knob of the door, with the patience of an Indian, with the care of a thief. Slowly he felt the pressure of the bolt increase, felt that it was giving to his touch. He tried to make the movement so slow that the thing which was in the room, even if it were at that moment carefully watching the knob of the door, would no more perceive the movement than the movement of the hour hand of a watch.

At length there was a sudden inward suction of the door, and Loring, feeling that the lock was free, hurled it open. He pressed his body against the wall as the shaft of light from the room rushed past him, and with his gun poised in his left hand, he peered past the jam.

There was no man in the room, nor any sign of a man, or weapon, or danger. There was only old Mrs. Mercer, who sat at his table with a bottle of his best Scotch before her and a siphon of his seltzer water. She had risen slowly to her feet, wondering at the open door.

But how had she dared to enter so boldly and sit there? Had she entered into the confidence of the Company? Did she know that Samuel Loring was supposed to cease to live on this day?

CHAPTER XXXVI

# THE WHISTLE

**LORING DROPPED THE** automatic into his pocket and stepped into view. The iron-hard face of Mrs. Mercer was contracted with fear and amazement. With trembling hands she caught at the edge of the table to support herself, and then made a rapid furtive sign of the cross.

"Begone!" breathed the old crone. "I had no part in it!"

Loring slipped into the room, and closing the door he put his shoulders against it, and smiled at her.

"I haven't begun to haunt you yet," he said cheerfully. "I'm not even a ghost, Mrs. Mercer. Later on, perhaps, but not now."

The fear passed gradually from her eyes. Presently she was looking at him with a squinted expression that reminded him of an ugly parody of Pete earlier on that same night. There was infinite cunning in that glance.

"Lord, Lord, Mr. Loring," she breathed, "but I'm glad to see you. They been telling me—the liars!—that you'd come to an accident. Poor young man, says I, so young and so unlucky, I says."

"I'll wager you did," murmured Loring.

He was tossing off the ragged hat and the old coat and slipping into clothes of his own.

"But I've given you a start, Mrs. Mercer, sit down. Sit down and have another drink!"

She stared closely at him, as though she doubted the ears which were telling her that he had no suspicions. Gradually the pallor left her face, and the color which the drink had given her returned. Hastily she poured a dram and tossed it off.

"Someone came in with news that the scaffold had killed me?" went on Loring, eager to smooth things over and take her off guard.

"Yes. A lying little thief of a boy from around the corner."

"That rascal Tommy, I wager."

"The very lad. He'll be coming to a bad end. So—"

Her eyes wandered as she hunted for a convincing lie.

"So you came in here to see if you could find the address of relatives, eh, to notify? That was thoughtful of you, Mrs. Mercer!"

"You're an understanding lad, Mr. Loring," she grinned, "And by the way I come on this bottle. It took me to heart, to think of the good whisky going to waste like this for want of an owner. 'Come,' says I to myself, 'let's sit down with the bottle and think of poor young Mr. Loring that was always so kind, so cheerful, that always had a good word both in the morning and at night! Let's sit down and think gentle about him,' says I to myself. And so I done it, as you see!"

"And yet, I should never have guessed that you have noticed me so much as all that."

"Would you not? That's because you haven't read me from the inside. I keep a hard face, Mr. Loring. I got to, don't I? Ain't I a weak and helpless widow woman? But inside I watch and see everything.

"There's Mr. Castor that's got the three rooms on the second floor, front. He pays me a handsome figure and he thinks he can take it out in talk. He no more sees me in the halls when he passes than he sees the figures on the wall paper. And when he speaks it's to order me about. I take the talk because his money is good; but I don't forget him, curse him! Mary Mercer don't forget!"

Her face twisted with devilish malice. Then she smoothed her expression hastily and resumed the wheeling tone.

"But you're different, lad. Oh, you're different. Always a

cheery word for the old woman when she passes. I been grumpy,
but a true gentleman don't mind a lady being grumpy. He's
always the same. That's the way my Jerry was, saving when he
was took bad with liquor, and then he used to beat me awful.
But Lord love him, that was the rum, not Jerry! Besides, mostly
I gave him as good as he sent. Oh, and better!"

She grinned at Loring joylessly.

"But I've had a mother's eye for you, lad! Because you're a
different kind."

He listened to her whining lies with a curious attention. Men
and women, the man with the opal had said, were agents of the
Company. And why not this cold-eyed virago? And Loring
remembered the mysterious manner in which the gas had been
turned on in his room on that first night. He would, if possible,
corner her suddenly with the truth. In the meantime, she was
serving him in another manner, for she was helping him to
while away a section of the night. There was no fear of becoming sleepy while the hatchet face of the crone was opposite him.

"A mother's eye?" repeated Loring gently. "Well, no doubt
you've been a mother. You've had your children and they have
grown up and left you."

"Children? Bah! I could never endure 'em—whining, snivel-
ing, dirty, noisy, ingrates—that's what children are! Haven't I
seen many a woman work out her heart on 'em and get cursed
for it later on? Oh no, Mary Mercer wasn't fool enough to tie
herself down with children!"

Loring rubbed his hand across his forehead to hide from her
the expression of loathing which had crossed his face in spite
of his self-control.

"No children," he echoed, "and I suppose you're right. They're
a burden. But then you had your husband to keep you busy. He
was a handful, no doubt."

"He was a fool, no doubt," sneered the old woman, and her
eyes glanced in an ugly fashion to one side, as though in the
shadow she saw the ghost of her departed spouse. "And it was

me that kept him busy while he lived. He married me by a trick, the idiot—and I paid him back for it. It took me twenty years to do the paying, and when I finished the balance was on my side.

"You can put your money on Mary Mercer, lad," she went on, cackling, "for there's never man, woman, nor child that ever wronged me but that wished sooner or later that they'd wronged the devil first!"

"I believe you," murmured Loring faintly. "Upon my soul, I believe you!"

"You're right to do so." She peered at him closely.

"And yet I've had my doubts of you, I confess."

"Now, what d'ye mean by that?"

"I mean what I say. That I've had my doubts of you, but talking to you to-night, I regain my faith in you—I think you may prove of real value to the Company!"

A strong tremor went through her, but then she set her face against the shock.

"What company?" she whispered.

"Very good," nodded Loring. "You do well. What Company, to be sure!"

He laughed softly.

"Merciful saints," whispered the crone, "d'you mean—"

"Exactly. I mean it."

"Give me a sign!"

Loring was staggered. Then he threw up his right hand with a stiffened forefinger and the rest of the hand closed to a fist. She blinked at him with a sort of breathless horror.

"You understand?" he asked.

"I—no! They haven't taught me that."

"To be sure! What am I thinking of? Of course they wouldn't teach you that as yet. However, you will learn in time. You see, you're new among us."

"Yes, yes. But—my head goes around!"

"You can't understand how I can be one of them? Is that it?"

She did not answer. With fox-like intensity she studied his face to find the deceit there, but Loring was enjoying the ticklish game. Also, he felt that he was coming close, close to the secret which he needed.

"Give me a proof—a proof—a sign that I can understand!"

"I'll do better. Mary Mercer, I was put here to test you. They wanted a proof of your ability and your zeal. That was why they gave you the order."

"To—"

"To kill me by fair means or foul."

She moistened her thin lips.

"Of course I was watching. And on the first night after your admission, I admired the way you turned on the gas!"

"God above!" gasped Mrs. Mercer, and he knew that the trap had closed on her.

Loring began to laugh carefully.

"Do you know," he said frankly, and still smiling, "that you were so cunning about it that you almost took me in? It was almost by accident that I discovered what you had done in time! Almost by accident! And when I opened the door to you—why, I admired the way you kept your face. It was a nice bit of acting!"

All at once she smiled with horrible glee.

"Ay, Mr. Loring, I can keep my face when there's a need. You'll tell 'em that?"

"I've already told them. And praised you. But afterward, lost faith in you because you did not more."

"But there was the order to leave you alone after that. Stronger hands than mine, they said—"

"Tush! Did you believe the order? Were you fool enough to believe that they meant it. My dear Mrs. Mercer, it was only a test of your zeal! You should have known that!"

She blinked at him again and nodded.

"I see," she muttered. "But—Lord deliver us!—did you take all that risk to try me and prove me?"

"Risk? When you're longer with us you'll come to know me better and then you'll see that I could not be in danger even from such a clever woman as you are, Mrs. Mercer."

"Are you so sure?" she said, with her grin of malice. "Don't be so sure, lad!"

"But you should have kept on."

"I tell you, it was an order. A strong order with the sign going with it!"

"What? Did they give you the sign, also?"

"They did!" she said triumphantly. "Now d'you think I'm such a fool?"

"No, but the man was a fool who gave you the sign. He exceeded his instructions."

"And how do you know?"

"Because I was directing."

"You gave the order?"

"Not I. I caused it to be given!"

"And he said too much? I thought at the time he was a rat-faced sneak! Take orders from you? I says to myself. But what could I do?"

"There was nothing you could do—if he gave you the sign. But I'll make things hot for him, the idiot!"

"Do it! Do it! I hated the sight of him, I tell you!"

"What was his name?"

"Eh? You so high and you don't know his name?"

"My good Mrs. Mercer, do you think that any one man can remember all the names in the Company?"

"That's true. Well, sir, his name was—"

She stopped abruptly. For a moment her eyes wondered at Loring, and then her face hardened.

It was not until then that he heard it—far away—as if it came from the street, or from the room below them. It was a whistle pitched high on the first note and breaking down in a short run. Twice it was repeated, and Mrs. Mercer got up from her chair and sidled toward the door. The malice in her face was a nightmare sight.

"You devil!" she snarled at Loring. "You cunning devil!"

She paused at the door with her teeth set in the excess of her hatred and rage, and then disappeared softly.

# CHAPTER XXXVII

# A NEW SIDE TO PETER CHARLES

**THE MOMENT THE** door had closed on her he knew that no matter what happened he must have some rest. Sleep was besieging his brain in heavy waves the instant the stimulus of the presence of the hag was removed. He decided to venture a short nap. Having been threatened by him so recently, he decided that the chances were that the Company would make no further attempt for an hour or so, at least. With all the lights still burning, and having first looked to the door and window wires, and turned on the electric switch, he went to his bedroom, set the alarm clock two hours ahead, and flinging himself on the bed was suddenly asleep.

Even fear of death could not keep him from some rest in that weariness.

He was wakened with the tearing, grinding clangor of the alarm at his ear, and knew that it had been ringing for some time before it could tear him out of his slumber.

Then he wakened with a start. Two full hours of sleep had braced his nerves marvelously. He felt fully rested compared with the nerve fag which had been his when he lay down, and he took a chair resolutely to spend the rest of the night reading. Ten minutes after he had composed himself there was a slight tug at the shutter of the living room window behind him—and Loring was instantly out of his chair and on his knees with the automatic in his hand.

No further sound. He waited through half a dozen heart-breaking moments, and there was no repetition.

But having pushed his chair back against the wall and settled himself in it with his eye facing the window, a new noise came to distract him—the stealthy sound of a footfall in the hall. It was not one of those ghost sounds which lived in the old house. There was all the difference in the world between the two sorts of noises. There was an unquestionable sense of weight in these stealing noises. Loring turned again and gripped the automatic hard. He looked to its charge; it was completely ready for service.

Then, with his eyes fixed on the door, he saw the knob turned—slowly, slowly, just as he had turned that same knob earlier in the evening. He set his jaw in a straight line and he poised the gun.

Presently the knob was released with a rattle; the stealthy sound went off down the hall, swiftly. And then Loring understood. They had not planned an actual attack with physical violence. They were purposely alarming him to wear down his nerves. He was sure of it.

But being sure of it did not quiet his nerves. At every alarm the beating of his heart set his temples throbbing. At every sudden and strange noise how could he tell that this was not the prelude to the real attack?

He managed to make coffee with his shaking hands and with that stimulant and a small dose of the strychnine he managed to wear out the night.

But by the morning he was a wreck. A nightmare can ruin a man's rest; but Loring had been through a waking nightmare. The fact that he understood the purpose of their maneuvers did not help him. No more than it helps the prizefighter who is stabbed and worried by the dancing, sparring tactics of a clever opponent, knowing that the quick footed man is simply wearing him down for the moment when he will leave himself open to a finishing punch.

The fourth day was gone. The fifth day was come. And what was this face that looked out from the mirror at Samuel Loring, athlete and adventurer? If he were not mistaken, the gray had spread upon his temples. The healthy color of his skin was changed to a sickly pallor, horrible to see.

Great shadows were pouched beneath his eyes and from his nose past his mouth ran deeply graven, long lines of pain and doubt. He looked, he told himself, like a man in the last stages of a struggle with some mortal disease—consumption, say. Hope was gone. Only the fighting instinct remained.

There was a knock at his door. Loring answered it, and opened the door with a jerk of his wrist, standing well under the cover of the wall as he did so, his hand grasping the automatic in his coat pocket.

It was only a messenger boy who started back and turned pale at the set face of Loring.

The message was unsigned, short:

"Courage, mon brave!"

Loring tossed the boy a fifty-cent piece and closed the door again.

It was Nicholas Zanten, of course, who had sent the message. The bold, free, careless writing was like an index to the character of the man. Courage! Loring could have broken into ironic laughter. It was like appealing to troops who have four times failed to storm the redoubt. For four days he had struggled against the Company. Three times he had thought that victory was in his grasp; and three times they had baffled him. If that had happened to Samuel Loring in the full possession of his strength, how could the shattered wreck which looked back at him from the mirror expect success?

He dressed hastily, and leaving the house journeyed first to a distant part of the city, where he tried to eat and made a miserable failure of it. Next he started to the prison.

It was not difficult to see the condemned Peter Charles. But once seen, Loring was astonished by the manner and the physical aspect of the man. Peter Charles, he felt, was a coward, but the man who shook hands with him was not the pale, cringing ghost which he expected.

His face had good color. His voice was steady. The clear eyes told that he had not been watching out the hours of the night. Death was four days away, but apparently the financier was awaiting it with calm patience. Loring had never seen him in such high spirits. And he had never dreamed that the man could have such an imposing calm.

"You look well," he muttered.

"I feel well. And—look at my hand!"

He held it out. It was as steady as the hand of a marksman.

"I've made myself be well," continued Peter Charles. "I'm going to fool them!"

It was as if all the pangs of the waiting had been transferred to Loring and his own usually indomitable high spirits had been poured into the frail body of Peter Charles. The thing was unbelievable. Was this the man who had collapsed in the court-room?

He was strangely, brutally frank about the whole thing. He talked of his treatment. He approved of it, and remarked on the excellent prison diet.

"I'm in training," he said, with a smile which Loring found hard to bear. "They say I haven't lived well. I'm going to show 'em that a Charles always dies well!"

It was the brazen carelessness of a man accustomed to executions—of some old revolutionary—of a Danton, say.

"There's no doubt of that," said Loring gravely. "I am glad to see that your spirits are high."

"You, on the contrary, look like the devil. What's this my daughter tells me about you? She'll always be talking of you. Gad, two words for you to every one she gives me. I think you've turned her head! But what's this she says about 'strange services' you are rendering me! What the devil does she mean by it?"

A grisly doubt had come to Loring while he listened to the condemned man. The same doubt was what had driven him to the prison in the first place. Now it shook him to his soul. Was not Peter Charles after all guilty? Was not this the calm of the hopeless criminal?

"Let me be frank, Mr. Charles. You see that I am no longer what I used to be."

"You look like a ghost—that's the straight of it."

"For four days I have been living in constant peril. It is a danger which I have invited in an effort to prove that you are innocent. It is a danger from which I can deliver myself if I choose. As long as I have the faintest hope that I can discover the truth about you and free an innocent man I shall persist, although to be frank, I have an almost hopeless task before me. I have come to you to-day to beg you, Mr. Charles, to tell me the truth."

"The truth about what? Come, come, if you're in danger, you're a fool if you don't get out of it if you can."

"I've tried to explain. Mr. Charles, your time is short. You are hopeless, I know, unless I am fortunate enough to discover the truth in the short interim and that truth proves your innocence.

"I have come to beg you to tell me frankly whether or not you are innocent or guilty. If you are innocent I shall persist. If you are guilty you see that my persistence can do you no good. The truth I discover will only doubly damn you, and in the meantime it brings me close to almost certain destruction."

Peter Charles looked at him in amazement.

"So they've sent you to me, have they?" he sneered. "Do they think that I've lost the last bit of sense in my head. They send you to me with this cock-and-bull story in the hope that I may admit guilt in order to keep the wrinkles out of your precious face? This is too much! I'm to admit it to you, and you go out and spread the news?"

"Sir, I swear to you on my honor that no matter what you tell me, not a syllable shall ever be repeated."

"And what is your honor, eh?" said Peter Charles brutally. "So far as I know, you're a nameless adventurer, Loring. How am I to trust in your honor?"

"My honor kept you from some danger in the trial, sir! You must be aware of that."

"Bah! How do I know that you and Lorriston didn't put your heads together to play the trick on me? If you didn't tell him, how did he even know what sort of a gun I was supposed to use? How could he get a copy of it to play the trick?"

"If I had been on his side, don't you suppose that I would instantly have given him the real weapon and told the story that would have damned you without any trick?"

"I don't know. The law is full of holes and tricks. How am I to know what went on inside his clever head? No, sir, I won't trust you and I won't trust any man."

"Mr. Charles, think that over before you make it an irrevocable decision. I tell you, it condemns me to the gravest danger!"

"I'll say nothing; I'll admit nothing!" cried Peter Charles in excitement. "No matter what they think, I'm going to walk out with a firm step and a high head. 'Gentlemen,' I'll say to 'em all, 'here stands Peter Charles, an innocent man done to death by the force of circumstantial evidence. Pray for my soul!'"

He walked up and down, saying this, and Loring knew that it was a scene which the other had rehearsed many a time. It was for this last effect that he was hoarding and husbanding his strength.

"You refuse to speak a syllable that will take me out of my doubt?"

"Not a sound! Get out of your trouble, if you can. At the best you can't help me. At the worst you'll die like a fool and the world's already too full of 'em. Mr. Loring, you take my strength and I need that for myself. Good-by!"

And Loring left, burdened by the newer and greater doubt.

Innocent men were not apt to refuse even the shadow of a hope. With his own lips, it seemed, Peter Charles had condemned himself without a hope of reprieve. And for a moment Loring lifted his head to the sky and took a great breath of relief. Had not the condemned man with his own selfish lips freed him from any shred of duty? Could he not go freely to Nicholas Zanten, now, and tell him that the thing was done?

With his mind made up, he hurried back to Manhattan, and straight toward the house of the man with the opal he took his way. But Fate, it seemed, was against him. Nicholas Zanten was not at home, and when Loring went down again into the street he heard, through an open window which he could not locate, a girl's voice singing the last thrilling phrases of Gounod's "Ave Maria."

The thought of Beatrice Charles rushed back upon his heart. Was it not worth all chances and all danger in order to lift the shadow from her face? He paused until the singing ceased. When he walked on again he knew he was doomed to fight the battle to the end.

# CHAPTER XXXVIII

# LORING CONFESSES

**AN HOUR OF** broken slumber on an elevated train was his only portion for the fifth day, and before the gloom of the evening settled over the city he was back at the lodging house. Mrs. Mercer, her face set like iron, was in the hall when he entered, and when he turned, after passing her, he saw her smiling with silent malignance. There was something peculiarly devilish in this setting of a woman on his trail, and keeping her there, openly; as though they had read his character and knew that his hands were tied against a woman.

From the hall she watched his cautious entrance to his room, and he closed the door, shutting out the sound of her racking laughter. There began again that preliminary search with which he went over the apartment always before he settled down to the long battle with sleep.

Midnight came, and as it passed he had entered upon the last and sixth day of the waiting. By midnight of the following day the period would have elapsed and then, if the Company kept faith, he was free!

But he was beginning to have a shuddering feeling that he had not yet met the full strength of the Company. Those keen brains of which the man with the opal had told him had not yet been put in operation against him. A feeble old woman and the brutal mind of Pete, what were these as antagonists for him? They were merely the foils with which the Company tried him out, measured his strength. They were the crude weapons with which he was being worn down.

And at the last, when he had come within an hour of delivery and freedom, a real antagonist would step into the arena and strike him down with polished finesse. They were only delaying until his mind was reeling with weariness, drunk with sleep. Then the blow would fall.

As if he had read their minds, he knew the truth with certainty, but still that was no help. This night was a repetition of the night before—the succession of alarming noises which tried his nerve power again and again and turned the night into a horror.

How he endured until the morning he never really knew. The strong black coffee and the repeated use of the drug helped him through, and then came the cold dawn with its feeling of chill and death.

The last day had begun—his last day on earth, Loring was reasonably sure.

When the sun was high he went out. On the steps he stumbled like a drunkard. Why did they not strike him then? He was helpless against even a child's force, he felt. But no, they would wait until the very end. They would make him drain the last drop from that cup of despair, and then the blow would fall.

He was so sure of it that he passed the day almost carelessly.

One thing remained for him to do, he felt. He must see Beatrice before the end, tell her good-by, assume some good cheer to deceive her, and then go back to wait for the finish. But without that final interview he felt that it would be a death without the sacrament. Twice he tried to reach her on the telephone; in the late afternoon he succeeded and went to her apartment.

He found her pale but very calm. She, too, had been waiting all these days, and the trial was beginning to tell on her. Certainly the bloom was gone and another man would not have found her even pretty, but to Loring she was divine. He would have talked to her about herself, but she was too shocked by his appearance to let him. She placed him in the biggest chair in the room and propped his head with a pillow as if he were an invalid.

"What have you been doing?" she kept saying. "What have you been doing to wreck yourself like this?"

"I've tried my best," answered Loring, "and I've been beaten. That's why I've come to you."

She closed her eyes; when she opened them he knew that up to that moment she had still been placing some trust in what he might do for her father. Now that trust was gone. She brushed it away with a generous gesture.

"We'll forget about the past," said the girl. "We'll think only of the future. You understand? We'll think only of the future. And how to get you back on your feet. You're only a ghost of what you were! Only a ghost!"

"You have troubles of your own," said Loring gently, "and yet you think of me? But I'm stepping out. That's why I've come here—to tell you that being beaten, I'm going to shake myself clear of the whole matter."

"You're going away?"

"To the ends of the world," said Loring steadily. "I've no wish to stay near the place of my defeat."

She drew up a chair opposite his and leaned a little toward him.

"I wish I could explain to you," she said, "that I feel you haven't been beaten. Exactly what you've done I don't know, but I can see that you've given every ounce of power in your mind and body to the service of my father, without hope of any reward. And because you have done that, do you know what I feel?"

He shook his head.

"That it's a triumph! A great triumph for you! Defeats like that are victories!"

Loring shuddered.

"That's because you're proud," she said eagerly. "But look at it with my eyes! If I ever lose faith in men and their courage and justice and clean hearts, do you know what I'll do? I'll think of you!"

"Hush!" said Loring. "You see, you let the idea sweep you away! The most I ask of you is that you forget me entirely and my failure with me. But I'm afraid that the time will come when you'll remember me as an egotistical fool who thought he could succeed where a great many clever men had failed. Don't deny it. I know you will out of your large heart. I think that's the divine part of a woman like you—your mind follows your heart, and your heart is always following your sympathy."

He laughed faintly.

"Lord, Lord, I'm a poor sort! Here I come with a pair of hollow eyes and a thin face and a yellow skin and let you pour out your pity on me. I tell you, if you keep on talking as you have, I'll begin to despise myself more than ever!"

He shook himself out of the chair and rose.

"I'm going now. Why I came here I don't know. I must have felt that I would cut you up. I begin to think that all men are babies around women. They like to boast and brag, but down in their hearts they hope to be admired and petted and pitied all at once. Good-by."

She sat with her head bowed, and at the door he wheeled and came back to her.

"At least," he said, "I'm going to have the courage to tell you the whole truth, now that I'm leaving for good. You've admired my generosity in doing all that I've tried to do for a man I hardly know—your father. But let me tell you that from the first I have done it all for you. Don't stop me!"

She had straightened and turned to him with something like fear in her face.

"Do you know what I was going to do? I knew that you were engaged to another man; that you loved another man; but when I started on this adventure I said to myself: 'I'll do this thing and when I've done it—who can tell what her gratitude will be? And what it will do? Perhaps it will make her give herself to me!' For you see, I've loved you from the moment I laid eyes on you.

"Do you remember when I first saw you, in the hall when you came smiling to Geoffrey? That's the way I remember you. And I could sit here perfectly contented in this room if I were blind, simply to listen to your voice. That's the way I've loved you from the first. That's why I've tried to do these things.

"Have you ever heard of a man who's unselfish when he's in love? No more am I! And—the best I can ask is for you to forgive me and forget me and my failure. Good-by again!"

A cry from her stopped him. She started up before him.

"Are you going to leave without asking for a single return?"

"What return can I ask?"

"Hold out your hands."

He obeyed, and her own hands slipped into them.

"Whatever I can give is yours. All of me!"

"Beatrice, you don't know what you say!"

"Oh, my dear, haven't I done this over and over again in my dreams? It is the truest thing I have ever done in my life!"

His arms were about her before he could stop the impulse; but with her face upturned beneath his, waiting for his kiss, he fought himself away.

"I'm not such a thief," he stammered. "Do you think I'd steal your happiness? Why, your whole life has been built toward your marriage with Geoffrey!"

"My father's plan—not mine!"

"It will break his heart; and knowing that you'd never forgive yourself!"

"Let me tell you my faith. Whatever I could do for him out

of my own power I would do. But I love you, don't you see? And because that's true it is a thing over which he has no claim. I have tried to be loyal to him. I have fought honestly against loving you. I have tried faithfully to think of Geoffrey as a husband. But I can't. Let me tell you if I can. When I began to care for you I no longer belonged entirely to myself. All the best part of me was yours."

"Ah, but you don't know. A nameless, heedless adventurer— that's the best I can say for myself."

"Do you think I would care for you more if you were rich?"

"But poverty—it is an anchor around the neck—a torture of which you don't dream."

"But I dream of this and know this: I can't take my wealth into my love any more than I can take it into the other world after death. My father will disinherit me as far as he can. Let it be done altogether. We shall respect his wishes. Whatever comes to my share we'll give away together. Then we'll start alone and clean-handed, empty-handed. You say you are going on a long journey. I'll follow; around the world, through jungles—why, if we have each other, all the rest is not a handful!"

But with a last great effort of the will Loring pushed himself away.

"Where I am going," he said hoarsely, "you cannot follow me."

"Then it's no place on earth." Her voice rose to a cry. "What do you mean?"

"Nothing I can explain."

"But I know. There's a danger."

"If I am worthy of you," said Loring heavily, "the thing which is ahead of me must be done. And if you care for me, Beatrice, don't try to dissuade me. God knows I'm weak and easily bent. I command you not to speak.

"Only give me this promise: that if I fail to return you'll carry on your life as your father and you have planned it. You'll marry

Geoffrey; you'll build your home together; you'll keep your father's fortune. Will you promise?"

"Will you let me say one thing?"

"Nothing you say can stop me. Promise me, Beatrice!"

She bowed her head, and before she raised it, Loring had fled from the room.

CHAPTER XXXIX

# GEOFFREY CHARLES: FRIEND

**HE DESPISED HIMSELF** bitterly for having ventured on that interview, not that he could have guessed the state of Beatrice's mind, but for having allowed himself to appear in such a pitiable plight. Yet he left the place stronger. It was not that he hoped, in spite of the fact that he had more to hope for. But the interview had roused in him a stern pride and a determination that he would die fighting to his uttermost.

That pride strengthened his step as he reached the street. And it kept his head erect on the way back, through the early evening, to the lodging house of Mrs. Mercer. With his hand on the front doorknob he turned abruptly, and across the street he saw the squat form of Mr. Gregg hurrying away.

That was sufficient for Loring to know that the net was about to close on him. The enemies were aware of his return and they were about to step in for the final act.

As far as he could, he had prepared himself physically for the test. He had bought some new coffee on the way home and he had the remnants of the strychnine. If there remained any resiliency in his will and his nerve and muscular force, the stimulants would bring it out. He began as usual, with the search of the apartment. He studied the shutters and the doors. He saw to it that the electric alarm was in working order, and then he sat down to begin his vigil.

The night deepened.

It was as he expected—they were saving their blow for the

very end of the six days. And yet through his mind went a half wild, half frantic hope that the whole thing might be a tremendous hoax. The memory of Pete and Mrs. Mercer was enough to wipe away that hope.

The night wore on. It was eight. Then it was nine, with a prodigious interval between. There remained three hours, but in three hours what could not be done? The split part of a second was long enough to destroy a life!

It was a little after a quarter past nine when he heard a loud knock at his living room door. And instantly he decided that the crisis had come. Suppose he should be foolish enough to open the door, would they try the force of numbers against him—an overwhelming rush?

"Who's there?" he called, and expected no answer.

But a deep, strong voice answered: "Geoffrey Charles!"

Geoffrey Charles! Suddenly he yearned to have that calm-eyed young Hercules beside him There was a man! His heart fluttered with gratitude to Beatrice. She undoubtedly had sent him, and yet he was a little angered, also, that she should have persisted in attempting to keep in touch with him after he had so solemnly forbidden it.

"I can't see you," said Loring.

He felt that he dared not meet Geoffrey face to face; the temptation to beg him to stay would then be too great. But with Geoffrey at his back, what could he not face?

"The devil!" he heard Geoffrey mutter. Then: "Hello, Loring!"

"Yes?"

"I tell you, I've got to see you."

Loring went to the door.

"My dear fellow. I'm terribly sorry, but I can't see you. To-morrow—"

There was an exclamation of impatience.

"Don't be so mysterious, Loring. I've got to get in to you!"

"Charles, for your own sake—"

"Of course, that makes me absolutely determined. Loring, if you won't open the door, I'm going to take things into my own hands and break it down!"

There was nothing left. With a shudder of self-loathing for his weakness, but with a feeling of infinite relief, Loring unlocked the door and opened it. At once Geoffrey, as though he feared he would be shut out again if he delayed, shouldered past his host into the room.

"Door locked, eh?" he growled. "Now, what the devil is this, Loring? I don't make it out! Not a bit! And who's the old hag with the face of a witch that I passed in the hall. She was watching this door of yours the way a cat watches a mouse. Who is she?"

"She was watching my door?" said Loring faintly.

"She was. Good gad, man, you look sick! I'm going to go out and bring in a doctor."

Loring put out a trembling hand and caught the arm of the other. What an arm it was! The huge corded muscles rolled and tightened under his touch.

"Don't do that, my friend. For God's sake, don't do that!"

"Why not? I give you my solemn assurance that you need a doctor's help. Take a mirror and look at yourself! By the Lord, I'd say you haven't had a sound night's sleep in a month."

"That's exactly it. Insomnia. A rotten weakness of mine. No rest for a week. You know how that cuts a fellow up?"

"I don't knew it; but I can guess from the look of you. Man, you seem to have been through hell!"

"A dozen hells, Charles."

"Then, you idiot, let me get a doctor. He'll put you to sleep fast enough."

"Sleep?" cried Loring in horror. "Sleep? God in heaven! Sleep now? Not for all the treasures in the world!"

He broke off, for he saw that Geoffrey Charles had changed color and was eyeing him sternly. "I don't mean to alarm you. Let me explain. I dabble in chemistry, you see? I have a little experiment which I consider of importance. To-night I try it. And I can't have anyone here to disturb me."

"Insomnia—then chemistry. The devil!"

Geoffrey deliberately seated himself in a chair and crossed his legs.

"I give you my solemn word," he said calmly, "that I'm not going to leave the room until I get at the bottom of this."

For a moment Loring studied him, the clean, healthy skin, the bright eyes, the exuberant strength of an unwasted youth. What a man this Geoffrey Charles was! He was glad that he had made that last demand upon Beatrice in favor of such a fellow as this with gentleman written in every line of his face, every tone of his voice.

And what a reënforcement he would be. Yet Loring set his teeth and beat back the impulse to ask help. At least, he would not be guilty of the sin of involving Geoffrey in his fall. He began to play for time.

"I'm afraid Beatrice sent you," he said.

His companion frowned gloomily at the floor.

He answered heavily: "Yes. She sent me."

"I'm sorry. I—I shouldn't have called on her."

"Do you know how I found her? Weeping her heart out. 'Geoffrey, go to him and save him. He's in danger, and he's in danger for our sakes.' Well, that's why I'm here."

"I shouldn't have gone near her to-day. But I forgot that I look so out of shape."

"The point is that you *did* go to her. The point is, Loring, that she sent me to save the man she loves. I won't beat about the bush. As a matter of fact, you know everything I could tell you. I love her. I've always loved her. But I'm not the sort to stand between her and another choice."

Loring bowed his head.

"I've made a mess of everything," he answered. "I won't insult you by saying that I'm sorry for you, Charles."

"Thanks."

"But I'll give you this assurance. I'm going on a long journey and I won't come back. You'll pick up where you left off with her."

The face of Geoffrey went black.

"That shows you don't know her. A nunnery is nearer to her than I am, now. She isn't the sort to love two men. But let's forget about me and my affairs. She has the right to command me—God bless her!—and she's commanded me to look after you. And I'm going to do it. You can put your last cent on that cold fact!

"To begin with, what's all this rot about the long journey? You've about broken her heart with your queer talk."

"It is something I can't talk over with you, I'm sorry to say."

"Like the insomnia and the chemical experiment, eh?" said Geoffrey, without mirth.

Loring brushed his hand hastily across his face, digging in the tips of his fingers to straighten the twitching muscles.

"Charles," he said, "I can only tell you this. My nerves are about gone. I'm nearly used up. I can't stand having you here much longer. I don't want to appear ungentlemanly—I hate to be brutish—but—if you don't get up and leave this room I'll throw you out of it!"

"So!" said Geoffrey Charles. "So!"

His glance traveled leisurely over the tall, trembling body of Loring.

"You're a good deal of a man, Loring, but between you and me I don't mind saying that I think you'd have quite a time throwing me out."

"If not by physical force," added Loring, "then at the point of a gun, if—"

There was a faint scratching sound at the door, and Loring, wheeling, sprang lightly back against the wall, his automatic leaping into his hand at the same time. There he crouched, braced, ready for any action that might be necessary, sure that the time had come.

"Guard yourself, Charles!" he gasped.

But big Geoffrey, after casting a glance of bewilderment at his host, heaved himself out of his chair with a frown.

"What nonsense is all this?" he growled.

He strode to the door.

"If you value your life," panted Loring, "don't open that door!"

"The devil take your womanish nonsense!" answered Geoffrey, and turning the lock he cast open the door.

Loring braced himself, either to see the tall form crushed to the floor by a blow, or to hear the report of a gun. But there was only silence. Geoffrey disappeared into the blackness. Presently he came back, closed the door, locked it, and faced Loring point-blank.

"Nothing out there. Not a solitary thing."

He advanced to the center of the room.

"Sit down in that chair," he said to Loring, "before you topple on the floor."

Under that commanding gesture, Loring could do nothing but obey. He sat watching the face of Geoffrey with twitching lips. Oh, for a tithe of the cool strength which sat in the face of the younger man!

"This has gone far enough," said Geoffrey Charles solemnly. "Personally I've an idea that you've been given some sort of jolt that has knocked your brains askew. But no matter what it is, out with it. You see that I'm going to stay on now until I get at the truth."

"I can't talk to you, I say! God knows that I want to!"

"Then I'll tell you what. This whole business looks queer to me. There's something rotten about it. And unless you talk out, I'm going to ring the police. I have some influence in the department and I can get half a dozen men to come up and take charge."

It pulled Loring out of his chair.

"Not that, Charles!"

"Then, will you talk?"

For a moment of silence, Loring listened to the pounding of his own heart. Then: "You win. Sit down and listen—and God help you!"

# CHAPTER XL

# "YOU ARE THE MAN"

"**CHARLES,**" **HE BEGAN,** "every moment you spend in this room is a moment of mortal danger to your life!"

Geoffrey whistled long and low. "Well, well, that's an amiable beginning."

"It sounds like a fairy story?"

"It sounds as if I ought to put in that ring for the police after all. Why haven't you done it yourself?"

"Because the first policeman to answer the call would be the man I fear. Because I'm fighting a force which has a thousand eyes, a thousand arms. You understand?"

"Hardly."

"You smile? You think it's a jest? Charles, it's the truth. I started to find the true murderer of Joseph Wilbur. Who it is I don't know. But in following that trail I've brought the danger of murder on my own head—and on the head of you, because you're in this room. Now take my advice. I've set my mind on following this thing through. You can be of no help. Go back to your home.

"In the morning, if I have disappeared, you can do your best to find me. That's the most help you can be. But I won't let you leave this room until you swear by everything holy that you'll keep my secret. Will you?"

"I relieve you from that anxiety by giving you my oath by everything that's holy that I don't intend to leave this room."

"Charles, for the sake of pity and good sense, are you going to damn me by letting me drag you down?"

"Tush! I don't intend to be dragged down. You're doing this for Peter Charles. Why, man, if you have an obligation to yourself, I have an obligation to the man to whom I owe everything except life. If you're able to stay here and meet a danger, I'm able also. Sit where you are. I'm going to sit where I am. And by the eternal, if they try to murder us it will take more than two men to turn the trick!"

As he spoke, he calmly took from his pocket a Colt forty-five and laid it on the table.

"What's more, I can use the gun. Now, Loring, I guess this is settled, but I still don't see why we shouldn't call for the police."

"Take my word. It would be suicide. I'd rather put my gun to my own head and pull the trigger."

Geoffrey shrugged his shoulders. Blood told in that crisis. His color had fallen a little, but he was superbly at ease, lighting a cigarette and watching the pale blue clouds drift toward the ceiling. Loring watched him in silent envy and admiration, "A thoroughbred," he decided.

That thought had scarcely flickered through his brain when he received proof that his companion was filled with a hair-trigger alertness in spite of his pretended calm. There was a faint sound at the shutters and instantly Geoffrey was out of his chair and had bounded to the windows, landing on noiseless feet in spite of his bulk. There he crouched and waited, with the gun which he had scooped from the table in his hand.

At length he stepped back.

"I think I saw a shadow cross the shutter," he said softly to Loring. "If it passes again, I'm going to fire!"

"Don't be a fool! One shot will bring the neighborhood about our ears and spoil everything. You see, Geoffrey, the whole point of the matter is that we're trapped, but we are also a trap. And the man who, sooner or later, but certainly not later than mid-

*He turned and faced them doggedly, a beaten man at last!*

night, makes an attempt upon my life, will be a man connected with the organization which, I think, killed Joseph
Wilbur."

"And in return, do you know my solemn conviction?"

"Well?"

"That the murderer of Joseph Wilbur is the man who is going
to the chair for it—Peter Charles! It's not an easy thing to say,
but we're men enough to talk frankly. Personally, I think that
you're playing a fool's part and risking your life for nothing."

Loring bent his head in an agony of doubt.

"Charles," he said, "I've never been a religious man, but I've
prayed for some sort of guidance in this affair. Life isn't cheap
with me, but somehow I can't give the thing up. Go if you want
to. It's not too late. But I'm going to see this through!"

"You're speaking for both of us, then. I won't welch. How
about the entrances? How many rooms have you?"

"The two. That's all. I've laid electric wires which I tested a
little while ago. No one can enter this room without setting off
an alarm. In the meantime—for ten minute's sleep! It would
make a new man of me!"

"By all means lie down. I can waken you instantly."

Loring fought out the temptation.

"I can't do it. I've a premonition that when the blow falls it will come like lightning. Nothing but work in the split part of a second will count then—and I'm not going to sleep."

Geoffrey sighed.

"I think you've told us that you're poor, Loring, but you certainly have a wealth of conscience. Well, do as you see fit, but you'll be propping your eyes open in a little while."

Indeed, Loring's eyes were heavy as lead. He took the hint, and starting up the little gas heater, he soon had a pot of strong coffee simmering. He served it to Geoffrey with sugar. He took it himself with only a touch of the deadly strychnine. And he explained the drug to his companion.

The latter shook his head in wonder.

"And you've been going through all this for the sake of Peter Charles?" he said. "Without a word to me or to anyone who might help willingly?"

"Because I haven't dared to speak. Two men can't hold a secret that's safe with one. In spite of yourself you might have let a word fall that would have ruined everything. Beside, I had no right to involve you in this horrible mess.

"Then," he added, "I have to confess that there was Beatrice as an inspiration!"

"Aye," nodded Geoffrey, turning gloomy again, "there's something deadly about every pretty girl. And to think that this, after all, is Beatrice's work!" He shook his head in mute wonder.

In the meantime, the hands of the clock moved. They had reached half past ten—they passed with incredible slowness toward a quarter to eleven, and in spite of the stimulants, Loring felt his head faltering with sleep.

But when would they strike?

He took another cup of coffee and moved to the table where Geoffrey sat with his cup.

"Charles," he said, "the time has almost come. Within the next hour the blow is going to fall. And there's an odd feeling of horror in me that tells me it is going to fall almost in the next minute."

Geoffrey shuddered.

"It can't possibly fall without some warning. Not if that alarm will work."

"It will work. But there are always mysterious ways of getting at a man's life, it seems. It's easier to guard anything than life. And when the blow comes on me it will come from the least expected direction."

"True enough—but don't talk about it. You give me the creeps, man, and we need our nerve!"

"Ah, my friend, and you're this way after an hour! Think of six whole days of it!"

"How you've borne up I can't imagine! What's that?"

Loring whirled; there had, indeed, been a faint noise at the door. He waited.

"It's nothing," said Charles.

He added, "and in the meantime your coffee is getting cold."

Loring turned and found that his companion was touching his cup.

"It's warm enough," said Loring. "I'm not drinking it for pleasure, and I don't want to use more of the stuff than is absolutely necessary."

"Of course that's right," admitted Geoffrey, and he settled back in his chair with a sigh. "An hour and a quarter left!" he muttered.

Loring was buried in profound thought. That the Company should have waited until the last hour to strike him was not strange. It was entirely explicable. That it should have allowed him to be reinforced by a power so great as that of Geoffrey Charles was, however, a mystery.

From the man with the opal he gathered abundant conviction that this was no ordinary society. It was one which, to effect its ends, stepped into families, between brother and sister, mother and son. There was no tie which it would not corrupt by its insidious influence.

And yet this all-wise power had allowed plain Samuel Loring, adventurer extraordinary, to keep it at bay for six whole days, and at the end of that period take another man, as strong in every way, it seemed, as himself, into his confidence and into his company. Two men were twice as strong as one. Considering the mutual support and vigilance they afforded one another, they became instantly ten times as formidable as a single person.

Nothing was, indeed, as mysterious as this oversight in allowing big Geoffrey Charles to enter the room. And certainly Geoffrey had from the first been such a probable ally of Loring that the company, were it all-wise, should have watched every move of both.

Why had they allowed Charles to come!

Suddenly the terrible thought rushed upon the mind of Loring with instant conviction—the danger was already in that room. It was a danger from which Geoffrey could not shield him. Long ago the Company must have planted that danger there. Long ago they were aware that when other expedients failed this last resource was certain to have effect.

What was it? Had they planted a powerful bomb with a time fuse beneath the flooring?

It seemed improbable. Geoffrey was no enemy of theirs. He was an obstacle, but from what he knew of it, the Company worked with a neat-handed precision, killing only where it was absolutely necessary to destroy. Could it possibly be guilty of work so raw, so randomly murderous, as the explosion of a bomb in a house full of people?

The thought was ridiculous.

Then where was the danger? Beyond doubt, thought Loring, with the sweat pouring down his forehead, that danger was already in the room. The sense of it was so strong that he dared not mention it even to Geoffrey Charles. It would seem like a mad intuition.

"Coffee isn't half so stimulating when it's cold," murmured Geoffrey at this point.

"True," nodded Loring, and raised the cup.

As he did it his eyes turned to the face of Geoffrey; and the horrible conviction burst in on him in a blinding flash of intuition: "You are the man!"

Luckily Geoffrey's eyes were lowered and he could not see the sudden convulsion of Loring's face. Else he must have started up in alarm.

And Loring thought swiftly: "By a human agent's hand, certainly, the society will strike. And considering all things, it is foolish to suppose that the Company would try to break through all the guards in upon two strong, armed men. Therefore, its agent was already there. And that agent could be no other than Geoffrey Charles himself!"

# CHAPTER XLI

# THE ATTACK

**IT WAS IN** vain for Loring to reason against his instinct. It was in vain that he searched the calm, clean-featured face of the younger man. It was in vain that he recalled how he had tried every possible human persuasion to induce Geoffrey to leave the room and how only irresistible courage and good nature had kept Geoffrey with him. It was in vain that he even remembered how Geoffrey had rushed to the window at the suspicious noise, his revolver poised for instant use.

In spite of all those thoughts, in spite of all reasonable self-argument, the horrible thought swept back with renewed assurance upon Loring: "You are the man!"

And another thought came to him. It was a coldly malignant suspicion, and he shuddered as it entered his mind. But he remorselessly tested it.

He deliberately raised the cup of coffee to his lips and pretended to swallow a mouthful.

"Odd taste to this stuff," he said thoughtfully. "Try a spoonful, will you, Geoffrey, old man?"

"Taste it? No, I've had enough. You make your stuff infernally strong, Loring!"

"But just a spoonful, Geoffrey. I want you to get this odd flavor."

"Curse the flavor," said the other with pronounced aversion. "I couldn't cram any more of your brew into my mouth just now. Later on, old man, when the effect of this wears off, perhaps."

"Well," said Loring softly—and he lowered the cup to his saucer—"I'm not going to drink any more myself."

But so doing, his eyes crossed the glance of Geoffrey, and for one burning instant their glances held, clashed against each other, burned into one another's brain.

And Loring swore to himself: "This is the man! His guilt is in his face."

But it was impossible! Geoffrey Charles? Absurd!

Deliberately, rising from the table, he murmured: "I'm feeling sleepy as the devil. I think I'll walk about a bit."

And so saying, he turned his back on his companion and stretched luxuriously. But in stretching he turned his head just enough to keep Geoffrey, or the shadow of Geoffrey, in the corner of his eye.

And in that corner he saw the face of the younger man change marvelously, harden, set, and his eyes narrowed to slits of light. He leaned forward, his hand stole to the revolver, caught it by the barrel, and suddenly he half rose, clubbing the heavy weapon, and struck at the head of Loring.

Until the very instant that the hand of Charles rose, Loring, paralyzed with the horror of it, continued with his arms stretched above his head. Then, whirling on his heel, he crashed his left fist into the face of his guest.

It caught Geoffrey off balance; the impact split the flesh beneath his right eye and the weight of the blow thrust him staggering back against the wall. As for Loring, the nervous energy of a wildcat had fallen upon him. Madness had turned him into a mass of electric power. Around the table he darted and leaped without a word on Charles.

Instantly he realized the folly of that action. In the grip of the latter, unbroken by the vigil of a week of sleepless nights, he was little more than a child. He found himself crushed in a vast pressure, lifted, and hurled down; but in falling, he twined himself around Geoffrey and the fall hurled them both to the floor.

And there, in deadly silence, they writhed and struggled until Loring found his opening. Geoffrey, struggling back to his feet, left his throat unguarded, and in a flash, Loring, the practiced wrestler, had leaped upon him with a strangle-hold. There was one convulsive struggle; but after the first terrible pressure of his arm against the yielding flesh, Geoffrey's body went limp. His head whipped back, and he gasped with a harsh whisper: "Enough!"

"Listen to me," said Loring through his teeth, relaxing his paralyzing hold a trifle. "Lie flat on your face and lie motionless. If you stir, I blow your brains out."

And he gathered up Geoffrey's revolver as he spoke.

There was a convulsive effort for the last time on the part of Geoffrey. Thrice he struck out blindly, and thrice his heels struck heavily on the floor.

"No more," said Loring. "Noise will bring a crowd—and I want you either alone or dead—I hardly care which!"

"By heavens," gasped Geoffrey, "you *are* mad—just as I guessed when you sent that terrible look at me at the table. The thing has got on your mind until you've gone mad!"

"Perhaps. Now, being a member of the Company, you've heard that I shoot fairly well, and my hands were never steadier than they are at this moment. I'm crossing the room—don't lift your head—the least motion is your last!"

He came again with cords and trussed his captive in them. Hands and feet he tied securely and then lifted the burden with nervous ease and planted his man in the chair.

"So here we are!" smiled Loring.

"Ah," snarled Geoffrey, "you'll sweat for this, you thick-headed fool!"

"Perhaps."

He went hastily through the pockets of Charles. From a vest pocket he extracted two small papers, one empty and one partly filled. He examined the contents—compared them with his strychnine—and then turned to Geoffrey with a spasm of horror.

"What in the name of God influenced you, Geoffrey? What could make you mad enough to try this? Was it Beatrice? Was it the loss of her?"

"Attempt what?"

"Charles, this is strychnine. And the other little paper held the same stuff. You dumped the contents into my cup of coffee at the same time that you asked me why I didn't drink before it became cold, eh?"

"Loring, you *are* mad!"

"Perhaps."

"Hasn't a man a right to carry strychnine without being a murderer? And where is my motive in killing you?"

"The order of the Company."

"What company?"

"The Murder Company."

"A ghastly name. Did you make it up?"

"You're too cool, Geoffrey. Your very coolness damns you. Why? Because it proves that you have the nerve which can face the music, Mr. Murderer Charles."

"I can't answer you. Call the police, then, and we'll have an end to this madness."

"Call your friends? No, no! I'll tell you what proves your guilt and your complicity with the Company. It's the fact that you thought of strychnine. Their devilish information bureau discovered the stimulant I was using. They conveyed that knowledge to you. Then your plan became simple—to bring the dose, foist yourself into my company to-night as a protector, and then poison the coffee I have to drink to keep awake.

"The doctor is called after my death. He pronounces strychnine poisoning. Then the doctor who gave me the prescription is summoned. He admits giving me authorization for getting the poison as a stimulant. The verdict is that I killed myself with an accidental overdose. Is not that simple and perfect? Ah, there's brains in your Company. Zanten was right!"

"Loring, in time you'll shudder at the memory of what you're saying. You could never convince a jury."

"Why, you idiot, you can disprove it yourself by saying that you are willing to taste this cup of mine."

He held it to the lips of Geoffrey and for the first time the latter lost color. But he kept his voice under control.

"And if I refuse to fill my stomach with your abominable coffee, what does that prove?"

"Why, Geoffrey, it proves that there's enough poison in that cup to kill six men. Because there's enough strychnine in the other package to do the same. I am simply going to keep this cup and have it analyzed."

"A remarkable way of proving that I wish to—kill you. Gad, the word sticks in my throat!"

"I tell you again, Geoffrey, you're too cool to be innocent. And your eyes, in spite of yourself, are positively wolfish."

"Excellent stuff to put before a judge!"

"You think it rests on a small thing? Listen to me! I have a doctor's prescription for the drug; I can show the amount I received from the druggist. The total quantity I received from him was not so much as you have put in this cup. Now, Geoffrey, if I could not have put the poison into the cup simply because I did not have it, who did put it there? You, my friend!"

"You go on the insane assumption that the coffee is actually poisoned!"

"Exactly."

"And you expect to have me arrested until it is analyzed?"

"I hope to do so."

"Of course I'm helpless."

The glance of Geoffrey wandered to the clock. It was nearing midnight.

And Loring, stirring a little, saw that the forehead of his captive was bright with perspiration. If there had been a single doubt in his mind it was removed now. The guilty man was before him!

"There is one way for you to escape from the immediate danger," he said. "I told you that I was trapped here and that I was also a trap? It happens that the trap has worked. I have caught a rat. Now, Geoffrey, you go scot-free as far as I am concerned if you write out and sign a full statement concerning the manner of the killing of Joseph Wilbur."

Geoffrey had become, all at once, deadly quiet.

"You bring that home to my door?" he said softly.

"I bring it home to the door of the Company."

"Pure madness. You accuse yourself of insanity by simply mentioning such a grisly organization. Do you really dream that Wilbur was not killed by my poor uncle?"

"I am as certain of it as I am that I stand in this room. Why? Because I have been through the same torture that Wilbur passed. For six days, Geoffrey, I have been a living clew. I have walked in the shoes of the dead man expecting death every moment. The horror has worn me down until I am what you see!

"If I stood here and the ghost of Wilbur as he was on his death day were to appear beside me, a witness would think us blood-brothers! It is the terror of the Company that has wrecked me. It was the fear of the Company that wrecked Wilbur. I had the nerve to fight back; he submitted. That's all there is to it!"

"Don't you think that if ever a man were damned by all evidence, my uncle is he?"

"Listen! Your uncle, strange to say, told the truth. I am perfectly convinced of it. Not the story he told in the courtroom, but the tale he told his lawyer about the door opening slowly and the hand appearing carrying the automatic. Have you heard that story?"

"I understand about it. It's absurd. Who could have wished

to saddle the murder on my uncle? Who could have known in the first place where his automatic was?"

"A man with a nerve of iron and a soul of ice. A man who was an intimate of the household. A man who had made it his business to learn every detail of the life and habits of Peter Charles. A man who had found it necessary to kill Joseph Wilbur, and who was determined to saddle that guilt on Peter Charles."

"An excellent theory. Who could it be?"

"Why, the person whom the death of Peter Charles would most benefit. The heir to his estate, the prospective husband of his daughter, the cold-blooded hound who had been fed out of the hand of Peter Charles since his boyhood—in a word, you are the man!

"It is impossible that it should be anyone else. It is impossible that any other person should have united in one the perfect knowledge of the house that enabled him to get the gun of Peter Charles and the key which opened the study door, and on the other hand, who had a motive to wish the death of Charles, and who, at the same time, was an agent of the Company. And I say again, you are the man!"

Conviction had come to Loring as he talked, and now his voice rang low and clear through the room. And Geoffrey Charles was silent.

"But," went on Loring, "I cannot hang those proofs on you. I can prove that you are here to-night in the rôle of a murderer. That is all."

"And my motive, if you please?" asked the businesslike voice of Geoffrey Charles.

"Your motive was Beatrice."

Geoffrey closed his eyes; when he opened them his face was still wrinkled. The stroke had told.

"I knew you were a dangerous snake the minute I laid eyes on you!" he said softly.

"What I want you to see, Geoffrey, is that I can put you

behind the bars for this attempt. What I offer is this: sit down at that table. I'll liberate your right arm. Then you can write out in full a confession telling how you killed Joseph Wilbur and liberating Peter Charles. With that confession in my keeping, I shall make no attempt to prevent your leaving.

"I will even give you all the time between now and the day set for your uncle's execution. In that time you should be able to put a thousand miles behind you and be on your way to liberty. At least, the chance is good. Stupid fellows have been able to hide successfully. A man of your brains, and with your support, should be able to pass instantly out of view."

The face of Geoffrey was working, and his eyes roved uneasily. He was cornered.

"You expect me to incriminate this mythical Company of which you have been speaking?" he said at length.

"By no means. I am not entirely a fool. And I understand perfectly that even a fellow of your desperate, cool character, Charles, would not dare to betray the Company. I shall go farther. I shall promise you that I myself shall never refer to that Company by word, hint, or deed. What I want is the personal confession which will liberate Peter Charles."

"What witness will you have to the truth of the confession?"

"Your handwriting will be known. For the rest, the document will be too extraordinary to be doubted. The tale will be too damning to be a lie."

"Then"—and here again Charles glanced at the clock—"give me the writing materials and liberate my right arm."

"Very good."

Loring put aside his automatic and the revolver of Geoffrey, and crossing the room, he picked up his fountain pen and a sheaf of large paper. But here a faint sound of a fall made him whirl. The key which he had placed in the lock of the living room door had fallen to the floor!

CHAPTER XLII

# THE TURNING POINT

**THE OLD LORING** of the days before the long duel with
the Murder Company began would have moved like a flash to
secure a weapon. But the Loring who stood with the paper in
one hand and the pen in the other was a different man. Weariness and long waiting had sapped his vitality. Far away, the
midnight hour was being rung by the chimes of a big clock in
the house, or the adjoining house, very faint and small.

And before the dulled nerves of Loring could react, the lock
turned with a click, the door was cast open, and three masked
men crowded into the room with their guns ready. Loring had
whipped toward his own gun, but too late. The sharp, quiet
command of the first man to enter the room stopped him and
he turned and faced them doggedly, a beaten man at last!

He was aware, with annoyance, that his alarm was working,
faintly, imperfectly to be sure, but he was glad when the door
was closed behind the last of the three and the noise of the bell
ceased. The clock, also, had ceased chiming.

"Gentlemen," said Loring calmly, "you have done very well.
I was so expectant of a flank attack that this move in front
disarmed me."

He bowed to them.

"I am done. I only ask you to get your business to a conclusion as quickly as possible!"

But they had no eye for him; their masked faces were turned
to the bound form of Geoffrey.

"Well?" they asked him.

"Not in such a hurry," he smiled. "Untie me first. Cut these cords!"

"The time's up. It was up before we got to the door."

"No one will question us about seconds. Beside, this is my order. Untie me first."

A few touches of a knife did the work.

One of the men gathered up the fragments of the cords and made a suggestive gesture toward Samuel Loring.

"No," said Geoffrey, rising and shaking himself to restore the circulation of his blood. "He doesn't need tying. A beaten dog doesn't fight back. He's done. Spirit broken, my friends."

He turned with a smile to Loring, and the latter saw a face white with controlled rage and shame. He understood. The shame was that of the leader who had been exposed to his subordinates in the rôle of a conquered and helpless man.

"The time, I tell you, is up," insisted one of the masks.

Geoffrey silenced him with a glance of rage. He advanced upon Loring.

"Before you die, my friend," he said, "I want to give you the satisfaction of knowing that from the first you were right. What devil worked inside of your head I don't know, but every deduction you have made is completely correct. I killed Joseph Wilbur; I threw the automatic into the room; I came here to-night to put a quiet period to your life because you, like an idiot, had made Beatrice promise to marry me if you failed to return.

"And now, Loring, I want you to review your work. I want you to remember all the agony you have passed through in the last six days. And remember that it was all for nothing. Peter Charles hangs. Beatrice is thrown irrevocably into my arms by the wishes both of you and her father. Think of it! The deathbed wishes of both of my victims are for my prolonged happiness through life. And the world at large shall see in me the honest young man who quietly lives down the shadow which had fallen over the family fortunes!"

He broke off and laughed softly.

"But having seen so much, Loring, it would be unfair if you had not foreseen your own death and the manner of it. Let us go back. The coffee is now cold. But I believe you said that hot or cold, the effect of it would be the same. Let us see. The coffee is now—yes—quite chilly. But drink, my dear fellow, and let us see if the effect is not quite sudden and painless."

Without a quiver of his nerves, Loring stepped to the table and raised the cup.

"Gentlemen," he said calmly, "to our future meeting in hell!"

"No speeches, curse you," whispered Geoffrey.

And there, like the stroke of doom, came a knock at the door.

"You!" snapped Geoffrey swiftly, catching up his revolver. "Take the door. Now, Loring, drink!"

Two of the masks had jumped quickly to the door, but one of them turned and raised his hand.

"Listen!" he whispered.

The knock was repeated. It fell in a broken rhythm—a tap, a pause—two taps, a pause—three light taps, and then silence.

"The signal," nodded the man, who had raised his hand.

"This first!" said Geoffrey through his teeth, turning on Loring.

"Nothing first, Mr. Charles, on your life!" cried another of the masks sternly and softly. "I am about to open the door."

He did as he had said, and into the room in a black overcoat and glimmering top hat, very pale in contrast with his black mustache and the black silk neck cloth, stepped the man with the opal, Nicholas Zanten.

He stood for a moment looking calmly from face to face. In the meantime he removed his scarf, slipped out of hat and coat, and having laid these on a chair, he stood removing his gloves.

"Mr. Charles," he said, "it is a pleasure to see you again. Loring, I seem to find you embarrassed. Gentlemen, your names are known to me, but apparently you do not wish them re-peated."

He had finished removing the gloves and was rubbing warmth into his long, pale fingers.

"Zanten," said Geoffrey, "what your arrival means I don't know. I present my respects and must request you to leave the room again. We have business—short business. I'll rejoin you outside in a moment."

"So curt?" smiled Zanten. "So very curt? Tush, Mr. Charles, won't you be frank enough to tell me your business? Have I proved such a chattering confidant?"

"Our business?" said Geoffrey, and he turned with an ugly sneer on Loring. "It is this!"

"You indicate Mr. Loring? I am sorry to appear ignorant—but what earthly business can you and these associates of yours have with Mr. Loring?"

It took Geoffrey Charles aback. He looked at Zanten with wonder first and then with a scowl.

"Are you interfering?" he asked gruffly.

"Interfering?" smiled Zanten. He waved his hand apologetically and the opal flashed on the white fingers. "How little you know me, my dear young chap, to think that I could ever interfere—where it is not my own business that is concerned."

"Then be satisfied. We have nothing to do with your business."

"To be sure, then. Very good. Go ahead with whatever you have on hand."

"Excellent. In that case—I was in doubt of you for a moment—but in that case, kindly turn your head and the business will be done instantly."

"Turn my head? And why?"

"While I turn this ass into a carcass," said Geoffrey, his teeth glinting under his lifted lip.

An expression of pain crossed the clearly chiseled features of Nicholas Zanten.

"My dear fellow," he murmured, "my *dear* fellow, your vocabulary really needs attention. It needs pruning and regrowing. There are always pleasant words for *the* most unpleasant things."

"Say it for yourself, then. I've neither the time nor the will to hunt for fine phrases. But this work has to be done."

"I begin to gather that your work is with Loring?"

"Of course. You know that."

"But, my dear Charles, anything that concerns Loring now concerns me."

"Since when, pray?"

"Since midnight, to be exact."

"Zanten, this is a commission from you. Do you mean that you are interfering?"

"Interfering? I object to the word. Let us go back to that commission. Six days and a little more have passed since I placed in the hands of a gentleman of our acquaintance a commission of some importance. It was a commission concerning a friend of mine."

He paused and bowed to Loring with a smile. And for the first time, not really understanding the drift of this strange talk, hope sprang up in the breast of Loring. He bent a feverish eye upon Zanten.

"At that time," resumed the smooth-tongued man with the opal, "I particularly impressed on my mutual friend that I was sharply interested in the outcome of the affair. I begged him to see that the greatest efforts should be made to deliver the required results *inside* the specified time. At the moment I had reason to become excited. I even declared that if the work were not done as required I should myself undertake the work.

"Since that time I have had reason to change my mind. I have had occasion to perceive that I was wrong in my first conception, so that, so far from attempting to complete the work with my own hand, I have determined to see that nothing is attempted after the designated period came to an end."

His voice changed a little.

"Mr. Charles, the period ended before these men entered the room. Kane, am I right?"

"You are, sir," nodded one of the masks.

Zanten sighed with relief.

"I was not sure. Now I see that I am right. What did you find when you entered? These two amiably chatting, I suppose?"

"I should say not! Charles was tied hand and foot!"

"Ah," murmured Zanten, and his glance sought out Loring and rested with a gleam of fire upon him. "Is it possible?"

"Mr. Zanten," cried Geoffrey, "I know you and respect and esteem you. But I wish to know what your intentions are."

"Can you ask? Can you really ask?"

"You've heard me!"

But Zanten still rubbed his hands together, still smiled on Geoffrey.

"Of course, I intend to see that the situation is restored as it existed at midnight sharp."

"My God!" breathed Geoffrey. "Do you think I will submit?"

And Loring saw him gather the revolver more closely in his hand.

"You will submit."

"Take him!" cried Geoffrey suddenly, pointing to Zanten. "Take him and hold him while I attend to—this!"

There was a stir among the three as they closed like so many hounds around Zanten; but Loring noted that their movements were excessively slow.

As for Zanten, a remarkable change swept over him. He seemed to grow, on the instant, whole inches taller, and to expand in size. His head was tossed back with a singular, leonine gesture that Loring was never to forget. One of the lean, pale hands slipped into a coat pocket and appeared to be balled there like a fist, or grasping something. Color burned into the white face of the gambler, and there was a flash in his eyes.

"Is it possible that I am Nicholas Zanten?" he said through his teeth. "Is it possible that you dare to show your teeth to me? You bloody dogs! Keep back! Charles!"

Geoffrey Charles, whirling away from Loring, put his back to the wall and glared at Zanten with a desperate menace. As for the three, they shrank as if from a fire.

"Lower your gun," commanded Zanten. "Lower your gun, Charles, or by everything that's sacred I'll kill you where you stand!"

"Gentlemen—friends—" groaned Geoffrey, flashing a glance of appeal at the three masks, "are you with me?"

"By the Lord," said Zanten, growing more terrible. "Are you staying to talk after I've ordered you to move? Over to that table, you cur, and put your gun on it!"

He jerked his head toward the three without moving his eyes from Geoffrey.

"And you—put up your weapons!"

To the astonishment of Loring, the three masks obeyed, slowly, but as men in fear. Not even a glance had been needed to quell them. As for Geoffrey, he still hung in his tracks, fighting the eye of Zanten. Then, with dragging steps, he crossed the room to the table and slowly laid his weapon upon it.

"There'll be a reckoning for this!" he said savagely to the man with the opal.

"You're right. There'll be a reckoning. You three, get out from this house. Go back to your directors. Tell them that Nicholas Zanten wishes to know how they have dared to cross him? How they have dared to deal lightly with him? How they have had the consummate impudence to go behind his back?"

"The time was up at midnight. They had failed in the commission I gave them. They dared to overstep that commission. Or—was it possible that the fault was not theirs, but the willful crime of this dog-eyed scoundrel, Geoffrey Charles? In that case I forgive them. But let them establish the truth. Has Charles dared to take their business into his own hands to execute in the time and manner he himself chooses? No, go and tell them what I have said."

There was a faint cry from Geoffrey and he was starting forward when a glance from Zanten checked him like a blow in the face.

"Sit down!" said the man with the opal, and Charles obeyed. He slumped into a chair as one from whose body the will to live has passed.

One of the masks approached.

"I, personally," he said to Zanten, "reminded Mr. Charles that the time was up!"

"I believe it, Kane," said Zanten, relenting a little, "and if any mischief springs out of this matter I'll see that no harm comes to you. That goes for your two companions as well if you answer for them."

"I do, sir. We acted only on the express orders of our superior, Mr. Charles."

"Then you are exonerated. You may go!"

And like animals escaping from a trap, they flocked through the door and were gone. Zanten turned to Geoffrey Charles with a smile of implacable cruelty that curdled the blood in the veins of Loring.

"Now, Geoffrey Charles," he said, "your hour strikes! The situation comes to an end; say your prayers, for I'm about to leave you, bound, in the hands of Loring!"

Geoffrey caught his breath like a man drinking. Then, unable to meet the terrible glance of Zanten, he dropped his head into the palm of one of his big hands.

"Mr. Zanten, do you leave me?" asked Loring anxiously.

A change slipped over the face of Nicholas Zanten. He stepped to the side of Loring and laid his hand on the massive shoulder of the younger man; yet at that moment Loring

seemed, with the six days of agony upon his face, ten years the
senior of the two.

"Leave you, Loring? Let God be my witness that I shall
never leave you so long as there is breath in my body and
strength in my mind. Someday I shall ask you to forgive me
for allowing you to pass through this horrible trial. Do you
know why I allowed it to run out its limit and come to a natural
end without my interposition? Because I wished to test you—
in the fire!

"And now I have something to say which you can take up
or let pass like wind. I have lived in myself—cruelly and self-
ishly. I have never loved a woman; I have never given to a man
the hand of friendship. I have never admitted a partner and a
companion. But to you, Loring, kind heart, staunch hand, I let
down the bars. I have played the part of devil to you so far.
Forgive me for it, and you can use me henceforth like a brother
or a father or a son.

"Weigh it in your mind. Think it over coldly. Then—either
take this hand of mine as a pledge or shake your head. If you
do the one we are bound together forever. If you do the other
I give you my word that I shall have forgotten you by morning—
and bear you no malice!"

For a moment Loring hesitated, knowing that much of his
destiny would be foreshadowed by his action in the next instant.

"Zanten," he said gravely at length, "I began by fearing you.
I went on to respect you. To-night you have saved my life. But
it is something more than that that makes me take your hand."

Quietly they shook hands with their eyes studying one
another solemnly. Then Zanten turned.

"And this?" he said.

"His death means nothing to me," said Loring calmly. "What
I want is the freedom of Peter Charles. I have never left the
trail that I started at Buttrick's, you know? When I left on the
heels of Joseph Wilbur? That trail brings me here. I've paid for
the truth and I'm about to get it.

"If Charles will write his confession of the manner in which he shot and killed Wilbur, I let him go as free as the wind. If he refuses, I hold him for attempted murder! Speak up, Geoffrey, which shall it be!"

Unquestionably Geoffrey had been thinking many things. When he raised his head from his hand he fixed his malignant eyes on Loring.

"I have a reason for desiring freedom," he said. "Give me the paper and I'll write the truth."

"The full truth," said Zanten, "for I shall read it and witness it."

For a moment Geoffrey glared at him, his mouth twitching. Then he bowed his head, finally beaten.

"Very well," he muttered, and sat down again, facing the table.

Before him Loring placed the writing materials. For a moment he chewed the head of the pen, thoughtful. Then he began to write. And as he wrote he seemed to lose consciousness of the presence of the others. Occasionally he tilted back in his chair with his huge hands locked behind his head. And on those occasions he often hummed softly to himself. And again, he would strike his hand lightly against his forehead and cry out softly.

"The joy of composition," murmured Zanten, smiling to his friend.

One by one they took the pages from the hand of Charles and with their heads close together read the confession.

CHAPTER XLIII

# THE NARRATIVE OF
# GEOFFREY CHARLES

"**TO BEGIN WITH,** let it not be thought that *brains* have beaten me. Luck and a truly feminine power of intuition with which I could not credit the man put me in the power of Loring. Even then I tricked him and had him in my power when the irresistible Zanten showed his hand. It is not shameful to admit the superiority of Zanten any more than it is for the pupil to bow to the skill of the master. Luck and Zanten, then, have beaten me.

"This will be published as my 'confession.' I detest the term. The initiated, however, who are not afflicted with panic nerves and soft heads, will understand that it is a character portrait. Words become colors; my hand puts them on; I draw myself for the eye of the wise men who may blunder upon this statement. And even the prejudiced and stupid, when they understand my aims, will be aware of some ability, perhaps, and ends which justify the means.

"Since this is a character sketch, let me go back to a beginning.

"I was born poor; I was raised poor. But circumstances which would have stunted the mental growth of most men were a fertile soil for me. While I was still too young to express myself properly, I determined to be stronger than circumstance. There was only one way to accomplish this: that was to appear other than I was at heart."

"It was not difficult for even my child's eye to discover that all people are upon a stage and act to the world behind foot-lights. The beautiful girl sets off her beauty by an ample careless-ness, as if she is not aware that her smiles have a point and a sting that disturb men; her cue from the days of Cleopatra has been artless simplicity—which is the highest art. The rich man masks his wealth with an assumption of bonhomie; his great care is always to talk of something other than money; he sur-rounds himself with furnishings of art and chatters small talk.

"The artist, on the other hand, that most patient and painful of laborers, wears his hair long, gives himself a rapt expression, and wishes to convince the world that his works are the result of inspiration; dashed off briefly, without labor—after conver-sation with God. To continue, the old man wishes to appear young; the young man to seem old and bored. The good man hugs a few vices to his breast and loves to be called 'dangerous.' The consummate villain poses as a saint.

"In short, I saw these things clearly while I was hardly more than an infant and resolved to apply my lesson. What was I to do? Money was the thing which above all else I craved. Ac-cordingly I determined to act as if money was nothing. I de-liberately hunted out a family yet poorer than mine and made them a present of the little silver that was in my pocket. I wished my generosity to be much talked about, and therefore I took care to offer my gift in the greatest secrecy.

"The result, of course, was that my offer was refused and instantly published abroad by those who had refused it. I es-tablished at a stroke a reputation for generosity; people who passed me threadbare on the street turned to look after me. I was instantly considered the most worthy boy in the village where I lived.

"My mother was already dead; and when my father died a short time later I was instantly taken into his family by a man of good standing in the community. He had two sons. One of them was well on the way toward becoming a drunkard before he was twenty; the other was a hard-working lout on the farm.

"I instantly took a halfway position. I refused to touch even the beer which the family drank and which was offered to me, although I was only a child; and I constantly lived with the books which I was studying, or pretending to study. The farmer saw in me a happy exception to the faults of both his children and at once buckled me to his heart.

"But another great step was opened before me. To the house of the farmer one evening came a great man—great in wealth— his name was Peter Charles. I had heard my father speak of him, his money, and the distant relationship. I was in bed when Peter Charles arrived that night; I made it a point to slip out of the bed, and stealing downstairs, I listened and heard him relate a number of anecdotes concerning his life and his experiences. I immediately put him down as a fool for talking so much about his own cleverness, and since that time I have never had occasion to change my mind concerning his folly.

"The next day I saw Peter Charles. From the first I had known that I must be the occasion of his visit. And a great hope had inspired me to the guess that he might have come to take me into his family, for I had learned the night before that he had no son.

"I framed my conversation accordingly. Having heard him often refer with pride, during the overheard conversation, to the length of his family tree, when he spoke to me the next day with sympathy about my lonely position in the world, I assumed an attitude of pride. I said that I felt that I had a great opportunity before me, and that I started into the world with a valuable heritage. He asked me what I meant. I told him that I meant the good old name of Charles.

"He was instantly delighted. He attempted to mask his emotion, but I saw it beaming at me from his eyes, and from that moment I knew that I had acquired a great power over him.

"He talked with me a long time. He had apparently formed a good opinion of me from his talk with the farmer and the farmer's wife the night before. I took care to enlarge his good opinion of me by saying never a word about my exploits in the past and telling him only what I expected to do in the future. To begin in a small way to save money, I told him, and patiently accumulate until I had a good-sized sum.

"In a word, Peter Charles was delighted to hear from my childish lips the very wisdom which he had foolishly scattered before the farmer's swinish family the night before and which he was certain I could not have heard. I was wise enough to give him back the sense of what he had said without attempting to imitate the phraseology, and the poor man never suspected the deception.

"He sent me about my business after some time and went into the village. There I afterwards learned that he made extensive inquiries. What he learned enchanted him. He was referred to the poor family to which I had offered the money some time before. They spoke of me and described my virtues with tears in their eyes. And when Peter Charles came back to me his face was lighted. The moment I saw him I knew that I had Peter Charles and his wealth at my command.

"Accordingly, when he told me he wished to take me home with him, I offered many objections. The farmer had been gratuitously kind to me. I wished to repay him, I said, for his kindness. Also, there was a charm in starting with nothing and building myself into an important man, whereas if I went to him all the credit would be his.

"He heard me out with attention and then began an argument to which I gradually submitted. In short, before the afternoon we were on our way to the train together.

"My new life was all that I could have dreamed. The plan of Peter Charles to marry me to his infant daughter when we arrived at the proper age was quickly apparent to me, and I began a steady course of action from which I never deviated. Of Peter Charles I was reasonably sure. Of the girl I could never be sure. Accordingly I patterned my actions after hers. I made myself her inseparable playmate.

"She loved the outdoors and its sports. I learned to read the points of a horse as others read books; to skate, to box, to run, to wrestle, to shoot. I studied the woods with the devotion of a hermit. I crammed myself with field lore of herbs and flowers and continually brought bits of information to the girl. When she walked or rode I was always with her, because I made the hills and meadows and hedges and woods into books whose pages I turned and gave her delightful glimpses here and there.

"Also, these attainments of mine delighted Peter Charles. The simple man, feeling that he had made money enough, now wished to devote the rest of his life to establishing the family on a firm footing among the gentry of the country. And these studies of mine he felt to be the proper sphere of the country gentleman. I readily took the cue. From that time I apparently lost all interest in the making of money, and the more careless of finances I showed myself the more pleased was Uncle Peter.

"So my life study continued to be Beatrice. Perhaps it was nearness that did it; at any rate, as I grew up I found myself in love with her. Why? She was neither lovely nor very wise. The truth is that I could never understand her. At the very moment when I felt that I had the clew to her character, she thrust me away and baffled me.

"As a matter of fact, the nearer a man is to a woman the less he understands her. A woman is too bright a light to be looked at closely. That is, a good woman. Without morals they step to a different plane and become like men. They are then only silly and weak. But a pure woman is as impalpable, as removed from understanding, as an angel.

"Beatrice, in short, was an angel to me. I loved her. I adored even her moody times. I delighted in wooing her out of a cloud into brightness. I slaved for her. And the result was that when she reached a marriageable age Beatrice, who in reality did not understand me at all, felt as familiar toward me as if I had been the house dog. That was my great mistake. I had planned a campaign as faultless as Napoleon's Marengo; but on the battlefield, like Napoleon on that great day, I executed my maneuvers clumsily and invited ruin. In short, I failed to preserve that native strangeness which must fall around a man if a woman is to be taught to love him. It is impossible for a woman to be both a friend and a lover. Beatrice was my friend and companion. For that very reason she could not love me.

"It was about this time that I, through a freak of circumstance, became involved with a great power which cannot be referred to more than vaguely from this point on in my narrative, though it must be frequently mentioned.

"But let me now advance directly to the heart of my narrative—that portion in which Mr. Loring, particularly, is interested."

CHAPTER XLIV

# THE NARRATIVE OF GEOFFREY CHARLES (CONTINUED)

"**IT WAS ON** the occasion of a dance. The night began as the happiest in my life, for on that night I had talked seriously with Beatrice and she had confessed that she looked upon our eventful marriage as a certainty. She confessed it as a friend; she also told me that she did not love me.

"Now, in the middle of the festivities, one of the servants who was, like me, a member of the society of which I have spoken, came to bring word that Joseph Wilbur had entered the house, had insisted upon seeing Peter Charles, and was at that moment closeted with my 'uncle.' But that was only part of his message. The remainder was to the effect that the death of Joseph Wilbur had been decreed and that I was the agent selected for the task.

"It was a bolt from the blue that stunned me. For some moments I was unable to rally from the shock. Then I prepared my mind and submitted to my fate. In fact, after a little examination of the case, I arrived at the conclusion that the affair might be beneficial to me.

"When I first became a member of the society I knew that at any time I might be called upon to strike some member of the household. I had therefore long ago made myself familiar with everything in the physical composition of the house and its people. Among other things, searching through the room of Peter Charles, I had discovered his automatic pistol in the silly hiding place which he used for it.

"The memory of this pistol now rushed back upon my mind. I saw in it a means not only of killing Wilbur, but also of advancing my own interests in the highest degree by destroying Peter Charles with the same blow, and with his death marrying by his will Beatrice and becoming the sole heir to his property.

"At this point the foolishly scrupulous reader will perhaps shudder, but the initiated—I mean those who have felt the touch of the spur of ambition—will understand how it was that when the great idea came upon me I became drunk with it. I sank into a chair, and resting my head on my hand, I saw the future as a rosy cloud. The world was mine!

"So thinking, I at once left the ballroom, hastened up to the room of Peter Charles, and removed the automatic. I came downstairs again and once more mingled with the dancers. I was never gayer. My heart leaped and I felt my happiness shining in my eyes.

"And truly it was a small thing to do for such great results. To kill Joseph Wilbur was to kill a dog. To kill Peter Charles was to remove from the world a clever sneak, a petty, trifling fellow, a cold-blooded schemer without bigness of mind even for a crime. He was even less than Wilbur.

"I was about to go to the study and execute my mission when word was brought by the servant who was my comrade in the society that a man was at the door asking to see Peter Charles in the most solemn terms. I asked for a brief description. A bold-faced, active, big man was described to me—an adequate man of action.

"For a moment I thought that it might be some high agent of the society. I determined to see him without being seen, and leaving the ballroom again, I entered a wall passage—built in as a freak of fancy by the architect who wished to imitate in everything his Tudor model for the house—and I came to a little panel door opening into the hall.

"Opening this carefully, I looked out upon a strong-faced man of about thirty, or perhaps more. If I could have guessed it, in the very moment of my triumph I was now looking upon my Nemesis!

"But I could not guess. I only knew that I had not recognized him as an agent of the society, and coming around into the main hall, I talked to him. He told me at once that he had followed a man who seemed in terror of his life—and that man was Joseph Wilbur. He had traced him to this house and he was determined to see that the man was given due protection.

"I put him off with some coldness and some mockery.

"Fool that I was! When I came up behind him in the hall I had seen him sounding the panel which I opened. I should have known that I had a rare man on my hands. Instead, I merely took him for an adventurous fool. That was the great mistake. Had I known him then as I have come to know him since, I should have seen that he had his interview with my 'uncle,' and bided my time to effect my scheme later on with this dangerous antagonist out of the house.

"But I continued to mock him until Beatrice came into the hall. I left him to talk to her and went on my way. Again I might have read my fate. I had of my own free will abandoned the woman I loved to the society of the man who was to usurp my place in her affections—and more than my place!

"I went back into the ballroom. I danced one dance. Then I came out and went to the door of the study. Peter Charles had just entered. I heard him talking to Wilbur; I made out that they were both in a highly emotional state—and that both were unarmed.

"Then I decided. Should I kill both Peter Charles and Wilbur, throw the weapon into the room, lock the door, and leave it to be understood that one of them had killed the other and then committed suicide? I determined on the negative.

"Let no one think that I was influenced by a foolish tenderness for Peter Charles. Neither was I moved by a recollection of his so-called generosity, which I well knew to have been merely a form of sublime selfishness. But I was possessed with an eager curiosity to see Peter Charles in the toils of the law, just as a chemist wishes to see the germ under the microscope wriggle at the touch of the acid. It was, if you wish, a scientific interest in the reactions of this common-minded fellow under the acid test of fear, fighting for his life.

"So I opened the door, advanced the automatic through, and shot Joseph Wilbur through the heart. I was rejoiced to find that my hand was as steady as steel. A singular pleasure such as I have never known before came over me as I felt that I had, in the slightest beck of my forefinger, the power to summon the soul of one or both of these men out of its body.

"And, carelessly, I decided to summon forth only one soul. I shot Joseph Wilbur through the heart, closed the door, and locked it with the master key which I carried, having first tossed the automatic on the floor of the room.

"Then I hurried around into the hall and ran for the door of the study. I found the interloper, Samuel Loring, blocking the doorway, and before him, on her knees beside the dead man, was Beatrice. And the automatic was not on the floor!

"I wished to stay and make private examination of the room and perhaps be told by Peter Charles what he had done with the weapon. But again Loring interfered. Ever he was the stumbling block. He made me stop the rush of guests which I had hoped would pour into the study, and send them back.

"Then, that done, I returned to the study and heard the story of my 'uncle.' It was, I knew, true, except that he left out the throwing of the revolver into the room. With this exception he was letter-perfect. But the omission of the automatic would destroy him if I could only see that the weapon fell into the hands of the police. His name was inscribed upon it!

"But who had the gun? I decided that my uncle did not. He could not, for the police came to take him and up to that time I had watched every move he made. Then there was the possibility of Loring, but he had arrived at the door of the study only a fraction of a second before me—and already the gun had disappeared.

"It must be Beatrice.

"That night I dogged her out to the terrace and was about to trail her closely when I saw another figure, shadowy and silent as a black panther, slipping over the lawn behind her.

"It was Loring? For the first time I began to see that the fellow was inextricably entangling himself with the mystery. From a distance I saw him catch the hand of Beatrice and take from her a shining object which she was about to throw into the lake. I knew, of course, that it was the automatic. Loring now had it.

"He remained for some time in talk with Beatrice. Would he play the part of are honest man and turn over the weapon to the police and thereby send Peter Charles to the chair? I could not be sure. It was an unromantic and vengeful thing to do and Loring was, if nothing else, romantic.

"He came in shortly after Beatrice, and the fear grew upon me that he intended to keep the automatic until it suited his pleasure to give it up. My own mind was instantly determined. I would get him drugged with liquor, and while he slept heavily I would enter his room and take the weapon.

"But the man had the eye of a fox. He saw me stinting my own measure of the whisky, grew suspicious, and refused to taste another drop. He went to bed. But he had enough under his belt to make me sure that he would soon be asleep, inasmuch as he had just completed a strenuous evening by his own account of it.

"But again I mistook my man. I allowed enough time for him to fall asleep if he were an ordinary fellow; but Loring was not ordinary. I learned that to my cost. In the meantime, having got out of my clothes and into pyjamas, I slipped to his room, found that he had locked his door, opened it with a master key, and approached his bed. Had he stirred I was determined to brain him and take the key. Would to God I had done so!

"My object, having stolen the pistol, was to have myself searched by the police the next, confess that it was my uncle's weapon, and thus be the 'unwilling' means of delivering up the damning testimony. For without the weapon I foresaw that the case against him might break down.

"But Loring, as I leaned over him, did not stir in his sleep. He was too cunning for that. He waited until I had made sure by his deep breathing that he was sound asleep. Then, as I went through his clothes, he leaped at me. I turned in the nick of time and gave him all my weight in a straight right that rang on the button. I wish it had snapped his neck!

"I jumped through the door, then, locked it again from the outside, and was in my room. Then I composed my face and when he stumbled out into the hall I rushed out to lead the hunt for the fugitive, who was myself!

"But Loring had beaten me again!

"The next day, as I left for town, I had the servant who was my comrade in the society ring up the police and advise them to search Loring for the weapon with which the shooting had been done. Accordingly, our machine was stopped, Loring was taken to headquarters and searched. But the automatic was not found. How he managed to secret it is, to this day, a mystery.

"That event convinced me that I had to deal with a man of parts.

"In the meantime the trial approached. I had had the prosecuting attorney carefully advised as to the part which Loring played, and I had been able to advise him through a second party to center his case on the testimony which he could extract from the adventurer. What Loring would do in the witness stand, however, I could not tell.

"He was a strange fellow. I had already gone to his room and attempted to bribe him for the weapon. He took it as an insult, though I offered a huge sum. Had he given me the weapon it would have been in the hands of the police within one minute, for I had arranged to have myself arrested and searched as soon as I left him.

"That conception of bribing Loring for the gun was one of the high points of cleverness in my schemes. For the spending of the money would have been accepted by Peter Charles and Beatrice as a proof of my boundless devotion, and the unfortunate outcome of the affair would not have been attributed to any fault of mine.

"However, once again I had failed, and once again Loring had been the cause of the failure."

CHAPTER XLV

# THE NARRATIVE OF GEOFFREY CHARLES (CONCLUDED)

"**THE DAY OF** the trial came. All hung, for the prosecution, on the testimony it could extract from Loring. The world knows what that testimony was. He lied, in short, with the finesse and adroitness of the most accomplished villain. Never have I admired a man as I admired the honest, simple face which Loring assumed while he told that astonishing tangle of falsehoods! I could have clasped his hand and hailed him as a brother had I not begun to hate him with all my heart.

"Our case was ruined. Peter Charles seemed saved. And then, at the recess, he extracted from Beatrice the promise to marry me if he were convicted. It then became absolutely necessary for me to secure that conviction.

"I had already had a vague idea and secured an automatic pistol exactly like that of my uncle to be used as a bluff in case of need. I now wrote a note to the prosecuting attorney, enclosed the automatic, suggested how it be used, and the world also knows how the ruse succeeded.

"At sight of the gun Peter Charles, as I had hoped from his shattered nerves, thought that all was lost and collapsed. He condemned himself by that instant of weakness. It was a great triumph for me. With the battle lost, I had stepped into the breach and wrested victory from crushing defeat. The fortune of Peter Charles was mine, and the hand of Beatrice was mine!

"But in the very time of triumph the first blow fell, the prelude of disaster—when I reached Beatrice shortly afterward in her apartment I found her changed. I had met Loring going out as I entered. And in the interview that followed she told me frankly that though she intended to execute the will of her father and marry me before his death, she really loved Samuel Loring.

"Why? The question bewildered me. I can only guess that it was the dash of romance with which that remarkable character was seasoned, that very element of headstrong carelessness which is conspicuously absent from my make-up. But that day, while I was assuring Beatrice that I wished her to make her own conclusions, I determined that sooner or later Samuel Loring must die.

"Shortly afterward he was thrown into my power. He invited upon his head the danger of the society to which I have already so often referred. The society, knowing that I had already clashed with him, put the case into my hands.

"After that I devised everything. On the first night of the six I corrupted my first agent, a woman, to attempt his life by turning on the gas.

"The attempt failed!

"The next day Loring saw Beatrice. His changed appearance excited her. She begged me to have him watched. The opportunity was a golden one. I sent the second agent on his trail. But the cunning devil hunted the hunter, struck him down, and made him take him, Loring, to the home of the man who had hired him.

"They entered together. Wholly unexpectedly I found my near-victim facing me gun in hand. Luckily my lie was ready. The man was in reality an agent of a detective bureau. I told Loring that at Beatrice's request I had had him followed. He was convinced and left.

"But once more I had failed.

"I went to incredible exertions. In the restaurant where he usually ate I arranged to have his food poisoned. But he changed his habits and never entered the place. He seemed to penetrate my plans with a power akin to second sight.

"My next formal plan was to place near the house a man who was to cut down a scaffolding if Loring should ever pass that way. Eventually he did, the platform descended, and only incredible speed of eye and strength of limb enabled Loring to escape a horrible death.

"He not only escaped; he followed and located his would-be assassin. That fellow, from the house where he changed his clothes, had telephoned to me that everything was accomplished. He was going to his home in a different state. I passed the word everywhere through the society that the fact was accomplished. It was a happy moment for me, but I had foresight enough to have two men follow my agent to his home.

"They arrived in the nick of time, truly. Loring had followed, trailed his man to his home in the country, and was about to force a confession from him that would have ruined me and everyone when my second pair arrived. They cut that confession short with a bullet through the man's head and then swung a gun on Loring—and missed! His return fire wounded one of them.

"They retired to watch the door, but Loring jumped out the very window through which the shots had been fired, and took them by sufficient surprise for him to escape before they could drop him.

"Once more I had failed to stop Loring!

"Another danger came at me on this night. One of my agents, the woman, having heard of Loring's death, had gone in to look over his effects, but got no farther than his whisky. And while she was testing it Loring arrived, instantly guessed at her character, and stepped into a clever rôle. By the merest luck the danger was called to my attention, and the whistle of alarm which called the foolish woman out of the room came to her ear as she was on the verge of uncovering all names and places connected with the affair.

"This time Loring had come within an ace of bringing ruin on me!

"I now decided to let everything go until the last moment of the time allotted me. The interim I filled with slight annoyances aimed at breaking down Loring's nerve. And then, rising to the greatest moment of my life, I, the destroyer, stepped into the room of Samuel Loring as his protector, a rôle which I played, as Loring will testify, with no little skill. The strychnine which he was using as a bulwark for his broken nerves during the hideous waiting of the six days was my cue. I came with enough of it to kill a brigade and poisoned his coffee while we sat chatting together over the table.

"And then—how it was I shall never know unless there is such an actuality as telepathy—I found his eyes blazing at me across the table while he lowered the cup untasted from his lips.

"I knew I was discovered in the rôle of destroyer!

"What could I do? I could not risk a shot which would alarm the whole house. My plans were rent to pieces. Luckily Loring pretended not to have understood my plans. He rose and pretended to yawn, and while his back was turned I clubbed the revolver to strike him down where he stood.

"But the fox was watching me from the corner of his eye. He whirled as I rose—the rest is common history, and here sit I, Geoffrey Charles, facing the consciousness that I have failed in the first great episode of my life.

"I have failed. But not miserably. Uncommon forces operated against me, and the interposition of the great Zanten was a thing against which no man could have armed himself.

"I have failed. I lose the great fortune which would have been a terrific weapon in my hands. I lose the woman I love.

"But is there no recompense?

"By all means! Out of failure I learn the great lesson which only defeat can teach. Hereafter I shall be invincible. And by the very confession at which the vulgar will shudder I gain the means of freedom out of which shall grow a new strength. The future shall know me!"

**THE LAST** page was completed. With a sigh Geoffrey laid down his pen and passed his hand across his eyes. Then he arose and shook himself. Going to the window, he cast open the shutters and breathed deep of the cool air of dawn.

"I have underrated myself in one respect," he said, turning gayly to Nicholas Zanten, "I have overlooked my merits as a writer."

"Of fiction?" said Nicholas Zanten calmly.

Geoffrey started violently.

"What do you mean by that?"

"Ah, that's the question! What do you think I mean?"

"You infer that I have not written the truth?"

"You have written enough of it to serve the purpose of my friend Loring."

"Your friend Loring has turned into a staggering tottering wreck," grinned Geoffrey without mirth.

And indeed, Loring lay back in his chair with closed eyes, breathing heavily. He was in the last stages of mental and physical exhaustion.

"Ah, for one moment alone with him, eh?" smiled Zanten. "And now, Mr. Charles, good-by!"

"Good-by, sir. No malice?"

He held out his hand, but Zanten drew himself to his full height.

"Sir!" he said coldly.

"Tush! Play-acting without an audience, Zanten? Well, be it so. Farewell!"

He waved his hand gayly from the door and was gone.

# EPILOGUE

**ON A CERTAIN** morning Nicholas Zanten—for the game had lasted all night—laid down his cards, went to the window, and drawing the heavy curtains let in the slant, rich sunlight.

"My friends," he said, "the game is over for me. I warned you last night that I'm busy to-day. But if you wish revenge, I shall welcome the resumption of the game to-morrow with the same stakes."

"You're breaking in on your own game, Mr. Zanten."

"My dear sir, my engagement is most important. This morning I am to be godfather at a christening!"

He bowed, murmured his farewells, and left.

"There seems an excellent chance of Christ and the Devil shaking hands, then," said one.

# ABOUT THE AUTHOR

**MAX BRAND IS** a Californian who saw the West first in the central valley of the State, where the Coast Range ran low on one side and the Sierra Nevadas on clear days were green and brown over the foothills, and blue or glass-white above. He learned something of cattle and cattlemen among the great grasslands of the foothills, but he never was so deep in that Old West which is a golden legend to-day, as when he spent a few weeks with two old trappers near the Diablo Mountains, close to El Paso, in Texas.

Nick and Alec had fought Indians, ridden range, prospected for gold, made fortunes for others, and had never been able to spend all the wealth that had poured in upon their minds. Some of the glory of mountains and desert remained with them as a perpetual heritage. Nick, at seventy-eight, had a body bent and twisted by age; Alec at eighty was straight as a stick, with no visible sign of the passage of time about him. But Alec was apt to blame his inability to read upon a defect of his eyes.

They quarreled constantly. To Max Brand, Nick reported that Alec was just a touchy old idiot—who could not even read! And what is a man capable of when he cannot read print? Alec, with equal fervor, reported that poor Nick was not to be blamed for weakness of temper and mind, for, said Alec, when a man's body is bent his brain is sure to sag also! But in spite of their wrangling, the two loved one another with a perfect devotion. And the long tales which they told in the evenings, making

sixty years of Western history breathe
and repainting mountains and deserts,
have never been out of the mind of
Max Brand. Nothing is more vivid to
him than the memory of the little
shanty near the "tank," the small
stretchers on which the skins of coyotes
and bobcats were drying, and the
wrangling voices of old Nick and Alec.

Max Brand has been a traveler for
a great many years, from the Pacific

*Max Brand*

Islands to the deserts of northern Africa, but when he search-
es for stories, he most often goes back to that shanty in Texas,
and the voices of the two old men pour up in his mind. That is
why Western themes generally have come off his typewriter
during the last sixteen years. In fact, he has written more
Western stories than any other author. He is forty years old,
was born on the Coast, spent twenty-three years in California,
and since that time has lived east and west in diverse parts of
the world.

# THE ARGOSY LIBRARY ™

SERIES 2 INCLUDES:

\* **BRAND** \* **BRENT** \* **ADAMS** \*
\* **MacISAAC** \* **ROSCOE** \*
\* **GIESY & SMITH** \*
\* **BECHDOLDT** \*
\* **MONTGOMERY** \*
\* **FARLEY** \*
\* **DAVIS** \*

THE BEST FICTION
FROM THE FRANK
A. MUNSEY LINE

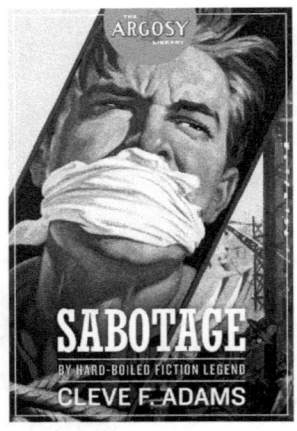

**SABOTAGE**
BY HARD-BOILED FICTION LEGEND
**CLEVE F. ADAMS**

**CHAMPION OF LOST CAUSES**
WILLIAM F. NOLAN
**MAX BRAND**

**DOAN AND CARSTAIRS**
THEIR COMPLETE CASES
BY BLACK MASK MAGAZINE LEGEND
**NORBERT DAVIS**

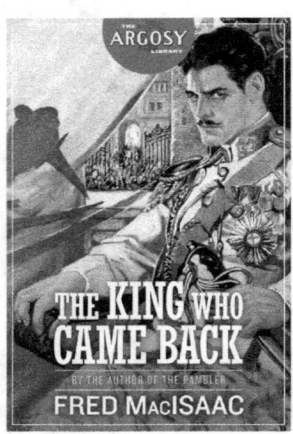

**THE KING WHO CAME BACK**
BY THE AUTHOR OF THE RAMBLER
**FRED MacISAAC**

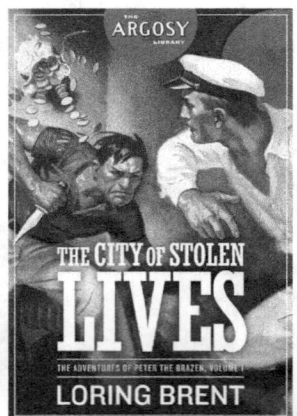

**THE CITY OF STOLEN LIVES**
THE ADVENTURES OF PETER THE BRAZEN, VOLUME 1
**LORING BRENT**

**THE RADIO GUN-RUNNERS**
BY SCIENCE FICTION LEGEND
**RALPH MILNE FARLEY**

**BLOOD RITUAL**
THE ADVENTURES OF SCARLET AND BRADSHAW, VOLUME 1
**THEODORE ROSCOE**

**THE SCARLET BLADE**
THE RAKEHELLY ADVENTURES OF CLEVE AND D'ENTREVILLE, VOLUME 1
**MURRAY R. MONTGOMERY**

**SEMI DUAL**
THE COMPLETE CABALISTIC CASES OF
THE OCCULT DETECTOR: VOLUME 2: 1912–13
**J.U. GIESY AND JUNIUS B. SMITH**

**SOUTH OF FIFTY-THREE**
BY THE AUTHOR OF THE TORCH
**JACK BECHDOLT**

SERIES 2 • AVAILABLE SPRING 2015

www.ingramcontent.com/pod-product-compliance
Lightning Source LLC
Chambersburg PA
CBHW051636050726
47502CB00011B/556